Reduced Ransom!

Second Edition

Reduced Ransom!

Second Edition

Mike Faricy

To Teresa
"The more you eat,
the harder you are to kidnap.
Eat cake and stay safe."

Acknowledgments

I would like to thank the following people for their help and support:

Thanks to Roy, Steve, and Julie for their creative talent and not slitting their wrists or jumping off the high bridge when dealing with my Neanderthal computer capabilities.

Last, I would like to thank family and friends for their encouragement and unqualified support. Special thanks to Maggie, Jed, Schatz, Pat, Av, Emily, and Pat for not rolling their eyes, at least when I was there, and most of all, to my wife Teresa whose belief, support and inspiration has from day one, never waned.

One

Mickey leaned over and half-whispered into Dell's ear. "So, you're in with me on this. I mean, if we figure it out and play our cards right, you'd be willing to do more than just consider it?" Mickey half-whispered into Dell's ear. He glanced around the darkened barroom, then straightened up and arranged his swizzle sticks along the edge of the bar.

If he'd ever had a prime, Mickey Donnelly was past it. He'd done a lot of living, more than a little of it in smoke-filled bars within easy reach of a stiff drink or a cold beer. He'd put on three to four pounds annually over the last twelve years, ever since he got out of the Lino Lakes Correctional Facility, placing him on the far side of solid, heading toward fat. His once dark, curly hair had begun to gray, at least the hair that remained. With more than the hint of an extra chin, plus a natural disdain for ties, he had converted to the open collar look a number of years back. Today, he was wearing a button-down, black, rayon shirt. A flock of pink flamingos standing on one leg were wrapped around the base of the garment.

He took another sip, "Dell, you on board here? " He asked again, drawing close, giving Dell the conspiratorial nod.

"Yeah," Dell said and took a sip before nodding to Cookie, the bartender, for another round. "Yeah, count me in. Come on, Mick, we go back a long way. Christ, we were crawling when we first met. You know I'm in. I'm with you, man."

Dell tossed a twenty in Cookie's direction as she set the next round in front of them. This was finally it, this was going to be big, and wouldn't you know, his old pal Mickey, the guy he'd known longer than anyone, had dumped it all right in his lap.

"Amen, brother, I'm in," Dell said and toasted Mickey." To success, baby. Long may it last."

Dell had been rocking since he was thirteen. Not in a band. He'd been hanging it, sheetrock, and he was damn tired of it. He knew he was on borrowed time, aches and pain wise. But he didn't know much else. He supposed he could go back to school, get his GED, take a computer course or some damn thing. Guys did that all the time. But he'd have to learn how to type first, and besides, he never, ever liked school. But now old Mickey had a plan that would land them both on 'Easy Street.'

They were a Mutt and Jeff team. Mickey, always the idea man, an extrovert, quick with a joke. He knew everyone, cops, girls, all of the bartenders in town. Dell was Mickey's opposite, almost whip thin, but muscled, not in a pumped iron way, just hard, angular, sinewy strong. He had a full head of salt and pepper hair with a razor-sharp part. He kept to himself, always content to watch, listen, then just nod and do the damn job, whatever it was. People around town knew him as 'that guy who was always with Mickey.'

They did have one thing in common. They'd never had any money. Dell dreamed of spreading money all over the bed and sleeping on it. He loved the smell of money, and he thought he could almost smell it, big time, with Mickey's latest idea. He had no real problem with breaking the law, providing they didn't get caught and no one got hurt.

"See, I figure," Mickey said, standing in the rear of the War Bonnet Lounge, his arm draped over Dell's shoulder." Who's to even know? I mean, where guys usually screw up is they get greedy. They think they need the high profile, the fancy car, the big house, and the women."

Dell nodded.

"But, you and me, Dell. Hell, we've been living on a five-dollar cushion most of our lives, just a paycheck ahead of the sheriff. So, now we'll just continue to take it low key, keep it quiet. It's as simple as that." Mickey clinked glasses with Dell. "To our new, simple success."

Dell narrowed his eyes for a brief moment, and Mickey caught the look.

"What is it?"

"Mick, when you say women, you're not talking kids here, right? I can't grab any kids, okay?"

"Jesus, Dell, are you kidding me, kids? You mean like little kids? What's wrong with you?" he punched Dell in the shoulder. "They'll be women, not kids. Women rolling in the dough. Their old man has to be able to get the cash. What we call in business, disposable income. Once we get the money, everyone goes off happy. The guy has his woman back, and we'll have one hundred thousand dollars. Think of it, Dell, a hundred thousand bucks, you and me. Us two schmucks! A hundred grand, cash! And no one tells the cops. It's perfect, brilliant, pure genius, even if I do say so myself. Here's to us and our newfound success," Mickey said and raised his glass.

"Mick, why are you so sure they won't go to the cops?"

"That's the beauty of the plan. A hundred thousand is nothing to these guys. They just get a second mortgage on their house. Hell, it's almost paid off, anyway. I can check all that out. It's enough money to work for you and me, but not too much that the guy goes nuts. And, we warn them. They go to the cops, something worse will happen. We can work out these smaller details later. I got a couple of thoughts to guarantee our safety, but don't worry, nothing that would hurt anyone."

Dell nodded, pushed his baseball cap back a notch, and smiled.

"Plus, I've been doing research, watching all those cop shows and stuff. Learning things like she should never see our face, so we wear a mask. We keep them at your joint because there's no one around, no nosey neighbors, and besides, you got that bedroom downstairs next to your workshop. Oh, and here's just one of the beautiful points, just in case someone goes to the cops, we repaint the bedroom at your place after each one. I mean, some woman says she was in a white room, whoops, excuse me, officer, this room is green. See, Dell? It's all in the details. Well, and not getting greedy, of course."

"Look, you're working days, I work nights, we don't change our schedules. We just slowly get rich and quietly change our address to Easy Street. Speaking of which, I better get to work now. We can talk tomorrow and don't say a damn thing to anyone. Got it?"

Mickey shook his head as he pulled into the parking lot, ready to go to work. At this hour of the night, there was never anyone in the office. He parked next to the door, gliding into the spot reserved for Claudia Cummings, Manager. He'd never met Claudia. He guessed she was probably a nice person. But she'd be pissed off if she knew Mickey was parking in her spot, even after hours, which made parking in her spot fun.

He liked to tell folks he'd been cleaning up in real estate for the last couple of years, and that wasn't too far from the truth. He cleaned up the office most nights between midnight and two. Just vacuum, empty the trash, clean the break room, hit the bathrooms, a little dusting around the front desk. He cleaned Claudia's office, of course, and a few obvious heavy hitters. Then he just sat back, relaxed, raided the fridge in the break room, and wasted time while on the clock.

That's when he first started to put the key elements of his plan together, while he was wasting time. He'd been on one of the computers, looking for porn sites it turned out they didn't have access to. Lucky thing for him because he started snooping at files, checking out what folks were worth. Average folks who hadn't done a damn thing different than Mickey, except buy a house on the cheap twenty-five or thirty years ago, make the payments, and do the responsible routine. Now, all of a sudden, they were sitting on all sorts of market value. That started Mickey thinking.

All the information he needed was stored on a secure system, but it's funny what you pick up, picking up after people. At least three of the associates had their passwords taped to their computers. The sneaky ones, like Claudia, the manager, had their passwords stored in a Rolodex, usually filed under 'C, 'for computer. With Claudia's password, he'd been able to look at files from all the other branches around town. Once he could look at files, he began checking on people he knew, and then it just started— his grudge list.

He had never been aware he even kept a grudge list, it just bubbled out one night. It started with Huey Evans, an older kid he knew growing up. Huey beat up Mickey every day after school for two years, just for fun. Fun for Huey, anyway. It got to where he would just run out after school, trying to clear the playground before the beating began. That's when he learned Huey could run faster.

He hadn't thought of Huey in years. Yet, there he was, and Mickey could hear the taunts, feel the punches, the kicks, see the faces of the other kids, none of them really knowing what to do. So, they all just watched. Except for Dell, he stood by Mickey, and then there were two guys for Huey to beat up, a double your pleasure deal.

It turned out old Huey had 'market value 'and was worth some bucks, and that had started the ball rolling in Mickey's mind. At first, it was just a day-dream. But the more he thought about it, the more he saw real potential. For possibly the first time in his life, Mickey was going to work a job he enjoyed. It was going to be payback time, get even and get rich at the same time.

Janice continued lecturing as she carried two bags of groceries from her car. "I said no. What part of that no, don't you understand?"

"But, Mom," whined her daughter, Ashley." You don't get it. Everyone can go, except me. It's just because you never have any fun in your life. You just sit around the house. That's why you never do anything because you don't know what it's like to have fun."

Her daughter was half-right. A single mom at thirty-two, raising a fifteen-year-old daughter. Janice Evans McGregor couldn't remember the lst time she actually had fun. She was working two dead-end jobs, getting five and half hours of sleep on any given night, and she still couldn't make ends meet. The grass needed cutting, eve-rything in the house needed repair, paint, or both. For Janice, life had become one big sleep deprived blur. Do anything fun? How about eight hours of uninterrupted sleep on a set of clean sheets?

"No, that's final, young lady," Janice said and pushed through the kitchen door. She scratched her fore-arm on the torn screen as she stepped over shoes, then stumbled on a backpack before sidestepping the empty dog dish on her way to the cluttered counter. "Hey, Ash, I got some microwave popcorn in here somewhere," she said, digging around in one of the grocery bags.

Ashley rolled her eyes. "Yeah, right. Like I want to be around this dump eating some crummy popcorn to-night. Mom, I'm not a kid anymore. I'm fifteen. God, why do you have to be so mean? Don't you want me to have fun, to have a life? Do you want me to end up like you?"

"That's enough, young lady," Janice said, still rum-maging around in the grocery bag. "Don't push me, Ash, I've had a really long day."

"But Mom, everyone gets to go except me. It's just not fair, and it sucks. You suck, and this stinky house sucks big time."

"All right, that's enough, young lady. You haven't done a damn thing around here all day except make more work for me. Look at this mess, did it ever cross your mind to clean up any of this?" Janice swept her arm around in a wide arc encompassing domestic devastation in every direction.

"Do you think that maybe just once, I could come home and not have to battle with you about something you want? What about me? What about what I want? Oh no, I can't think about that, can I? I'm just put on this earth to serve Ashley and to make sure she has fun. Well, I've got news for you, young lady, life isn't about having fun. We're starting a new regime around here. Right now. You're going to start pulling your own weight. You're—"

"No, no, I'm not. It's not my mess. I didn't make it. I hate you! I hate this sucky house, and I'm going to go live with Dad," she screamed and ran out the kitchen door.

"You get back here, young lady. Do you hear me? Oh, shit," Janice said, wishing she could run away as well.

TWO

Mickey and Dell had spent the past two months getting every detail of the bedroom ready. Dell's location was perfect, out in the country on the backside of Ramsey County, almost to Stillwater. No close neighbors, a tuck under garage, and the basement bedroom with an attached bathroom and one small window, too small and high to crawl out.

"We'll cover that damn thing up," said Mickey, using the royal we and pointing to the window. "Disguise this room, so next time there's no window, after that maybe two windows. That way, anyone ever puts this together, their description won't make any sense."

Dell had to give Mickey credit. If anyone knew about things that didn't make sense, it was Mickey. "I'll put up two walls, shorten the room by four and a half inches, but it'll look like there isn't a way out, except this door."

Dell had removed all the furniture, except the metal-framed bed, which he bolted to the floor. He pulled up the carpet and laid down two boxes of black and white self-stick tiles. Another of Mickey's brainstorms, whoever was in here would remember the black and white tile floor. Once her old man made the payment, Dell could rip it out and lay the carpet back down. The cops ever show up, they pull back the carpet and there's the floor that had been installed back in 1953. Gee, sorry guys, wrong house.

Just to be sure, Mickey actually spent a night in the room to see if he could pick up sounds or anything that might help identify the place later on. He'd seen a number of cop shows where the cops got their forensic clues from the drain trap below the kitchen sink and the shower drain.

"Point is, we gotta pour bleach down the drains. I saw them do it on a show. They poured bleach down the drains after they cut up some dead gangster guy with a power saw," Mickey said.

"Why didn't they just put all new pipes in?" Dell said. "New plastic down past the water trap, get rid of it completely. A guy could plumb it for about thirty bucks and change. Ditch the old stuff. That way, no sign or trace of anyone for sure."

Mickey took another sip from his beer and looked at Dell. "You think of that or did you see it on TV? It's brilliant, Dell, that's what we do. We'll re-plumb the joint, put in new pipes and, we don't leave the old pipes out back. We get them out of here the same day, drop 'em in another county. We buy the new stuff over in Minneapolis, pay cash. Buy it at a different store every time. Brilliant, absolutely brilliant."

The next night at the War Bonnet Lounge, Mickey sprung his little surprise on Dell. They were sitting alone at the far end of the bar, on the outside edge of a circle of dingy pink neon light. To be on the safe side, Mickey stopped talking every time some guy went in or came out of the men's room. "Who's the biggest jerk we knew in grade school?"

"That's easy, Huey Evans, he kicked the shit out of both of us all those times. I'd like to run that guy down if I ever see him," Dell said.

"How'd you like to go it one better and have him give us a hundred grand? No questions asked, and we make him sweat a little?"

"You kidding me, Huey Evans? That's who you're going after? Won't he know it's us?"

Mickey waited as a fat guy wiping his hands on his jeans exited the men's room. "What's to know? Huey hasn't thought of or seen us since we were kids. He doesn't even know we exist, Dell. I think it's time old

Huey gets taught a lesson. If he was that big of a jerk in grade school, it's a pretty safe bet he hasn't changed. The list of people who'd want to get back at him has to be a mile long. No one's gonna come looking for us, Dell. Two kids from way back when we were under the radar."

"I hear he runs with some pretty rough crowds, uses his liquor store as a front for a lot of bad stuff."

"Hey, he could be the damned Godfather, for all I care. We'll be so careful he won't even know we exist. Besides, Huey Evans is such a jerk they'd have to rent the damn stadium just to house all the guys he's screwed over the years. He ain't gonna be thinking of two kids from grade school."

Janice Evans McGregor was too tired to care. Working double shifts just to try and get a little ahead, and now the brakes went out on her damn car. They'd started to make a grinding noise about two weeks ago. That's when she'd turned up the radio. Earlier this week, they were barely working. Now they had just flat out failed, and she sailed through the intersection and wrestled the car to a stop against the curb.

Right now, she didn't have enough money in the bank to cover the tow, let alone the repair. She didn't know how to reach Ashley's father, not that he'd help, and she didn't dare call her stepfather, Huey. She hadn't spoken to him for almost a year, hadn't spoken to him civilly in almost five years.

She was deep in thought, searching for a way out of this current dilemma, and failed to notice the faded green El Dorado, parked just fifty feet away. Damn it, she thought, who could she call? One of the many problems with working double shifts was it left no time for a boy-friend. Boyfriend? God, it left no time for a life.

Sometimes, Mickey thought, sitting in his car, you make your own breaks, and once in a while, they're made for you. He watched the woman, Huey's kid Janice, from a discrete distance. He'd actually been following her to and from her waitressing jobs for the past week, trying to find a place and possibly a time when they could grab her. Now, it looked like she had car trouble, and Mickey was suddenly thinking he might be hearing opportunity knock.

An hour and three phone calls later and still no tow truck, Janice was beside herself, pacing back and forth on the curb. She was late picking up Ashley, who would make sure there was hell to pay. She was late for her sec-ond job, which was already hanging by a thread. She had to use a bathroom pretty soon, and she didn't know how she was going to pay for the tow, let alone the car repair.

"Excuse me, ma'am, is there something I can do to help?" Mickey asked as he pulled alongside her. He immediately violated three of his cardinal rules of kidnapping, showing his face, his car, and letting her hear his voice.

"No, I've got some help on the way, at least I think so, thanks all the same," she said, not sounding at all sure.

"You Huey's little girl, Janice?"

"I am," she said, sounding surprised. "My stupid car broke down, and I've been waiting for a tow for over an hour. It's taking so long. I don't know what to do. I'm late to pick up my daughter and still get to my job. God, I just hate cars."

"It's simple," replied Mickey, violating his fourth rule when he climbed out of the car to walk toward her, providing her with a complete physical profile should she ever be asked to identify him. "Just toss your keys on the floor, leave a note, and I'll give you a lift home. It's not like someone can steal it, besides, anything for Huey. I owe him. Come on, I got a pen and paper in my car. Once you're home, you can call the service station. It's after four," he said, pretending to check his watch, "and they aren't gonna work on it tonight. Cars, you can't live with 'em, and you can't live without 'em. I tell my own kids, girls, keep those damn things tuned up and operating, but they never listen to me. They're always thinking about a new pair of shoes, braces for the kids, or some damn thing. I guess I don't have to tell you about that."

"You sure don't." Janice said, wondering how this guy knew her, grateful at the same time that her luck was about to change.

As she slid into the passenger seat of his El Dorado, Mickey opened the rear door and rummaged around. "Should be a pen and paper in my glove compartment," he said, finding a roll of duct tape beneath the bowling shoes he thought he'd returned last spring.

"So, where do you know my stepdad from?" Janice said, focused on writing a note to leave with her car.

"I knew your father some years back," Mickey said, and tore off a length of duct tape." He used to beat me up every day after school." As he said the last few words, he wrapped the length of tape over her eyes and around her head, quickly reclining the front seat and pinning her down. "Quit fighting, lady. I'm not gonna hurt you," he said, holding her down while frantically glancing around to see if anyone was watching them.

Janice pulled at the tape, but not too hard, seemingly resigned to what was about to happen.

"You better behave if you ever want to see that kid again."

"What do you want from me?"

"I don't want to hurt you. You'll be fine. Just let me put this on your wrists. It's just some tape," he said, quickly wrapping a length around her wrists. "Now slip into the back seat here and stay on the floor," he said and hoisted her over and out of the reclined passenger seat and into the back seat. He helped her roll onto the floor of the car as gently as he could. "Careful, now. Watch your head, ma'am, just stay there, quiet like, long as there's no trouble from you, I won't have to call my partners. The ones who are watching your daughter."

"Ashley, you've got Ashley?" she screamed, suddenly kicking the inside of the door from the floor of the back seat.

"Hey, take it easy. She's fine. They're just watching her. But if I get any trouble from you, any trouble at all, then they might have to grab her, too. Now, I'm sure you don't want that to happen. So, you just lay real quiet like, and we'll all get along just fine." As he slid behind the wheel, he spotted a bright red tow truck heading in their direction.

Janice lay on the floor of the back seat, moving slightly, trying to get a bit more comfortable. There was a moldy smell, not too strong, subtle, but there just the same. Something was on the floor, beneath her, pushing the small of her back. Strangely, she wasn't frightened, as she thought this had to be the worst day of her life.

"You know, Janice," Mickey said, trying to sound calm as he passed the tow truck." We all appreciate your

help here. And, I want you to know, right from the beginning, that you won't be hurt, won't be harmed in any
way. We want to get you back with your family just as
soon as possible," he said, hoping he sounded sincere.

"Of course, that will all be up to your old man now,
just how soon you can go home, I mean. But we'll let you
talk to him. Let him know you're okay and that your
daughter is at home, so she's not alone and all. You don't
want her throwing any parties."

"No offense, but I haven't been married for six years.
So, if you think you're gonna get anything from my ex,
you can save yourself the cost of the phone call, because
he would probably pay you to keep me. He's eighteen
months behind in child support, and to tell the truth, I'm
not even sure where you would find him."

"Not your husband . . . I meant your old man, Huey,
your father."

Things just got worse, thought Janice, and she
banged her head on the floor of the car in pure frustration.

Dell's house had a hundred-and-twenty-foot drive
from the county road to the tuck-under garage. Mickey
didn't see Dell's van, which meant Dell was most likely
still on his way home from work.

"You just sit tight for a minute, let me tell these guys
everything is okay, so they can get the other guys away
from your daughter," Mickey said. He stood just outside

the car for a couple of minutes, carrying on three sides of a conversation, attempting to make it sound as if there were other people around. Eventually, he climbed back into the car and pulled into the eternally open garage.

He pulled the big overhead door closed, struggling the last few feet to keep the weight from slamming onto the concrete pad. The first thing he planned to do with Dell's share of the ransom was to buy a garage door opener.

"You just follow me," he said, carefully helping Janice out of the car. "We'll get you settled in. No one's going to hurt you."

He led her into the basement bedroom and over to the bed. "You can sit down here. I'm gonna take this tape off your wrists, and then, when you hear the door close, you can go ahead and pull it from your eyes. There's a bathroom that's private for you, with clean towels, and, there's clean sheets on the bed," he said, as he stepped out of the room. He locked the door, then stood very still and watched her through the peephole.

She sat on the edge of the bed and rubbed her wrists. She could still smell something unpleasant on her clothes from that junky car. With the tape still across her eyes, she listened for any telltale sign she wasn't alone. Strangely, she wasn't frightened.

She bit her tongue and pinched the tip of her index finger just to see if this could possibly be some dreadful dream. Failing that test, she sat a moment or two before cautiously removing the tape, then blinked with the sudden brightness from the overhead light.

She was in a small room with a black and white tile floor, the bed where she sat and an end table next to the bed were the only pieces of furniture. An open doorway led to the bathroom. She noticed there wasn't a door to close for privacy. Two folded white towels were on the bed, along with a toothbrush, toothpaste, and a bar of soap. *Very strange*, she thought.

"So, hey, what's up?" Dell said.

Mickey stood at the bedroom door with his eye against the peephole. "Shhhh, Huey's kid, she's in there."

"What the hell?" Dell pushed Mickey out of the way, pressed his face against the door, and peered into the small room. "You, you grabbed Huey's kid. How? Why? Mick, this is crazy. What are we gonna do?"

"Settle down. I've got it all under control. The opportunity just presented itself, and I took advantage of it. Just relax, Dell. I've got everything just the way we ant it."

"Relax? That's Huey Evans's daughter in there, just for starters. And you kidnapped her and then brought her to my damn house. Do you have any idea—"

"Stop it, Dell, get hold of yourself and listen for a minute. The opportunity presented itself. I was following her like I told you I would. Her car broke down. I got her into my car, she doesn't know where she is, doesn't know where your house is and doesn't know you even exist. So, just relax. Now, let's go upstairs, quietly discuss this over a couple of cold ones and move on to step two. Our plan is working perfectly. So, just calm down."

Over four or five beers, Mickey gave Dell the details of the abduction and kidnapping. Those weren't exactly the terms he used. He just told Dell she got in the car, he blindfolded her and then drove in a roundabout way to Dell's house with Janice on the floor of the back seat. He forgot to mention the tow truck, threatening her daughter's safety, nor did he mention that she would be able to describe and identify both Mickey and his car.

"So, how do we get paid? You gonna send Huey a note? If the idea is to get a hundred grand from him, he's gotta know we got her."

"Well, yeah, we're gonna send him instructions," Mickey said, not having really worked out the "how" aspect of things." You got some magazines here that we can cut up? You know, for the ransom note."

In short order, Dell brought a stack of hunting and fishing magazines to the kitchen table along with two more beers.

"Great. We'll need glue, scissors, and some rubber gloves. And don't touch any of this stuff," he said, pointing to the table.

An hour later, Mickey threw down the scissors. "This really sucks. Damn letters are so small I can't glue 'em down with these rubber gloves on. Look at this. We've screwed up over a half-dozen attempts at making a ransom note. No wonder they catch guys. I'll just type the damn thing at the office when I clean tonight."

"Are you gonna mail the letter to him?" Dell asked, visibly calmer after his sixth beer.

"Naw, I'll slip it into the mail slot at his liquor store later tonight. He'll get it when he goes in tomorrow. But before that, we gotta have Janice call him. I acquired a cell phone at a bar this noon. We'll have her say a couple of words, so he knows we aren't kidding. Then we toss that cell phone, grab another one for our next call. That way, they can never trace us. Relax, I got all the angles covered. We just need to keep playing it smart and not panic."

"Now, here's what we're gonna do. We'll call Huey, have Janice say a few words. I'll write it down here," said Mickey, taking a pen and writing a note. "She can read this. She hangs up in less than a minute. Huey'll get the message. Then we get the dough and drop Janice off somewhere safe. It's simple."

Another beer later and outside the basement bedroom, Dell was suddenly feeling he might be having second thoughts. Mickey's plan had sounded pretty solid upstairs at the kitchen table, but here, peeking in and seeing her just sitting there, well, he wasn't quite so sure right now.

"You gotta go in, Dell. So she knows there's more than just me. I told her other guys were here, and more guys were watching her kid. So now, you gotta go in there so she can see you. And here, wear this, so she won't see your face," he said and handed Dell a brown paper grocery bag.

Maybe that was part of Dell's problem, the grocery bag, with eye holes cut in, and the big smile Mickey had drawn on the front.

"Come on, Dell," Mickey said. He opened up the grocery bag and placed it over Dell's head, one paper handle hung down on his chest, the other down his back.

"Okay, here are the notes. Hand her this one first with the directions. Once she reads it, you just press the button to dial the phone. Give me that beer," he said, and traded Dell's beer for the cell phone. "Then, as soon as Huey's on the line, she can read this second note. Once she's done, you grab the phone and hang it up. Then give her this note." He handed Dell the third note." It tells her dinner will be in about forty minutes, hope she likes pizza. You gotta do this, man. I know you can. You're only in there for a minute, then out. Don't say a word to her. Just hand her the notes. Okay, let's do it," Mickey said and knocked on the door to get Janice's attention.

She slowly looked up toward the door but made no effort to get off the bed.

Mickey pulled the door open and pushed Dell into the room. With the paper bag over his head, he half-stumbled as he attempted to see through the eye holes.

Now what? Janice thought and watched the idiot slowly approaching with a paper bag on his head. The way the day had gone, and now this, it figured. She'd been kidnapped by morons.

Dell handed her the first note. She had to hold it out at arm's length to read. "You're going to call my stepfather? This should be fun. I'm not sure he'll even take the damn call. Okay, go ahead," she said.

Dell pressed the send button on the phone and handed it to Janice. With the bag on his head, there was no point in trying to hear it ring.

"Yeah, hi, Marty, Janice. Let me talk to him. Look, Marty, no, you can't help. Just put him on, okay. No, Marty. Marty!" Janice yelled." Will you just put him on the damn phone, God."

Huey Evans ignored the beep on the line indicating a call waiting. "I understand we're way past 90 days on this invoice, but I pay for professional work, and the countertops you put in are not professional. So, I'm not paying. It's as simple as that." He had no intention of paying the man he was talking to. He had never intended to pay.

"Go ahead, take me to small claims court, I don't care. No, I'm not interested in finding a middle ground. I've got another call coming in, go do your substandard work for someone else and bother them," he said and hung up. He pressed the call waiting button. "Yeah."

"Hello, this is your daughter," Janice read." Do not attempt to contact the police. I'm being held. Instructions will follow. Pick up my daughter at home. I will be released as soon as you follow the instructions."

"Who the hell is this, Arlene?" Huey said.

"No, damn it, it's not Arlene. It's me, Janice. I've been kidnapped. They're going to give you instructions or directions, I don't know, just do as they say, okay."

Come on, Dell, Mickey screamed to himself, watching through the peephole as his hand squeezed the doorknob. *Grab the damn phone.*

"No, I'm not drunk, and I'm not kidding. Will you just listen, please?"

Dell pointed to the note he'd handed her, encouraging her to reread the message that Mickey had written.

Janice picked up on the hint and looked at the note, holding it again at arm's length. "It says here you're supposed to follow the directions that will came. Is that came?" she asked Dell, pointing to a word on the note. "Shouldn't it be come? Directions that will come."

"For Christ's sake!" Mickey screamed through the door.

"Jesus, what's that guy's problem?" Janice said, then screamed back at the door." Hey, if I could read your lousy handwriting, it would be a hell of a lot easier. You!" she shouted at Dell." Is this came or come? Ahh, God, directions will come later, I guess. I don't know. It could be come later or come in a letter. The damn writing's so bad I can't tell. Look, just do what they want and get me out of here. I'm gonna lose my job if I don't get back."

She paused, listened to a response, then said, "No! I'm not f-ing kidding. How do I know who the hell it is? One of them's kinda fat. Another one has a paper bag over his head. I don't know about the others. Oh, and get Ashley, she's got a dentist appointment tomorrow."

"Grab the damn phone, now!" Mickey screamed through the door.

Dell gently took the phone from Janice, fumbling for the disconnect button as he made his way toward the door. Mickey opened the door. As Dell exited, the paper bag brushed against the door frame, turning sideways on Dell's head and completely blocking his vision. He walked out of the room, feeling his way with his arms outstretched for the few final steps while Mickey slammed the door closed and checked Janice through the peephole.

"Hey, by the way, I'm lactose intolerant," she screamed at the door, waving the note about dinner. "Morons," she mumbled under her breath.

"What the hell was all that?" Mickey yelled and batted the paper bag off Dell's head. "Are you nuts? Did I not say it was to be a very short conversation? And you're in there afraid to interrupt her. I'm surprised she didn't hand you the phone, so you could talk to Huey. From now on, we stick to business. Next thing you know, you'll have her calling the cops and inviting them over for dinner. And let's get something better than this," he kicked at the paper bag on the floor. "Get a damn stocking cap and cut some holes in it."

"What color should it be?"

"Color? I don't care about the color, Dell. Just get an old one. Cut two eye holes in it and use that. Okay, I gotta go get us some dinner, Chinese since pizza is apparently out."

"You want me to ask her if she likes Chinese?"

"I couldn't care less what she likes," Mickey said, peering back through the peephole." She'll eat what we serve, lactose intolerant or not. Give me that phone. The sooner we get rid of this damn thing, the better," he said.

Three

uey drummed his fingers on the desk for a long moment then thought, 'What the hell?' "Ashley," Huey Evans said, leaving a phone message at Janice's house once he'd looked up the number. "This is your Grandfather, the one that talks to you. Give me a call as soon as you get this, no matter what time. Twenty bucks if I hear from you in the next half-hour ," he said, then hung up and drummed his fingers on the desk some more. This was too stupid to be the real deal.

Ashley returned his call fifteen minutes later as he drove home from work. "Hello? Ashley, turn down that damn racket in the background. I can't hear myself think. Put your mother on the line."

"I don't know where she is," Ashley yelled over the music. "She was supposed to be at Luther's two hours ago working the dinner shift until ten tonight, but I don't know if she's really there. She didn't bother to come home and make me dinner, and there's absolutely nothing good to eat here."

The noise thumping in the background was beginning to drive him crazy, and he yelled into the phone. "Ashley, turn that down. I can't hear what the hell you're saying. Is her car there?"

"Mom's?"

"For God's sake, Ashley. Turn that dreadful music off so we can talk." Things suddenly went quiet. "Thank you," he said in response. "Finally, you're gonna blow out what little brains you have, listening to that stuff. Now, is your mother's car there? Has she been home?"

"I already told you. She hasn't been home, there's nothing good to eat, and I don't know where she is. So there."

"I'll pick you up in fifteen minutes, but don't hold me up. I got a lot to do tonight." He hung up, wondering, *Could this really be on the level? God, the woman was over thirty and still a pain in the butt.*

Ashley was waiting on the front stoop when he pulled up. Now she was sitting in the passenger seat, staring at her feet. Her jaw was clenched, her eyebrows furrowed and her arms were crossed, and her headphones were around her neck as they drove in silence. Huey was more than a little uncomfortable in her presence. Ashley was thinking *There wouldn't be anything to do at his house, and she was going to miss out on whatever fun might happen tonight.*

"Did your mother mention anything about where she might go, a doctor's appointment or anything?" Huey asked.

"I already told you, she didn't say anything. Besides, she's so worked up about her stupid old job. She doesn't even care about me." She gave a quick glanced sideways to see if he reacted.

"So, as far as you know, she's at work. Any guys hanging around lately?"

"Guys? You mean men? With mom? Oh, gross," Ashley said and shuddered.

Huey couldn't quite put his finger on it, but there was something about the kid that made him want to hit her. Right here in the car. Perhaps it was the sense he really shouldn't that made the idea seem so appealing. He pulled into the driveway, turned off the car, and climbed out.

"Come on, Ashley," Huey said, waiting for his granddaughter to catch up to him at the back door. "Now, I've got just one rule. It's my only rule. Don't touch a damned thing."

"Whatever," Ashley said and slipped on her head-phones.

Huey called Luther's restaurant and learned that Janice had been fired effective immediately for not showing up. He still wasn't sure this might not be another Janice stunt, stick him with her kid for a night while she was out on the town. Right now, all he wanted was a cold beer and a shower before he went out for the night.

"Look, kid," he said, forty minutes later. "Here's twenty bucks. Get yourself a pizza, okay? I got a meeting I need to get to. I'll be back as soon as I can."

"Twenty bucks?" she said, looking at the two ten-dollar bills he handed her. "I'll be lucky if they put cheese on it for twenty bucks. It's more like thirty, especially if I want something to drink with it."

He peeled a twenty off the stack of bills." Save me some," he said and walked out the door.

Ashley watched as Huey backed out of the drive-way, then waited at the window for a few more minutes, just to be sure, before she began to explore.

His house was certainly nicer than home. No junk was piled on every available flat surface. The kitchen counters were clear. None of the furniture cushions were torn. There weren't any broken springs in the couch. Even the the walls were clean.

She searched through his bedroom drawers but found nothing of interest. She looked under his bed and only came up with empty suitcases. She pawed through his office, finding nothing much but stacks of papers and boring pictures of Huey with rows of dead ducks, dead deer, and some old car. She found a five-dollar bill in a desk drawer, which she figured he would never miss, and then there, way in the back, a gun.

She carefully pulled it out of the drawer, set it on the desk, and looked at it from a number of different angles. She held it in her hand, surprised at the weight of the thing and the coldness of the steel against her fingers. She held it out directly in front of her, aiming. It was heavy and kept sinking toward the floor. She steadied it with both hands, extended her arms, fighting to keep the pistol level.

She struck different poses in front of the full-length mirror downstairs. "Freeze, gorgeous," she yelled at her reflection. She stuck the pistol in her waistband, but it was so heavy it fell onto the floor. She put it back in her waistband, rested a hand on the grip, and struck different poses, angling her hips. She imagined walking into a bank and getting a hundred dollars. Or, into a designer store and just taking all their really cool tops. Maybe she'd get a gun tattooed on her back.

Of course, a lot of kids had probably held a gun, but how many could say they had actually pulled the trigger? Looking out the window, she figured it was dark enough.

She stood in the driveway, her back to the street and in her mind, completely hidden. The shades were pulled in the house next door. The garage was off to the side, and all anyone would see from the street was a fifteen-year-old girl standing in the driveway.

Still, she would have to be fast about it. Wouldn't it be cool to wear the bullet she shot around her neck, like, well, forever? Beautiful and dangerous. Get a bullet tattooed on her back. Maybe that could be her new name, Bullet. Everyone would know her name. Even her stupid teachers would be afraid of her.

She quickly brought the pistol up with both hands, aimed at the double garage door no more than five feet in front of her. She turned her head to the side, closed her eyes, and began to squeeze the trigger. She squeezed the trigger hard, and just as she was thinking, *this sucks . . .* BOOM!

She stood still for a very long moment before coming back to life, thinking, *Oh. My. God.* She was thrilled with the rush of excitement. She had seen enough movies to know she should walk slowly and quietly back into the house, not rush, and not hold the pistol out in front of her for everyone to see. She knew all that, but she ran anyway, banging the gun a couple of times against the door as she hurried to get back inside.

Once inside, she wondered who she should call first? Well, of course, Tara. She returned the gun to the desk drawer. Then decided to get the bullet before she called everyone and got the word out, Ashley "Bullet" McGregor was in town.

The garage door was one of those wooden things, wide enough for two cars. Ashley's aim had put the round perfectly at eye height and just a yard or two to the right of center. This was so cool, she thought, seeing the hole, knowing her bullet was right there. She was more than a little disappointed to find out she could put her finger through the hole, but then, how cool was that?

Yeah, 'Bullet 'put her finger in the hole. She imagined long, red, manicured nails, one of her fingers wearing a bright gold ring sliding into the bullet hole. She had big boobs, a little top, and all these really cool boys were watching her. She had great designer jeans on, expensive heels. Real heels, not the old lady kind her mother or teachers wore, but real, sexy heels.

She walked around to the side door, wondering how 'Bullet 'was ever going to find the bullet. Hoping it would be rolling around on the floor, shiny, maybe gold or silver.

"Wow, cool!" she said out loud, stepping into the darkened garage as an automatic light immediately flashed on, and there directly in front of her sat the shiniest, reddest,' 56 Chevy she had ever seen. It was also the only one she had ever seen, and she had no idea it was a '56 let alone a Chevy. It was just this really cool car, and she forgot all about the bullet for half a minute as she stood in awe, gawking.

"Cool," she said out loud, and that was just about the time she saw the windshield, with the hole in it and the cracks radiating out from the hole in all directions, a spider web pattern. 'Bullet's 'bullet hole.

To say she panicked would be an understatement. She would have run home, hidden there, if only she'd known the way, but she hadn't a clue which direction to go.

Twelve years ago, Huey had told his wife at the time. This was about two years before she divorced him, that he got the '56 Chevy in honor of her.

"But I don't particularly like cars, and I can't drive a stick shift," she'd said.

"Yeah, I know that, but red's your favorite color, and that's what counts."

"Ahh, you're so sweet," she said, thinking he wasn't and taking an instant dislike to the car.

Truth be told, he'd paid cash for the thing in an effort to show off to a girlfriend. She dumped him a few weeks later when she learned he was already married. But in the process, Huey learned the car was a great chick magnet if you liked women who drank too much. Huey liked them just drunk enough so they couldn't testify and thus began his love affair with the car. The same car that was now sitting in his garage with the shattered windshield.

Whatever personality traits Ashley's long-gone father may have brought to the gene table fifteen years ago, they had been trumped by Huey's genetic cards. She quickly concocted a scheme, and with the help of a gallon of gasoline from Huey's lawnmower, she set the garage ablaze. Then ran in the house, jumped into bed at possibly the earliest hour in the last five years.

Huey knew nothing about any of this until he pulled into his driveway some nine hours later and was greeted by the smoldering ruins of his garage and the charred remains of his '56 Chevy babe magnet.

"Ashley, Ashley, damn it, wake up. What the hell happened out there to the garage?"

"What? What?" Ashley said sleepily, having practiced what to say. "Grandfather? Oh, Grandfather, I'm so glad you're here. I was so frightened, there was a fire and—"

"I can see there was a damn fire. What the hell happened?"

"The fire department came and put it out. They left a card and information. You're supposed to call in the morning. I left it all on the kitchen counter, so you'd see it. No one was hurt," she added, unable to resist getting a dig in, then switched gears. "Did your meeting go okay?"

A message, Huey figured, ignoring her question. These kidnappers sent a message. They knew he wasn't home. They were probably watching him all night, he thought, and began a mental rundown of the few faces he remembered from the bar. These guys aren't kidding. He'd been playing them for fools, but if they would burn his garage down with the chevy inside, they weren't fooling around.

It was a little after eleven the following morning when Huey drove Ashley home.

"You sure your school doesn't start until noon?"

"Yeah, gee, I already told you, some in-service workshop bullshit," she said, giving her best effort at educational doublespeak. "Why don't you ever believe me?"

She was barely out of his car when he growled, "Okay, I'll be in touch. Tell your mother to call me when you hear from her, kid," he said and drove off, leaving 'Bullet' standing at the curb. *Whatever. 'Bullet 'had the day off.*

"Huey," Marty called from behind the cash register as Huey entered the liquor store. "This came through the mail slot sometime after close last night." He waved an envelope with 'Huey Evans 'typed on the front in large block letters. Huey took the envelope without saying a word and hurried into his office just behind the gin and vodka shelf. Even before he opened it, he had a pretty good idea what he was going to find.

He opened the envelope and read the brief instructions.

'Get one hundred thousand in twenties, non-sequential numbers and await further instructions.'

Who in the hell were these guys? And, how did they know he had over a hundred grand on hand? How did they know the one thing that would grab his attention faster than anything else was to go after his '56 Chevy? Who were these guys that they knew nothing frightened him more than fire? Not a knife, not a gun, not a bomb, not threats, or physical violence, but fire scared the living daylights out of him.

He knew one thing, he was going to pay these guys, take his lumps, and hope to God they left him alone. He really didn't care about his stepdaughter, Janice. But the car, the fire, that made it very personal and suggested strongly that he would be next if he didn't play ball, now. A hundred grand, if it got these animals out of his life, a hundred grand was chump change.

Four

Mickey pulled the blaze orange stocking cap over his head as he thought, *That damn Dell. Damn thing smells like a tackle box, the eye holes don't line up, God.* It hadn't dawned on him that he was wearing the same clothes as when he first enticed Janice McGregor into his car, only now he was balancing a plate of scrambled eggs, sausage, and toast with a napkin and silverware stuffed into his shirt pocket.

He watched her through the peephole for a few moments before knocking softly on the door." Excuse me, ma'am, I've got some breakfast for you."

She remained still, lying in bed, her left leg clear up to her soft white thigh was exposed, she appeared to be sound asleep.

He quietly opened the door, set the plate and silverware inside the room, closed the door, and began to tiptoe up the stairs.

"What, no jelly? And I could use some coffee," she suddenly called.

                              * * *

All Huey had done since he read the note was sit at his desk drumming his fingers, trying to find a way out of this mess. He always arrived at the same conclusion, just pay these guys and hope they left him alone. He occasionally got out of his chair, opened his safe to check the hundred grand, making sure it somehow hadn't disappeared in the past ten minutes, then return to his desk, drum his fingers some more and wait for the phone call. When the phone finally did ring, he stared at it for a few moments before picking up." Yeah?"

It was one word, but from the tone, Mickey immediately knew it was Huey Evans, and for a moment, he felt like the frightened little boy from grade school.

"Huey Evans?" Mickey asked in a voice that sounded a lot like a cartoon character.

"Yeah."

"Did you read our instructions?"

Again with the voice, Huey thought, like this is some kind of funny joke to these animals." Yeah."

"Do you have . . ." Mickey had to pause and inhale more helium from the balloon he held.

Huey waited, straining his ears, wondering what in the hell was going on.

"Do you have the money as instructed?"

"Yeah," Huey said, beginning to wonder a little more.

"Excellent, we'll be contacting you in forty-five minutes." With that, Mickey hung up the phone, wiped the payphone receiver with a towel, and drove across town with a back seat full of helium-filled balloons.

Huey stared at the receiver still in his hands. *These bastards are so slick,* he thought. *It's all a funny game to them, animals, absolute animals.*

Thirty minutes later, Mickey called, this time from a payphone in the next county. He was more than a little bit nervous, and although he hadn't had a cigarette in sixteen years and four months, he had one going now.

"Yeah," Huey answered almost immediately.

"Are you ready to begin?" Mickey said.

Again with the voice, Huey thought. "Yeah, let's get this over with."

"Place the money in a box, drive to the corner of County Road B and Dale Street. There's a payphone. We'll call you," Mickey said, then hung up, not waiting for a reply.

Huey emptied a case of bourbon and placed twenty bundles of five thousand dollars each into the box. It worried him that whoever was behind this had as much information as they did. That meant it was someone close, very close. And, after the little warning they sent last night with the fire and the destruction of his '56 Chevy, he didn't want them any closer.

Mickey was making his third call to the payphone at County Road B and Dale before Huey answered.

"Yeah."

Mickey had to pause and quickly inhale more helium before he could talk.

"Anyone there?" Huey asked and looked around to see if he could spot a guy watching.

"I want you to drive to the Roseville Mall, ground floor, north end of the mall there's a row of pay phones. Leave your car unlocked, keys under the mat, come alone, we'll be watching."

Huey arrived at the mall pay phones and waited. Thinking this would be where they were going to grab the cash. Fine, he just wanted to get these animals out of his life.

"Yeah," was how he answered the phone.

"I want you to drive to the airport, the Lindbergh terminal, park in level E of long term parking. Go to the phones at door five, on the baggage claim level, and wait for our call. Leave the door of your car unlocked and the keys under the floor mat."

"Wait, now just wait a damn minute," Huey protested, but the line went dead. *Jesus,* he thought, *now the damn airport.*

Mickey watched from the floor below as Huey drove his white Cadillac up the spiraling ramp to the E level. It may have been years since he last saw him, but all the old pain and some of the fear rushed back. He watched as the elevator lights indicated an ascent and then eventually a decent from the E level. He watched Huey, now below him, as he walked through the glassed corridor down to the baggage claim area and door five.

Mickey slowly made his way to Huey's car parked on the E level. He walked past the car, glanced to see the liquor box in the back seat, and kept walking. He made a loop around the parking level. It wasn't deserted, but there was very little traffic up here, and all of it looked to be normal.

He slipped on latex gloves, made a beeline for the Cadillac, opened the rear door, dumped the cash into his backpack, zipped the pack shut, and took the staircase down to the transit level. He took the light rail train from the terminal to the first stop. Once off the train, he settled in his car and placed his call to Huey.

"Yeah," said Huey, answering on the first ring, nearly tearing the receiver from the cable, veins bulging in his neck.

"Go to the Delta counter, buy a one-way ticket for the eight o'clock flight to Seattle, get on the flight. We're watching."

"Seattle, are you . . . hello, hello?" Huey screamed, red-faced, and knowing he was about to head west.

Mickey let out a sigh, then opened his rear door and released the remainder of the helium balloons. On the drive back to Dell's, he tossed the cell phone out the window as he crossed the bridge over the Mississippi River. Now, just one more detail, return Janice.

* * *

"What do you mean, she doesn't want to go?" Mickey said. Dell was wearing the blaze orange stocking cap with the off-center eye holes. He'd just left Janice in the room, where she'd told him she really wasn't interested in going home.

"That's not an option, Dell. It's not how it's supposed to work. We took her, that idiot Huey paid us, now she's got to go back, that's all there is to it. It's, it's the rules," Mickey said.

Everything had gone so smoothly, the room, the woman, the instructions, the handoff, even sending Huey to Seattle. It had all gone so well, until now. Why were they even talking about it?

"Tell her, no, she's got to leave. Get back in there," Mickey said and pushed Dell back into the room.

"I already heard what you said," she yelled as the door opened and Dell stepped in. "And, I'm not going back, bills, my daughter constantly complaining, that dump I live in. I've probably lost one if not both of my jobs, and I've been operating on about four hours of sleep all day, every day for years. Let me know when we get to the good part. Plus, if you got any money out of my stepfather, you are either very sharp or you scared the hell out of him. And let's be honest, you guys aren't that sharp. Now he'll make my miserable life even more miserable, so I'm not going back. That's all there is to it, and I don't care what you do to me."

"You have to go," Mickey yelled from behind the door. "It's the way things work. We return you safe and sound, and you don't get to say you don't want to go."

"Well, it doesn't work for me, and I'm the one who's staying put. So, let me know when you come up with something that works for little old Janice."

"Jesus, this isn't, you can't just . . . Get back out here," Mickey finally yelled at Dell.

"See, I told you, she said she's staying put, she's not leaving," Dell said.

"We gotta get her out of here. I wouldn't want to go back either, but she has to. It gets very dangerous for us if she stays. We're suddenly supposed to feed her and keep her until *she's* ready? We're not running a spa here."

Mickey took out a pen and wrote a note on a piece of cardboard. "Go back in there and give this to her, see what she says."

Dell reentered the small bedroom, holding the cardboard note out in front of him.

"I don't care what you plan to do to me. I'm not going."

"Here," Dell said and handed her the note.

She read the note, shook her head, and yelled to Mickey behind the door." Nice stationery. It'll take more than that."

"How much more?" Mickey yelled back.

"A round number like eight," yelled Janice not evening pausing to think.

"Eight! No way."

"Now it's going to be nine," she yelled in response.

"Lady, you are off your f-ing rocker if you think that we're—"

"Now, it's ten. Are you beginning to see a pattern here?"

Dell looked like he was watching a tennis match, looking first at Janice, then the door with Mickey screaming, then back to Janice yelling, back and forth, back and forth.

"Okay, okay, ten," shouted Mickey." But you have to go now. And I mean, right now."

"Hey, baby, I'm all packed," Janice said. She jumped off the bed and held her wrists together. "Here, tape me up."

Mickey opened the door just far enough to roll the duct tape in Dell's direction. As soon as Dell taped her wrists, she spun halfway around.

"Just be careful when you go over the eyes, watch my eyebrows, Okay? And let me take these out," she said, deftly removing her dangling earrings and sliding them into her pocket.

"Okay, lead me out," she said. She raised her voice a notch, "I hope you cleaned that car since the last time I was in it. I can still smell the mold or whatever it was, phew."

Dell looked at the door, not sure what to do. Mickey opened it and silently waved them forward, gently taking Janice by the arm and helping her out of the room.

"So long, kidnap hotel, it's been real," she said.

They had been driving for almost an hour, Mickey taking the beltway all around the metro area, going almost full circle.

"You know," Janice said from the floor of the back seat," it would probably be best if you dropped me off in the alley, behind my place. It's pretty secluded, no traffic to speak of, and by the time I get this tape off my eyes, you'll be around the corner and gone. Not that I'd tell anyone about you, after our deal, I mean. Oh, and you ever do this again, you better get your car cleaned. I could ID you from the smell in this thing. It's like a gym locker at the end of the year."

Mickey drove twice around her block, then followed her earlier directions and cruised slowly down the alley. She'd been right, it was dark, and if he left her alongside the back of her garage, he could be around the corner and away in seconds.

He helped her up and out of the back seat, then slipped a thick envelope into her hands as she stood almost against the garage.

"Here's our side of the bargain, now you keep yours, count slow, to sixty so you don't risk seeing us, and we'll never, ever bother you again. I promise."

Janice counted to sixty, twice, before carefully pulling off the tape from her eyes. She used her teeth to unwrap the tape from around her wrists.

"Hi, Jan," a neighbor called, biking past her, oblivious to her taped wrists.

"Hi, Stevie," she called back, clutching the envelope with ten thousand dollars as she strolled into her back yard.

Five

A couple of weeks later. Mickey and Dell were in the War Bonnet Lounge. Cookie had just delivered another round of drinks. Once she left, Mickey opened the bag at his feet. "Okay, so I got you a little something," he said and pulled out a rubber mask.

"A dog mask?" Dell said.

"Not just any dog mask, it's a German Shepard mask," Mickey said.

"So, what's up with that?"

"Because we're on again. I've got this one really scoped out. It's a sure thing like before, only a lot less hassle."

"I didn't even know you were looking," Dell said.

"I didn't want you to know because I wanted to protect you. Anyway, you got the room ready, right?"

"Yeah, we went over all this last week. It looks completely different, new floor, fresh paint, no window."

"Just double-checking. I got a very likely suspect," he said, then lowered his voice and moved in closer to Dell. "I'm figuring it will happen in the next couple of weeks. I've got a plan figured out, just a few of the finer points left to finesse."

"What's the plan?"

"Un-uh," Mickey shook his head and waved his finger. "I'll let you in on it when the time comes. Right now, I'm just giving you a heads up."

Early the next morning, Mickey had everything cleaned, dusted, and scrubbed as well as it was going to be, and he wanted to be out of the office no later than three a.m., just forty-five minutes away. It had been a fluke when he came across Coach Buddy Belsmer's name on a note taped to manager Carol's desk.

At first, he had just been nosey. After all, how many guys with the first name of Thurlow could there be in town? But it wasn't a big leap from nosey to downright curious. It seemed the old high school coach turned out to be worth quite a bit, what with a home that had been paid off for years, his teacher's pension, and a huge stock portfolio.

"Coach Buddy is worth a couple of million? Who would have guessed?"

He recounted the zeros in the bottom-line figure, leaned back in Carol's office chair, put his hands behind his head, and thought some more. This could be a blow struck for generations of kids the coach had terrorized. Besides, how tough could it be to grab his old wife?

Mickey spent the next week following Candice Belsmer, which turned out to be another surprise. Apparently, the coach had remarried somewhere along the way because this woman was not the old battle-axe Mickey remembered chaperoning high school homecomings and proms, admonishing young girls not to trust young boys. This woman was younger than Mickey, which made her a hell of a lot younger than Coach Buddy.

He spent a good deal of time watching her and learned she was nothing if not dull. The wildest she seemed to get was attending daily morning mass and hanging around the cathedral praying for a few minutes after services. From there, she made the rounds at a variety of health food stores, where she did most of her grocery shopping. She volunteered at the elementary school Tuesday and Thursday, did Red Cross work every Wednesday, and served lunch at a homeless shelter on Friday. Monday seemed to be spent on housework. Mickey found her to be a moral, decent, no-nonsense, good Christian woman, four things he couldn't abide in a woman.

Over the course of his surveillance, he contrived a plan to grab her after morning mass at the cathedral. The following morning he parked next to her car in the nearly empty lot and waited until she came out of the church. He had dressed as a priest for the occasion and stood in the parking lot with the hood raised on the El Dorado, feigning car trouble. He glanced down and reminded himself not to wear brown, python skin cowboy boots the next time he dressed to look like a priest.

He was working out the details of how he would get her into his car without creating a scene. He had already torn appropriate lengths of duct tape and stuck them to the rear of his driver's seat, and placed an olive drab canister of pepper spray on the floor. He had to get her in the car somehow and hoped she wouldn't fight, scream, throw up, or try to run away.

He was deep in thought, wondering exactly how he was going to accomplish everything, wishing he had maybe planned these final details a little better before arriving when he heard the bells chiming and looked up to see she was suddenly no more than twenty feet away, walking directly toward him.

"Have a problem, Father? Can I help?" There was a soft southern accent to her sexy sounding voice.

"Yes, my child, it seems to be just a momentary difficulty. I wonder?" he asked, folding his hands as if in prayer." Could I ask you to try and turn the engine over, see if it starts while I make an adjustment here?"

"Sure, happy to help."

He opened the driver's door for her, catching just the slightest hint of perfume as she slid past and into the driver's seat.

"Let me just get a tool from the back seat. Let's see, ahh yes, here we go," he said, as he suddenly tore two strips of tape from the seat and grabbed the canister of spray. In the next few seconds, he sprayed her in the face and quickly wrapped a length of tape around her wrist and arm.

"Father, what the hell . . ." was all she got out before the spray hit her. She was immediately blinded, not to mention more than a little stunned, unaware at least for the moment that her wrists had been constrained.

It was all the time Mickey needed. As she assaulted her eyes with the sleeve of her blouse, he grabbed her by the lapels, hoisted her over his shoulder, and unceremoniously dumped her into the back seat.

She coughed and sputtered as she landed on the floor of his car.

"Just stay there and don't move," he said.

He quickly slammed the hood closed, slid behind the steering wheel, and drove off across the empty parking lot. He knew he couldn't drive all the way out to Dell's like this. He had to get control of this before she sat up, looked at him, jumped out the door, or signaled a cop. He took a side street off the freeway and drove west on a road that led to a park and a lake.

"If you'll just sit tight and be quiet, I'll get some water to wash those eyes. You took a pretty heavy dose back there. You'll be all right. It will wear off. Probably be best if you stopped rubbing those eyes. Listen, I don't want to hurt you or harm you in any way. You won't be touched, okay? Do you understand, you—"

Out of the corner of his eye, he saw her hands for just a brief moment on the back of the seat as she attempted to sit up.

"If you do that again, I'm going to really spray you with that stuff, lady. I just can't have you sitting up, lay back down, now," he shouted.

"Much better," he said as she settled back on the floor. "Just a few minutes, and we'll have some water for those eyes."

The lake area in the park was completely deserted at this early hour, and Mickey pulled in next to the cinder block public restroom.

"I'm going to get some water out of the trunk for those eyes. It will stop the stinging. Please, lay still for just a moment." He waited for half a beat, made some noise in the rear of his car, watched her for a second, then ran into the restroom and quickly filled up two empty beer bottles.

"All right, now hold still, careful. I'm going to pour this water over your face. Keep those eyes closed, just relax, you'll be okay. Just keep those eyes closed."

As he poured, the water began to ease the burning and stinging in Candice's eyes. She'd dealt with more than her share of creeps while dancing out in Vegas, and she half-wondered if this jerk was someone who possibly recognized her from the old days. Just now, she needed her eyes working, and the water, gently washing over them, seemed to be doing the trick.

"There, that seems to be a little better," Mickey said. "Please, keep those eyes closed, ma'am. Just let the water wash that spray away."

He slowly set the empty beer bottle down, picked up the roll of tape, and grabbed her wrists. He wrapped the tape around them and began to feel a little better.

She opened her eyes ever so slightly, saw his blurry figure, and took her chance, kicking both feet up as hard as she could, catching him solidly, right between his legs.

Mickey went blank for a moment or two. He gasped, forced himself to keep his stomach down, and fought to regain control. "Oh God, that really hurt. What'd I do to you?" he shouted at the bound figure on the floor of his car. He stumbled to the trunk of the El Dorado, opened it, yanked out the spare tire, and tossed it into the back seat on top of her. "There," he gasped, slamming the rear door." You can just lay there, and if I hear so much as the beginning of a noise, I'm going to empty that spray can on you."

He was only half paying attention to the route he took to Dell's. He kept his head slightly turned to the right, his ear cocked for the slightest hint of noise from the floor of his back seat. The canister of spray remained next to him, and at the ready should he hear the slightest hint of movement.

It seemed to take forever to get to Dell's. Due in no small part to the stress of driving while expecting her to crawl out from under the spare tire and either strangle him or jump from the speeding car.

He roared up the long driveway to Dell's house, pressed the button to open the garage door, then sped into the garage before jerking to a stop and knocking over a stack of paint cans onto the hood of his car.

Three identical gallon cans rolled across the hood of his car before falling to the floor, each revealing a fresh, two-inch crease where they had landed on the hood. He hopped out of the car, opened the back door, and stared at the pair of legs protruding from beneath his spare tire.

"Keep your eyes closed. I'm going to put this wool cap over your head, for your own protection. If you so much as think about kicking me or trying anything funny, I swear I'll hose you down with that spray and then let the dogs go after you. We'll let you get cleaned up. One of the other guys is getting in touch with coach, err, your husband. With any luck, you'll be back home in no time."

He pulled the spare tire off her, snugged the wool cap further over her face, then cautiously led her to the bedroom. He spoke, attempting to give the illusion they weren't alone.

"Clean out that car, fellas. You two, go down the road and keep watch. You guys get some breakfast cooked up, will ya'? And you, check the scanner, see if you can pick up anything."

Once they were in the bedroom, he said, "Keep that cap on until you hear the door close. There's a bathroom you can use to get cleaned up. I'll be out of here in a moment, so you can have some privacy." He loosened the tape on her wrists and quickly left, closing the door loudly.

He studied the fresh creases on the hood of the El Dorado then put his eye to the peephole. Her clothes were piled on the floor, and the towel was missing from the bed. It was on the way back to his car that he noticed a large pool of paint on the floor, splashed halfway up his front tire and two sets of footprints.

When Dell walked into the basement carrying a paper grocery bag by the handles, he was whistling an old rock and roll tune slightly off-pitch. He had just gotten to the chorus and was about to sing. He stopped and looked at Mickey on his hands and knees with a putty knife attacking what looked like footprints trailing across the basement floor.

"Mick, what the hell are you doing? Those look like footprints, you're . . ." Mickey's glance, his beet-red face and two sets of footprints suggested a new line of thinking for Dell.

"Oh man, don't tell me you went and grabbed another one?" He jumped over Mickey, still down on all
fours, raced to the door, and put his eye up against the
peephole. "Damn it, Mick. Why didn't you tell me?" he
said, staring at a blonde woman wrapped in a white terry
cloth robe, sitting on the bed.

Hearing the muffled voice, Candice glanced at the
door for a few seconds before getting off the bed. She
calmly walked over to the door.

Dell watched as she approached, struck by the way
she carried herself. She seemed to move like . . . BANG!

Dell's head visibly bounced off the door as she
struck it, and he let his bag of groceries fall onto the floor.

"Man, Mick, who is that woman?"

"Do you even have the slightest idea what it is I'm
doing down here?" Mickey asked, sitting back on his
haunches and ignoring the question. "Have you seen the
hood of my car? Have you seen the side of my car? Or
are you so used to these piles of junk you have all around
here that you're oblivious to the disaster?"

"What the hell are you talking about?" Dell said,
picking up his grocery bag. "What's with the hood of
your car?"

"Three new dents in it caused by your careless place-
ment of paint cans that fell onto the hood, spilled paint
all over the car, and now I'm cleaning up this mess," he

said, gesturing toward the paint trail. "Look at all this white paint. It's all over my car, the floor, it's—"

"It's Waterbury cream," replied Dell

"Huh?"

"The paint, it isn't white. It's Waterbury cream, the color."

"I don't care what the hell color it is, Dell. I do care that it's all over everything. And, you had better start paying attention to what's going on," he nodded toward the closed door. "Or we'll find ourselves looking at one another through a window with bars."

"Look, Mick, I come home, I find you here, in my house, paint all over the place, and a—"

"Shhh-shhh, keep your voice down, for Christ's sake!"

"Okay, okay. I'm just saying it would have been nice to get a heads up from you, so I knew what was happening in my own house. Now, who is that hot number?"

"What would you say if I told you it was Coach Buddy's wife. Would you feel like spanking her with one of those yellow wiffle ball bats he used to hit us with?"

"Coach Buddy? He's still alive? His wife? You sure it's not his granddaughter? I thought his wife was some old prune. That can't be his wife. Can it?"

"Well, the old prune is out of the picture, and the old coach has been running his plays up the middle of that,"

Mickey nodded toward the door again. "Hey, I'm starving. What'd you get us for dinner?"

"Nothing. Well, this isn't for you. I've got a friend coming out here. In fact, she'll be here in just a min—"

"A friend, are you nuts? You've got someone coming out here with all of this going on? What are you thinking?"

"I'm not a mind reader. I didn't know you were going to be here. I mean, the first I know about this, you've got paint all over everything, and damn Coach Buddy's wife locked in the room. How'd he end up with her?"

"How 'bout four million reasons. That's what he's got in the bank. And, if I can keep you from screwing things up in the next day or two, we'll get our share. Score something not only for us but for every other kid that deranged psycho terrorized at Kefauver High over the course of the last hundred years. Now, will you—" the doorbell ringing cut Mickey off.

"What was that?" Mickey said.

"The doorbell, it's—"

"Don't answer it," Mickey whispered.

"Mick, my car is out front. She knows I'm here. She said she'd be here ten minutes after I left."

"Who is it?"

"Cookie."

"Cookie? Are you crazy? Cookie. You didn't learn your lesson the last time you two went out? She was driving you nuts, Dell."

"No, Mick, she was driving you nuts. Me, I kind of liked it, so you just stay down here, quiet and out of sight. I've got an evening of activity to attend to," Dell said and hurried up the stairs as the doorbell rang again.

"What about me and the coach's wife? What are we going to do for dinner?"

"I'll bring you a pizza, but stay quiet down there. I'll get you fed. Just keep cleaning up that paint you tracked all over the floor." Dell said and closed the basement door behind him.

"Don't tell her we're down here, damn it," Mickey hissed in the direction of the closed door.

Six

From up on the first floor, Mickey heard Dell opening the front door." Well, look who's here, and aren't you a sight for sore eyes. Mmm-mmm, and that lovely perfume. Here, let me take that for you. You are so sweet. You didn't have to do this, Cookie."

Mickey's eyes followed the sound of feet walking across the floor above him.

"Let's open the first bottle right now, come on outside, Baby. I'll get the grill warmed up and jump in the shower. You just sit there looking great, relax, and sip a glass of wine for a couple of minutes."

Mickey could hear the tone of Cookie's voice, but he couldn't make out what she was saying.

"You sure don't waste time," Dell called, apparently back somewhere in the kitchen, probably opening the wine. "You just sip a glass of this, sit there, and enjoy the sunset while I get cleaned up. I promise I'll be right back.

Just give me five minutes, then we've got the rest of the night to ourselves."

The rest of the night, thought Mickey. He traced the copper water pipes across the basement ceiling to the point where they rose up and into the bathroom. He listened to Dell's footsteps heading into the bathroom above, heard the toilet flush a minute later, and then footsteps in the shower.

He waited a minute, then reached up to the shut-off valve on the hot water line and closed it. It took maybe five seconds before he heard Dell jumping.

"Whoa, Jesus, that's cold, what the . . . Mick, you son of a bitch. Mickey, do you hear me? Turn that hot water back on, or so help me, God."

Mickey turned the hot water back on, then waited another twenty seconds before turning it back off.

"Arghh. Mick, damn it, I'm warning you."

Suddenly there were footsteps walking across the kitchen floor, "Are you all right, Dell, is everything okay?" Cookie called.

Mickey quickly opened the hot water line again, then stood still, heart pounding.

"Dell, honey?" she asked, knocking on the bathroom door.

"Yeah, sorry, just singing in the shower. I'm out in a minute, Cookie."

It was about an hour later when Dell quickly ran into the basement with two large pizzas on plates. "Here, take these. I've got to get back outside before she misses me."

"This?" Mickey said, looking at the plates." We're supposed to eat a three dollar, paper-thin pizza while you're up there drinking? What are you guys having?"

"Steak, Mick, and that's not the point," Dell said and ran back up the steps.

"Not the point," Mickey exclaimed in barely a whisper, but Dell was already at the top of the stairs closing and then locking the door behind him.

It wasn't the first time they woke him up. Mickey was lying on the basement floor, on top of a sleeping bag that reeked of insecticide. He stared up at the ceiling and listened as Dell and Cookie wrestled in the middle of the night.

"Oh god, oh god, oh my god," Cookie kept yelling.

Thirty minutes later, Dell was barking like a dog. Cookie was barking back. Mickey tried to wrap the seat cushion he'd been using as a pillow around his head.

Sometime after that, he woke, thinking he heard the front door closing. He listened as a single set of heavy feet walked across the kitchen floor. He waited, following the sound of footsteps into the bathroom. The toilet flushed, and then he followed the footsteps as they traveled back into the kitchen. Cautiously he tiptoed up the staircase, peered through the keyhole to see Dell, in his boxer shorts, waiting in front of the coffee pot. He carefully knocked on the basement door a crack and softly called, "Is she gone?"

A moment later the lock clicked and Dell opened the basement door."Jesus, Mickey. Yeah, she's gone. Just left, doesn't like to wake up anywhere except her own bedroom."

"Wake up? From what I could hear, you two never went to sleep. I certainly couldn't. Thanks, I'll take a cup," he said, opening a cabinet door, grabbing a mug, and thrusting it at Dell.

"Tell me you got a plan with the coach's friend down there," Dell said. "You sure she's really his wife?"

"Not only do I have a plan, but we'll be putting that plan into action in just a few hours," Mickey replied. "Let him sweat out a night without her. He won't call the cops. He probably won't even miss her until he realizes no one's there to put his breakfast on the table. I acquired a cellphone," Mickey said with one of his all-knowing nods." We'll have her do the one-minute call later this morning."

"Mick, I can't help you. I got to get to work in a couple of hours, I—"

"Work?" Mickey stared at Dell with a look of utter disbelief. "I'm putting together a hundred thousand dollar deal for us, and you're traipsing off to an hourly wage job at exactly the time I need you? Oh, that's great, that's just beautiful, Dell. You keep me up all night riding Cookie around your bedroom, and now, when it's time to do some heavy lifting, it's up to me to get the job done. Beautiful, absolutely beautiful."

"Now, just hold on a minute, Mick. Weren't you the one who said not to alter our routine? Forget that I had absolutely no notice about any of this. Forget I came home from work only to find you have, once again, put me in the running for public enemy number one. Forget you're using my house. Forget you're eating my food. Forget you're drinking my coffee," Dell tried to snatch the coffee mug out of Mickey's hand but only managed to spill hot coffee over Mickey's hand.

"Ouch, damn it! Now look what you've done," said Mickey, shaking his hand. "All right, relax. I'll take care of everything, as per always. Sometimes I wonder why I even bother?"

Thurlow, 'Coach Buddy 'Belsmer glanced up at the clock on his fireplace mantel. He'd fallen asleep waiting for his wife to come home. It wasn't the first time he had done that, and he was going to confront her once she finally arrived. Just now, he was attempting to screw up the courage.

He rued the day he met her twelve years ago on his first and only trip to Las Vegas. He'd wanted to see the town. Just see it, not even partake in the evils of gambling, but just see the lights, maybe catch a big-name show.

He was celebrating the insurance check he had received from his first wife's passing, the victim of an untimely fall while carrying her laundry basket and receiving a gentle nudge from the coach as she stood at the very top of the basement stairs. She had done three perfect somersaults on the way down, and although she didn't move once she landed at the bottom, he hadn't been sure. So, he grabbed his jacket and spent the better part of the day running errands and making damn sure he was seen out and about by a number of different people. She was deader than the proverbial doornail by the time he returned home.

After mourning an appropriate length of time, he purchased an offseason, ninety dollar round trip fare including two nights lodging at the Red Roof Inn, packed a bag, and flew west to see the sights of Las Vegas.

He'd never been one to place much stock in alcohol and so, when he had the good fortune to strike up a conversation with what he could only assume was a fresh young college girl working her way through school, he followed her suggestion and ordered a Long Island Iced Tea. It was July, 116 degrees in the Vegas shade and, although the coach had a short sleeve shirt on, his tie was killing him. The Long Island Iced Tea was nothing if not refreshing, and he settled in comfortably with the innocent girl he had just met.

He ordered or, more accurately, he drank, and she ordered, at least six of the tasty teas, three that he remembered. Somewhere along the way, he knew he could trust her, and he confessed the dark secret of pushing his wife down the stairs, leaving her on the cold concrete basement floor for the better part of the day. He also mentioned receiving the insurance check for one point one million dollars.

For her part, Candy Dumbrowski, working that night as Candy Kane, knew a good thing when she saw it. With the help of a thousand-dollar cash incentive and a quick, final sample of her many talents, she rounded up a sometime client and full-time Justice of the Peace in the state of Nevada to pronounce her Mrs. Thurlow Belsmer, all legal and dated based on the paperwork she thrust in Coach Buddy's face the following morning.

Coach Buddy woke up in a lavender and pink honeymoon suite with a splitting headache, a wedding ring, and his new wife watching their honeymoon video, which included, among other things, his soul barring confession to murder. Candy cuddled up next to him and sweetly suggested that if he had any thoughts of changing the arrangement, she would take all his money and make sure he spent the rest of his life behind bars.

He had to give her one thing, the new Mrs. Belsmer. She had a knack for numbers and one heck of an intuition. Over the course of the next ten years, she parlayed the ill-gotten insurance money from a sizable nest egg to a small fortune. Coach Buddy and his bride were now worth upwards of five million dollars and growing at an amazing twenty-two percent annual rate.

But how much money did one retired coach really need? Last night wasn't the first time she had been gone for the better part of the night. It happened, occasionally, that her alley cat side seemed to get the better of her. Every time it did, Coach Buddy got his hopes up that some disaster had befallen his bride; a car accident, a collapsing building, perhaps she'd been struck by a meteor, only to have those very same hopes dashed when she arrived home at four or five the following morning.

This time it was a little different. It was after eight, and the Coach, pushing his breakfast around the plate, watched as the minutes slowly crawled past on the kitchen clock. His odds improved ever so slightly with every sweep of the second hand. He stared patiently, hoping this potentially glorious day wouldn't suddenly be dashed with her appearance at the back door. He dared not think beyond that, lest he jinx the whole deal, and she

suddenly flew in on her broomstick with marching or-
ders. And so, he sat, waiting patiently and hoping.

Dell had been true to his word and left for work
shortly before seven. Mickey rummaged and searched
through his car three times and couldn't find a trace of
the German shepherd mask he'd purchased. He had a
vague recollection of giving it to Dell. But where had
Dell put it?

He replayed the memory. Dell getting two more
beers out of the refrigerator and placing the bag with the
mask on top of the refrigerator. He hurried up the stairs.
The bag sat on top of the refrigerator, unfortunately,
empty.

He suddenly remembered one of the times Dell and
Cookie woke him, barking like dogs. He walked down
the hall to Dell's bedroom, there in the corner, beneath a
black thong, lay the mask. Time to come up with a different plan.

He had a pair of pantyhose in his car. He had vaguely
planned to wear them to hide his face when he was going
to grab her yesterday, but then realized that posing as a
priest and wearing pantyhose on his head might detract
from the believability of the situation.

It was nine-thirty, and he was already a little behind
schedule. He had typed up instructions and a short script
for her to read. He politely knocked on the door, waited
a moment, then strode purposefully toward her the the
hose over his head. He held a cell phone and the typed

instructions, which he thrust toward her as she lay on the bed.

Oh God, Candy thought, watching him come through the door. "Hey, pal, next time, cut one of the legs off before you put that on your fat head. If you want me to take you seriously, you better stop acting like an absolute moron. By the way, breakfast was barely okay. The eggs were a little too runny. I could do with some orange juice next time, and was that sawdust I detected in that sausage or just gristle? The coffee could be a bit hotter. You might try warming the mug first. I like to—"

"Shhh-hhh," Mickey signaled, finger to his lips. He handed the instruction sheet to her. He wasn't going to speak, hoping she would gradually forget what his voice sounded like yesterday.

"What's this?" she asked, holding the piece of paper at arm's length. "Get my glasses. They're in my handbag," she commanded, and nodded in the direction of her purse on the floor, making no effort to move off the bed.

He quickly did as he was told and handed her the bag.

Once she had her glasses on, she quickly read the directions he had given her, then she read the brief script and his warning to not stray from his prepared text. "Yeah, fine, let's get this over with," she said.

He punched the call button, waited until he heard the phone ring, then handed the cellphone to her.

Coach Buddy jumped from his kitchen chair at the sound of the first ring. He debated letting it record a message instead of answering. He finally answered after a number of rings, and his heart sank the moment he heard his wife's voice.

"I have been kidnapped," she read woodenly. "Do not contact the police. You will be given instructions later today."

Coach Buddy didn't say anything. He stood in his kitchen, exhaling through his nose, thinking slowly, gradually coming to a realization. *Kidnapped? He could live with that.* "Okay," he said and hung up.

Candy sat still for a moment feeling her face flush with anger before clicking the phone off and muttering, "Bastard," just loud enough so Mickey could hear.

Mickey took the phone, gave her a thumbs up, and backed toward the door, not sure why she was so upset.

Coach Buddy ran through a kidnapping playbook in his mind. The kidnappers would contact him, demand money, and if he refused to pay, they would kill his wife. It sounded a lot easier than pushing her down the basement steps while she carried a laundry basket. The first thing he had to do was create a series of alibis, make sure folks didn't think he had concocted this bit of good fortune.

He thought about contacting the police but decided to wait until there was a body. Best to just stay away from the whole thing and hope for the best. Maybe there was a game tonight at the high school. He could show up and make sure he was seen. He whistled as he left his house, nodded to a woman picking up fresh dog poop with a plastic bag over her hand." Morning, lovely day."

What's that old fart up to? she wondered.

Candy was still steaming, pacing back and forth in the small room, arms folded across her chest, fists clenched, talking to herself. "That old bastard. Okay? I'll give him okay. He had better get me out of this dreadful place and fast, or I'll tell anyone who'll listen that he killed his first wife. So help me, God. Even if I have to go back to Vegas and dance again. I'll do it, I don't care. Okay? I can't believe he said that. We'll just see how smart he is when I tell him the whole story is on the tip of my tongue, and I'd just love to sit down and tell the cops everything. Okay, my sweet ass!"

Seven

It was just past three in the afternoon. Mickey was back from the main post office where he had mailed payoff instructions to Coach Buddy three hours earlier. The instructions, minus any of Mickey's fingerprints, would arrive with tomorrow's mail and be one hundred percent absolutely untraceable.

He figured they could get the ball rolling today, have the bastard get the money, or at least start the process. Another day or two with this crazy woman storming around downstairs and who knew what would happen. He'd become pretty much of an expert when it came to pissed off women, and he was positive he had one on his hands now.

He stood in front of her with the pantyhose pulled over his face, thinking it would be a good idea to let Coach Buddy hear her voice for a moment, so he didn't panic and call the cops.

"There's still no damned answer," she said, thrusting the cellphone back to Mickey. "It just rolls into the stupid message center, like it did the last time and the time before that."

This wasn't making sense, and Mickey absently scratched the breathable cotton panel on the back of his head. Why wouldn't he be there to take the call? They told him to stay there and wait for the damn call.

"He's written me off. I know him," she said, shaking her head." The bastard has written me off. He probably hopes you're going to kill me, and save him the trouble. He's got me insured and, wait a minute." She glared at Mickey, thrust a finger toward him, backing him up one step at a time while she fired questions.

"You didn't plan this with him, did you? Is this all a plan, just to scare me off? Are you supposed to kill me, is that it? He'll just play stupid, not at all hard for him, and then my body is found, and he gets another insurance check. Is that it?" She backed him across the room until he bumped against the wall, with nowhere else to go.

"No, honest, I don't even like the guy," Mickey stammered. "I've hated him ever since I was a kid. I just, I mean we just, all of us, decided that it was payback time. Figured he'd never miss a hundred grand, not with all the money he has."

"A hundred grand," she shrieked. "That's it? That's all I'm worth? This is about a lousy hundred grand, and now you can't even get that from him? Get it from him? What the hell am I talking about? He won't even take the damn call. I've made that bastard millions, literally millions of dollars. He's just been along for the ride, the old fool. He'd never be worth a nickel if I hadn't diversified and invested for him, and now, he won't even take a damn phone call from me?" She walked dejectedly back to the bed, sat on the edge, arms folded, and quietly stared at the floor.

Mickey stepped away from the wall and stood in front of her." Look at it this way. He'll get the instructions I mailed last night. He can't ignore those," he said, sounding as if he was trying to convince both of them.

"And if he does?" she kept staring at her feet. "What if he does ignore them? Doesn't do a damn thing but hope that you carry out whatever threats you made. Are you supposed to send a piece of me to show him you mean business, carve off a toe, a finger, or maybe an ear? Then what, bury me in a hole with a limited amount of oxygen, and tell him he's got twelve hours to deliver? He'll sit in front of his damn TV, watching a game with two teams no one has ever heard of before, and just wait you out. Nice work. Looks like you really drew a losing hand on this one, dumb shit." A lone tear suddenly ran down her cheek.

"Sorry," she sniffled and shuffled into the bathroom. She pulled some toilet paper from the roll and then loudly blew her nose.

Mickey stood there wondering what he should do. "Do you think he'll go to the police?"

"The police?" she called from the bathroom, genuinely surprised at the question. "You gotta be kidding. No, he won't go to the police. He won't go there for two reasons. Like I said before, the best thing you could do for him would be to get me out of his life. The worst thing he could do to himself would be to get the cops involved. He doesn't want them to take another look at his first wife's death. He got away with that one."

"You ever meet her, his first wife?" Mickey asked as Candy reappeared.

"No," she shook her head." I told you, I met him in Vegas. He was out there with a sign on his forehead that said rich, stupid tourist, one-way ticket out of this town, and I took it. So, no, I never met the woman. He's got a picture of her in the front hallway. I know her name was Esther and she wasn't much fun. He never mentions her. In fact, other than the photo on the wall, there isn't anything of hers around, not one thing."

"I remember her," Mickey said. "She was one of those old-time religion types, you know, someone, somewhere might be having a good time, and if she could just find out where, she could put a stop to it. They used to chaperone the dances when we were kids, the two of them. You didn't play on one of his teams, you weren't worth shit. And, if you did play on the team, unless you were the star, he made your life miserable. You know," he said, suddenly sitting down next to her on the bed," in close to fifty years, however long he made life miserable for kids up at Kefauver High, he never had a winning season. Honest. He's in the state record books as being the worst high school coach in the whole damn state."

"He had this yellow wiffle ball bat," Mickey shifted and faced her. "You remember, those bright yellow ones, hard plastic, he even put black friction tape on the grips. Christ, he'd hit you across the ass going in or coming out of the shower. It makes a very distinctive smacking sound. And he always had that damn whistle around his neck, all the while yelling, 'move it, move it, move it.' He was a bully, picked on kids, and with that plate in his head, Christ, you were afraid he was gonna kill you."

"Well, news bulletin to you and all the other kids who thought he was a war hero," she said, half laughing. "He doesn't have a plate in his head. I've heard some of the stories. He was never in the service except for maybe twenty days before he got out on a medical discharge.

Never really did much with his life except terrorize children and push his wife down the basement steps for the insurance money."

"He met and married you."

"Yeah, he met and married me," she repeated half to herself, saying it like there was a lot more to the story but not offering up any other information.

"Sorry for the other morning," Mickey suddenly blurted out." I mean the pepper spray and all. I hope I didn't frighten you, and sorry you got sick."

"Yeah, well, let's just move on from that. Sorry about the kick to your sweet spot, but it seemed like the thing to do at the time."

He winced slightly at the memory.

"You mind if I ask how you plan to work this? Is he supposed to move this money into a numbered account for you? Or into some offshore corporation you've set up?"

"No, he gets it, we make sure he isn't followed, and he gives us cash. He doesn't hand it directly to us. We'll have him leave it somewhere. That's why we decided on a modest amount. One that could be obtained without the need for any authorities to get involved. It's not your typical million-dollar deal, but it was the desire of all of us involved—"

"You don't know what the hell you're doing, do you?"

"Well, now just a minute. We—"

"Yeah, I thought so from that first moment in your car. I knew I'd been kidnapped by a moron, no offense, but it figures. You have no idea what in the hell you're doing, and this old fool has just thrown you a curve," she said, biting her lower lip, and clearly thinking. "Give me that phone again."

He hesitated for a moment. She reached over, grabbed it from him, punched in a number, put the phone to her ear, and waited. He made a halfhearted attempt to reach for the phone, but she pushed his hand away and turned her back toward him.

"Yes, yes, this is Candice Belsmer. Could you connect me with Mr. Preston's office. Yes, thank you. Just wait," she said, turning to Mickey." I think I've got a way out of this for all of us, just— Yes, Bentley Preston, please. I see, well, this is rather urgent, this is Candice Belsmer, would you mind interrupting him and asking him to take my call. Yes, thank you. Meeting," she whispered." The guy's probably practicing hitting damn golf balls in his office with the door closed, these guys never . . . Bentley. Thanks for taking my call, so sorry to interrupt. Listen, I wanted to make a transfer before close tomorrow, the Grand Cayman account. You can check your records, but I believe the last time we did this was back in February. No, I'll be in tomorrow at say, eleven o'clock." She looked over at Mickey and nodded.

He wasn't sure how to respond.

"Yes, perfect. Oh, yes, I suppose you would need that, let's make it two million, even. Yes, wonderful, looking forward to seeing you tomorrow at eleven to sign that paperwork. Thank you, Bentley. " She pushed the end button and handed the phone back to Mickey.

She got off the bed, walked into the bathroom, and stood in front of the mirror. "I'm going to need you to take me home tomorrow morning before the meeting at the bank. I'll want to pack a few things, get some clean clothes for my flight."

"Did you just tell that guy two million dollars? What the hell just happened here?"

"Let's be honest. This whole thing has gotten away from you. You could be asking for a hundred bucks, and you still wouldn't get it from Buddy. He doesn't want me back unless it's in cube sized chunks from a butcher shop. The answer to his dream would be that you carry out whatever threat you made."

"I can tell you right now what he's doing. He's out running into people all over town, so they see him, making purchases, all under ten dollars, by the way, the cheapskate. So he can demonstrate if ever asked, that he had nothing to do with this kidnapping. Then, hoping I'll show up dead, he can sit all day in front of ESPN, eating

Cocoa Puffs and watching one mindless game after another. The only reason I'm even alive is that I made a recording the night of our wedding."

"Isn't he worried about that recording getting out there?"

"He might be, but to tell the truth, I'm more than a little tired playing the model wife. Big deal, I get out of town once every three months, kick up my heels and raise a little hell. I've been working on getting out for a while. It's a little sooner than I planned, but the more I think about it, this will work just fine. I've got the accounts set up, a condo, credit cards. I'm not taking everything from him, just half. Hell, by rights, I could leave him with the original insurance amount. After all, I'm the one who made all that dough for him, but I'm not going to do that. I'll be nice and split it, fifty-fifty. Oh yeah, and I'll give you a finders fee, your hundred grand. What do you care where it comes from? Deal?" she said and stuck out her hand for Mickey to shake.

He tentatively shook her hand, not sure what he had just agreed to.

"Great, now will you please take those stupid pantyhose off your head? They're really bugging me."

Eight

Dell was rotating his shoulder as he walked past Mickey's car and into the basement. Another long day, and at the end of it, his body reminded him in no uncertain way about the aches and pains of sheetrocking for a living. He worried about the rotator cup and planned to spend some time icing it down that night.

Of course, then there was Mickey, and this Candy woman, not to mention Coach Buddy. He noticed the door to her room was open at about the same time he heard the laughter and music coming from upstairs. He hurried up the staircase, taking the steps two at a time.

"So, he says to me," it was Candy talking and laughing." Well, can I just watch then, and I'm thinking this guy can't be that stupid, can he?"

Mickey was laughing, leaning against the counter with a beer in his hand, and there, standing in front of the stove, wrapped in a white terrycloth bathrobe, sipping a glass of wine and stirring a large pot was their latest project.

"Here, Mickey, now taste this. See what I mean about slicing the garlic really thin. You get that subtle little flavor. Go ahead, try it." She held a large wooden spoon toward Mickey with an open hand underneath, ready to catch any potential drip.

"Mmm-mmm, hot," said Mickey, blowing on the spoon for a second before taking another taste.

"What in the hell are you doing?" Dell said.

"Oh, Dell, hey, you gotta try Candy's spaghetti sauce, here, it's to die for, man. Really good," Mickey said.

"Oh, where, are my manners? Candy, I mean Candice Belsmer, my lifelong friend and pal, Dell Dolan. Dell, meet Candy."

"Hi, Dell, it's a pleasure," Candy said.

Dell just stood staring, a blanker look than normal on his face. After a long silence, Candy turned back to her pot of spaghetti sauce.

"Can we talk?" Dell said and headed back down the basement stairs without waiting for Mickey's answer.

"What in the hell are you doing, man? Are you nuts? You let her see you? You told her your, no, make that our names? I mean, Mick, what the hell?"

"Relax, I've got it all taken care of. We're paid, in full. She's going to do it herself. She's gonna ditch the coach and start off fresh, on her own. You don't have a thing to worry about. So, just calm down."

"Calm down!" Dell half-shouted. "Calm down? I'm stupid enough to let you talk me into being a part of your hair brain scheme, and now you want me to calm down? Mickey, you don't kidnap someone and then cook spaghetti sauce with them once they offer to pay you."

He thrust a finger in Mickey's face. "And you sure as hell don't tell them your name or show your face, not to mention mine. I'm going to end up doing hard time on this one, and it serves me right. I'm going to spend the rest of my life behind bars because I was stupid enough to get mixed up with you and this latest stupid idea of yours. Mick, I'm going to lose everything here, my house, my job, the lake place. It's gone," he said and shook his head.

"Take a deep breath and calm down for a minute, Dell."

" No. It's all gone. Federal charges. Then that other woman will come out of the woodwork, Huey's kid. Oh, this is just great. Huey will be on us like ugly on an ape. Only a matter of time before they decide what facility they'll lock us up in and just throw away the damn key. Perfect, just perfect, not only will they lock me up, they'll lock me up with you. And you know what? It serves me right. It just absolutely serves me right."

"Are you about through? Now calm down and just relax. She's the brains behind all the money. I didn't realize it at first, but it all makes perfect sense. Why do you think we haven't heard a peep from Coach Buddy? Hell, we played right into his hand. He wants her to disappear. Yeah, Dell, we'd be doing him a favor, a real favor, and he's sitting on all the money in the world. This way, she gets to start over, she's going to Florida, but more importantly, we get paid. It all works out, man. So, will you just relax? Let me worry about the details here."

"How do you know she's not going to hand you the money and have you arrested at the same time, or the next day or the day after that? Mickey, you don't just call the whole plan off because some woman can cook spaghetti sauce and tells you she'll pay the money. What's she going to do, write you a personal check, and then you can cash the damn thing? She can write the word ransom on the memo line, you can endorse the check, and meanwhile, I'll pack a toothbrush and spend the next twenty-five years in federal prison."

"Are you through with all the negative talk? Because we're going to be a hundred grand richer starting tomorrow. That's right, a hundred grand. Now, look at me,

Dell. Just like before, things have worked out in our favor. Is it exactly the way we envisioned? No, but, you see, I'm flexible, I'm adjusting to the situation, adapting. I'm not going around in circles playing 'ain't it awful', like someone else I could mention. Now, come on upstairs. I don't want to leave her alone any longer than we have to. So, come on," Mickey said.

The kitchen was empty, and for a long moment, Dell stopped halfway up the staircase and looked through Mickey's legs. Mickey seemed to be glued to the spot in the doorway, franticly scanning the room, not seeing any trace of a woman in a white terrycloth robe.

"Ahh great, just great, you idiot! See, I told you this would happen," Dell said. He rushed past Mickey and over to the kitchen window, scanning the pasture land for any movement. "God, she's probably already flagged down a car and is gone. We're toast, Mickey, burnt toast."

"Oh, gee fellas, I mean could you stir it once or twice, so it doesn't burn. I had to use the bathroom while you had your little lovers spat downstairs. I hope this sauce is okay," she said, pulling her robe closed and bustling back to the stove.

"Dell, get a pan out and fill it with water. Mickey, you said you two had some pasta around here. I'll be ready for it in a few minutes. I like linguine, the number seven if you've got it."

"Come on, Dell, get the pan of water, will you. Dinner in twenty minutes," Mickey said.

"You have any Kosher salt? I always like to use Kosher salt when I cook, and Mickey," Candy said, "set the table."

* * *

"Okay," Candy said once they'd finished dinner and Dell cleared the dishes. They were sitting around the kitchen table beneath the red and white Budweiser lamp Dell had won at a Labor Day raffle a few years back. "Let's talk about how you want to get paid. I can transfer the funds to an account, Mickey. You can take it from there, hide the trail, or we could do the negotiable bonds. Obviously, that would take maybe an additional day or two. If you don't mind me saying, and this is not a complaint, but it's almost too small an amount. A hundred grand sounds kind of cheesy, fellas. I've got girlfriends that spend more than that on cosmetic surgery in any given year."

"I was thinking unmarked twenties," Mickey said.

"Twenties? As in cash, a hundred grand, cash? You're kidding me, right? Oh God, but, I can see you're not."

"Look fellas, I love you both, but aren't you worried about a couple of things like maybe dye packs, tracing, marked bills, cut up newspaper, to say nothing of the distinct possibility of an arrest? I mean, what you're doing is illegal, despite our working arrangement."

"We got those things covered," Mickey said.

"Yeah, covered. Coffee'll be finished in a minute," Dell said, handing out paper-wrapped ice cream cones as he sat down.

"Is this a drumstick?" Candy said. "I didn't know they even made these anymore. It's been years since I had one, thanks. Now, boys, you really should have some accounts where you can transfer this stuff back and forth so you won't get caught, move it outside the country. Things have gotten a little tighter since the great recession, but you can still do it, and the small amounts you're dealing with, no one has time to track that. "

"We're more into the cash thing. It just keeps it that much simpler," Mickey said.

"Okay, we'll do cash if that's what you really want. God, these are good, Dell. Pure, one hundred percent, artery-clogging fat, it doesn't get much better than that."

Mickey was waiting in a coffee shop across the street from the parking ramp. It wasn't that he didn't trust Candy, but bottom line, he didn't, at least not completely. Even though she'd done everything just as she promised, there was still that element of doubt. He watched through the streaked windows of the coffee shop, smelling hot griddles and heart-stopping grease. He waited and watched so that in the event squad cars sealed off all the parking ramp exits, he could alert Dell by phone. If all went well, they planned to meet at Dell's lake cabin tonight.

"Would you care to see a lunch menu, sir?" the waitress asked. Her earlier request had concerned the breakfast menu. She was a heavy-set woman, not what you might call fat, but solid, with forearms that looked like they could deliver a hard slap or a sharp pinch in a nanosecond. Her plastic name badge read Marliss. She traveled in a cloud of perfume that reminded Mickey of the scented, pink toilet paper his grandmother used to have in her home.

"No, thanks, maybe just a little warm-up," Mickey said.

She reflexively poured steaming coffee into the cup, trailing a bit over the saucer and across the table, marking her territory before she left.

It had been more than an hour, but suddenly Candy appeared, strutting down the street calmly wheeling a small black suitcase behind her. She headed for the parking ramp, where she expected to find him sitting in his car. As far as he could tell, she wasn't being followed. He threw two dollars on the table and left, calling to her from across the street as he exited from the diner.

"Candy, hey, Candy."

"Aren't we clever," Candy said as he hurried over to her." Here, you drag this thing. I was in the bank and remembered I didn't have anything to carry your cash in. I had to buy this thing for twenty bucks. And let me tell you, it raised a few eyebrows in old Bentley's office. He wanted to send a guard with me. Where's your car?"

"This way," Mickey said and grabbed the plastic handle, wheeling the bag behind him.

They headed out of the parking ramp and drove in silence for the better part of the way to the airport. Candy busied herself looking through her purse, seeming to run down a mental checklist.

If she's got a gun, she'll pull it here, he thought.

"You okay?" he finally asked.

"Yeah, I'm fine. It's funny. I've been in St. Paul for over a decade but never felt like I lived here, more like just visiting. I pulled that door closed behind me at the house and never thought about looking back. I'm only sad because I'm not sad. I guess that says it all. I always called the house 'the Coach's', like I never made it my home. It was a nice place, clean. I tried to make it warm for him. It just was never home for me and, well, now it's time for me."

Mickey had heard those words before, 'It's time for me.' He'd heard them from a number of different women in his life. But he'd never heard them said so softly, so gently, and he thought he knew exactly what she meant.

"You sure you're okay with all this?"

"Would it make a difference? It's not like we're running off together. You're just driving me to the airport after you held me against my will for three days and forced me to pay for my own release. Which, even crazier, I did. Yeah, I'm okay, just fine, peachy," she said and turned to stare out the window.

They drove the remaining ten minutes in silence, and it wasn't until he was turning off the interstate, into the airport proper, that he began to worry. The blinking sign reminded motorists and anyone else to call 911 in the event of any suspicious activity. He kept checking his rearview mirror, thinking if it was going to happen, it would be here at the airport. Candy would step out of the car, and the next thing you know, he would be surrounded by police with guns drawn.

"What airline?" he asked.

"Anywhere is fine," she replied, not answering his question. "I've got plenty of time."

He pulled over to the curb, had a slight panic attack as a female traffic officer stepped off the curb, nodded, and walked past them. He watched her in the side view mirror as she continued to walk away from him, an unpleasant coincidence, but nothing more.

"Thanks," Candy said and opened the rear door to grab her suitcase.

"Don't take the wrong one. All that cash could be tough going through the security check."

She paused for a brief moment, just enough to get his attention. "It's been real," she said, then flashed a quick smile and headed into the terminal.

He didn't wait, didn't really look, just absently pulled into traffic, suddenly jolted back to reality by the screech of tires and the horn blast from the car he'd cut off. He shook his head, regained his bearings, and headed north toward the lake country and Dell's cabin.

Mickey didn't remember much of the four-and-a-half-hour drive until he passed the Elk Lake Tavern with the 'Fall In. Crawl Out 'sign over the door. It was the three-mile marker for Dell's place. He took the next right off St. Louis County pavement and onto a gravel road. A couple of miles later, he turned onto a logging road marked by a rusted mailbox pole.

The rusted pole was a fair indication of the condition of the logging road. Downed branches and the summer's crop of weeds and small saplings brushed under the car as he slowly groped his way deeper into the woods. The smell of damp pine and rotting birch hung in the still, humid air. Even in the car, he could feel a spongy texture to the ground.

He rolled the window down. It was silent except for the three or four large bugs that were batting their heads against the inside of his windshield, making a cracking sound. At the frequent high spots, the El Dorado bottomed out, scraping against the trail, causing him to slow to a frustrating crawl, and he arrived at the same thought he had every time he was up here. *God, he hated this place.*

Dell's cabin came into view as Mickey climbed a slight rise. Spongy rot gave way to a granite slab that begged to tear his muffler system from the undercarriage.

Cabin was a generous term. It was actually a faded orange school bus, driven back and discarded by Dell for the purpose of being used as a hunting shack for one season while he built a cabin. That was twenty years ago, and with inflation, fuel prices, and just life, Dell had only managed to attach a rickety screened entrance to the front half of the thing.

Inside, rusted scars were all that remained of the seats, long ago removed and dragged down to the lakeshore. In their place were cream and red painted kitchen cabinets Dell had scrounged from a remodel job, complete with a sink that drained onto the ground through a hole in the floor. The windows had been sealed shut twenty years ago with some silicone material that now curled up, leaving great gaps along the edges. To the rear, the emergency exit door was still in place, more or less, but the glass in the door had been replaced by a screen shrouded with a black plastic sheet.

Fifty yards behind the bus was the lake. Not a swimming lake, the burnt stumps, dead trees, rotting logs, not to mention all the weeds and the poison ivy precluded that kind of activity. To the best of his knowledge, Mickey was unaware of anyone ever catching a fish from the lake, and the last deer shot here was six or seven years ago when Dell bagged a ten-point buck while standing naked in the screened entrance.

He parked next to Dell's van. As he climbed out he caught sight of Dell down by the lake sitting on one of the old bus seats. Despite the stillness and the humidity, Dell was wearing jeans and a long sleeve shirt, protection against the mosquitoes and black flies.

"Everything go okay? Beer is in the cooler on the porch." Dell said, walking toward the bus.

"Yeah, fine. She's headed off to wherever. I got our cut in the back seat. I'll get it," Mickey said, suddenly remembering he had never checked the suitcase to see if the money really was in there.

He carried the suitcase into the bus, hoping the screening would do something to filter at least a few of the insects away. The inside was worse than he remembered, damp, smelling of mold and rot, the windows were grimy, and the floor seemed as spongy as the ground outside. He tossed the small suitcase onto the plywood counter, and when it thudded hollowly, he heard something scurry beneath the cabinet.

"You ought to burn this place."

"Damn near did," Dell said, handing Mickey a beer. He glanced up toward a charred and scorched scar running down the length of the ceiling. "Kerosene heater wasn't quite adjusted."

"You're lucky you weren't roasted alive or asphyxiated," Mickey said.

"Just open the damn suitcase, Mick."

He quickly zipped open the top of the small black suitcase, not immediately recognizing what he saw. It was the currency but packed sideways rather than face up. Instead of a suitcase full of Andrew Jackson's sitting on the front of twenty-dollar bills, they were looking at the side cut of neatly placed bundles.

"Man, I gotta tell you," Dell said." I really wasn't sure you would pull this off, but damned if you didn't. I thought we were going to be sleeping in orange jumpsuits somewhere tonight, compliments of the state. But you did it, man. Damned if you didn't do it."

"Yeah, well, we better count it just to be sure she didn't stiff us."

"I got some heavy-duty contractors bags. We'll bury the whole works. The dough from Huey is out in my trunk. We can wrap it all together in the bags for the time being. Go down deep, figure maybe we could build a fire pit over the top of the thing. Anyone looking would most likely take a pass on that spot. Mick, I gotta thank you. We got more money than I ever thought I'd see in my life."

Something scurried in the rear of the bus, larger this time. Mickey looked around, glanced up again at the charred scar on the ceiling." We better get it done, I have to be at work later tonight, and I'm already dragging from the drive up here. I didn't sleep all that great."

"You think maybe she was right, Coach's wife, about it being stupid to bury this stuff?"

"Yeah, it's stupid. We're stupid. That's why we pulled this off, twice, successfully, because it's stupid."

"I don't mean pulling it off. It's the burying I'm talking about. Maybe she was right, we should have bank accounts, and we could transfer the money, you know, like they do in the movies."

"You moonlight on the side, sheetrocking, you get paid by check. You deposit that check in the bank? Of course, you don't. You know it leaves a trail, and if the tax folks ever came after you and checked your account, they'd find ten to twenty grand you didn't pay taxes on, right? It's the same thing here. We're flying beneath the radar."

They dug the hole far deeper than Mickey would have liked with him on the business end of a shovel. It took two hours and four beers each to cut through tree roots, pull out half the rocks in St. Louis County, refill the hole and build a fire to cover the spot. In between times, they were swatting the air at a growing swarm of insects and flies drawn to the gallons of beer sweat.

"Want another beer?" Dell asked, tossing his empty can into the fire.

"No, but I'm gonna close my eyes for a half-hour. I don't want to end up in the ditch halfway home."

He squeezed past Dell rummaging in the bottom of the plastic cooler and climbed into the bus. He absently adjusted the pillow on the bunk bed, revealing a line of dried mouse droppings. Something scurried in the wall next to the bunk.

"On second thought, I better head back. I can grab a nap in a rest stop if I have to, but I need to be at work tonight, so everything looks normal. You staying up here?"

"We finished the job yesterday. I'm off 'til Monday, figure I'll stay here tonight, keep the fire going, so it leaves a lot of ash and trash, and head back tomorrow afternoon."

"See you at the War Bonnet tomorrow night?"

"Yeah, I'll probably end up with Cookie. She's got the weekend off. If her kids or grandkids don't hose it up for me."

Mickey jumped as something scurried behind a box under the bunk." Enjoy yourself up here," he said and left.

Nine

Janice stepped out of her car and absently stared across the street. She inserted her credit card, selected the fuel and placed the gas pump nozzle in the tank. She watched as the pump total quickly climbed. It was a hot summer day. Humid air, heavy with exhaust fumes that collected under the metal roof. Baking asphalt added more heat to the mix of noise and fumes from the street.

Her cell phone rang, and she rummaged in her purse only to see it was another call from her stepfather, Huey. She let the call dump into her voice mail. She'd lost count of how many times he had called her just today demanding his money back.

She told him if he wanted the money to get the cops involved, go to them. That had shut him up, but only for a day or two. Now, she simply stopped taking his calls.

At least things had eased up in the financial department with the help of the ten grand she had wormed out of those two clown kidnappers. Yeah, right, dumb and dumber was more like it. And her daughter Ashley had actually started to become a sweet kid, at least some of the time.

She stood there sweating in the heat, feet throbbing, ignoring the cell phone ringing. She felt a slight rumble in her stomach, the result of a curry dish she'd grabbed in the kitchen between serving tables. She thought briefly about dashing into the station restroom, but the rumble had all the earmarks of an unpleasant situation, and the privacy of her own bathroom held a greater appeal.

She was half-thinking about a bath, just soak, relax, maybe have a glass of wine in the tub, when she saw the car. It took a moment to reach her, why it was familiar. It wasn't the car that attracted her attention as much as the fact he was parking in a no-parking zone, a bus stop actually. And that's when she recognized the car and the driver at the same time. Her kidnapper, right across the street, ducking into a bar.

Cookie looked up from her magazine as Mickey entered the War Bonnet Lounge. Street heat rolled in the door along with him.

"Hi, Mick."

"When Dell shows up, tell him I'm in my office," he said, then strolled toward the end of the bar and a stool bathed in the dim light of a silent TV. She returned to her magazine after delivering his unordered bourbon.

Mickey and Dell were on their third or maybe fourth together, but then who counted on a Friday? Mickey arranged his swizzle sticks along the edge of the bar.

Somewhere during their conversation, Janice had quietly snuck in the door and slipped onto a stool in the corner. Her eyes slowly adjusted to the dim light. She pulled her baseball cap down over her face and ordered a glass of wine. She slowly looked around, scanning the bar over the rim of her wine glass.

It was the third time she checked the two guys at the far end, but it was so dark she wasn't one hundred percent positive. Still, it looked to be them, something about the way the heavier man moved. She wished she could get closer.

There was something familiar about the other guy, lean and quiet. He just sat there, not doing much but nodding. She suddenly pictured him in her mind with the paper bag on his head, remembered how he had bumped into the door frame, and she suddenly knew she was right.

She was on the bottom half of her glass of wine when she got the warning she needed a bathroom, fast. One of those warnings that eliminated the option of racing home. It was a sudden, immediate warning from that region well below her tummy. It told her things were going to be awful in about ninety seconds, her choice where, she had ninety seconds.

"Could you tell me where your restrooms are?" she half-begged Cookie.

"In the back, under the TV, hon," Cookie said, not really looking up from the drink glasses she was washing.

Her only option was to hope they didn't recognize her. She pulled her cap down and made a beeline for the ladies' room, not sure she would even make it in time based on the violent rumbling growing in her lower intestinal tract.

The ladies' room door had a painting of a sexy, squatting dog with eyelashes, labeled 'Setters.' The men's room door had a dog standing and peeing on a fire hydrant and labeled 'Pointers.'

Janice didn't have the luxury of time to critique the door art just now, let alone worry about possibly being recognized. She hurried past the two laughing men, cap pulled down low, head turned the other way, staring at the men's room door as if she was debating going in there.

She pushed through the door and thanked God the single stall was available. She could hear them out there laughing, just beyond the door, and prayed they wouldn't hear her.

Mickey paused in mid-swallow, not sure what he saw out of the corner of his eye. It was all so quick, out of nowhere, she looked familiar, but then again, no, it couldn't possibly be, not here. Could it?

Dell's back was to the restrooms, and Mickey said, "Hey, check this gal out in the can. You tell me, is it Huey's kid?"

"Huey's kid? You mean she found us? Let's get out of here."

"Hold on. It looked like her, but I can't be sure. It's just strange. Who comes here except us?" Mickey said.

"You sure you don't want to leave?" Dell asked again.

"Yeah, I told you, don't worry, probably not her. What would she be doing in this dive on a Friday night? Besides, you're not going to pass up Cookie, are you?"

"Not on your—"

"Shit," Mickey said, making direct eye contact with Janice as she exited the ladies' room.

"Oh, hi. Umm, w-w-what's up?" she said, like she was supposed to make casual conversation with the man who had kidnapped her, held her for ransom for two days, and then handed her ten thousand dollars cash when he dropped her off in the alley behind her house.

She moved a step closer. "I just wanted to say thanks for being nice. I know it sounds crazy, but what you did, the money, it really helped me, took the pressure off for a bit. Don't worry. I didn't tell anyone or anything. I just saw you when I was getting gas across the street and was kinda curious, that's all."

Mickey just nodded, dumbstruck.

Dell remained frozen on his barstool, his back to Janice standing no more than a foot behind him.

"I think you have me mixed up with someone else," Mickey finally said.

"You drive that car out front that's in the bus stop? You got a little room with black and white floor tile, and you like to wrap tape around girls who are having car trouble?"

Mickey's hands went up reflexively, and he shook his head back and forth, signaling her not to say these things out loud.

She moved in closer and lowered her voice. "I said I wasn't going to tell anyone, so relax." She turned and looked at Dell, who remained staring straight ahead, un-moving." Both of you, just relax."

"I think you must be mis—" Her look stopped him in mid-sentence." Buy you a drink?"

"Yeah, sure," she said and glided onto the stool next to him.

It was four or five drinks past the shift change. Dell had left with Cookie, running out the door as quickly as he could around nine o'clock. Mickey was still there, listening to Janice. He had pounded down the first two drinks just to calm his nerves but then dialed back and now found himself nodding for another, just so he could stay and talk to her.

She was a wise-ass, and he liked that. He liked the way she looked, pretty and not shy. At the moment, he had tuned out her voice and was envisioning the two of them on a beach. Janice in a very tiny bikini, and—

"Hey, Mickey, you listening? I said, are you okay? You got this look on your face like you were lost. If I want to hear myself talk, I can just go home and rattle around. Peace and quiet tonight, Ashley's at some sleep over. That's my daughter. You never met her. They'll probably sneak out and run around town until sun up, then crash until about three or four in the afternoon, get up, and wonder what's for breakfast. You got any kids?"

"Me? Good lord, no. Guess I never quite found the right person to settle down with. It never seemed to work out, or maybe they just came to their senses."

"You seem like a nice guy. If you forget for the moment how we met."

"Yeah, pretty strange," he glanced at the bartender, wondering where his drink was. "Harlan, that bourbon, you find it yet?"

Harlan nodded in Mickey's direction. Free poured a low glass with bourbon until it was just about full, no ice, then just stood there, joking with two girls.

"Watch, he'll end up driving those two home, does it all the time," Mickey said.

"That sounds kind of creepy," she said and shuddered.

"Actually, he owns the place, gives 'em a ride home, so they don't drive drunk. Or he calls them a cab. He's a real nice guy that way. Thanks," Mickey said, as Harlan suddenly pushed the full glass of bourbon across the bar.

"You need anything," he asked Janice.

"No, thanks, I'm taken care of," she said.

"Running the taxi again tonight, Harlan?" Mickey asked.

"I'm gonna give those two a lift right now. You watch the bar for me, Mick?" He tossed his apron on the bar, not waiting for an answer, and quickly herded the two girls off their stools and out the door.

Mickey lurched off his stool, carefully edged behind the bar, leaned across from Janice, and gave her his best glassy stare. "Get you anything, or did you want to wait for Harlan?"

"I think I've had about all I can handle for right now, but thanks all the same."

Mickey was thinking or trying to, but the sheer quantity of bourbon was beginning to take its cumulative effect. Harlan was suddenly there again, thanking Mickey and ushering him from behind the bar, then turning up the lights, locking the door, and pulling the dusty drapes closed.

"Looks like that's last call," Janice said, digging in her purse for her keys.

"No, he just locks up. We can stay here for another hour or two if you want, no problem. Harlan's real good about that. He keeps the place open if you're already in here."

Having poured himself a beer, Harlan stood at the far end of the bar talking to an older couple hiding behind a mound of losing pull tabs. The beer officially signaled he was more or less off duty.

"How 'bout I cook us some breakfast. I'm starving," Janice said.

Mickey seemed to think about the offer for a long moment "Sure, less go," he slurred, then slipped off his stool and lurched toward the door.

Janice quickly gathered up the bar napkin with his phone number, her purse, keys, phone, and spare change then ran to catch up.

"Should I follow you?" he asked out front. He was standing a little too close for conventional conversation, not that he was making a move. It was just the distance the better part of a fifth of bourbon allowed at two-twenty on a Saturday morning.

In for a penny in for a pound, Janice thought." No, that's my car across the street. I better drive us."

Mickey couldn't remember when he had last changed the sheets, but even with his eyes closed and the throbbing in his head, he could sense they were clean. The distant ringing of a phone was bringing him to the surface, pulling him from the depths of unconsciousness. He winced at the brightness of the room, yellow walls, not necessarily harsh on a normal morning, but then this was no normal morning. He was attempting to piece last night together while taking stock of the room. An antique chest of drawers, little red and white pillows lined up on the floor, the clean rug, the white door with the brass knob open just half-an-inch. He remembered talking to Harlan, Dell, and Cookie ducking out and then—Jesus Christ!

The far side of the bed appeared to have been slept in, but now it was cold to the touch. The pillow was indented and held just the slightest hint of perfume. The smell of bacon wafted in from somewhere on the other side of the door. He rolled out of bed as quietly as possible, found his clothes in a crumpled heap at the foot of the bed, and quickly began to dress. The top three buttons from his shirt were missing, and he sucked the last of the bourbon taste off his teeth. He contemplated the second-floor window as a possible escape, but the smell of bacon won him over, and he cautiously peeked out the door into the hallway. The door gave a slight squeak as he swung it open.

"There's a clean towel and a toothbrush laid out in the bathroom for you. Breakfast will be ready in about ten minutes." Janice called up the stairs from her position in front of the stove.

Mickey brushed his teeth, splashed water on his face, took stock of himself in the bathroom mirror, then took a deep breath and headed down the stairs into the kitchen.

"Morning, Mr. Party," Janice said, holding out a steaming mug of coffee. She was dressed in cut-off jeans, barefoot, wearing a t-shirt emblazoned with a Jameson Irish Whiskey logo, and braless.

Mickey's condition just now was still rough enough that he failed to appreciate the latter, and he gratefully took the coffee mug. He nodded thanks before sniffing the mug.

"What?" she said.

"I wasn't that keen on Jameson, at least this morning," he replied, nodding toward her t-shirt.

"You didn't seem to have any qualms with this package when we got home last night," she said, turning back to the bacon and quietly laughing.

It took him a minute to catch the meaning of her comment, and a picture suddenly burst into his mind, a lightning flash of naked flesh.

"Relax, you did fine, Superman. Now here, take this and sit down so I can eat, too. I'm absolutely famished. I could eat a small child after the workout we had. She threw toast on a plate of scrambled eggs then forked a half-dozen strips of bacon over the top.

"Well, I'm not so worried about me. But considering what you have at stake, you know being seen with me and all. What about your old man?" Mickey said.

"You mean my husband or my departed mother's husband, my stepfather? If it's the ex you're worried about, he hasn't been around except to call occasionally and tell me he was going to be late with the child support. If it's my departed mother's husband, we don't talk. He calls me a dozen times a day to yell and scream, tells me he wants the money back. Tells me I owe him, but that's not gonna happen. Oh, and Mick, I don't want any damn money. I don't want a handout, and that's not why you ended up in my bed last night. What you did for me when you dropped me off was actually sweet, in a weird way. I haven't always had this life of luxury I'm leading now."

"I hope you don't think I—"

"And, by the way, last night was not the dumbest thing I've ever done in my life, so there. I mean big deal, so you kidnapped me, wrapped me up with that shitty tape, threw me in the back of your stinky car, kept me in a small room with no door on the bathroom, and probably watched me through the keyhole, lots of girls meet guys that way. Don't they? There's no strings attached here. You're free to go."

"I wasn't worried about that. But, since I'm free to go, as you put it, I'll need a ride back to my car after breakfast," he said, then picked up a strip of bacon and took a large bite.

"Are you kidding me?" Mickey yelled. He pulled the parking ticket off his windshield and waved it at Janice as she drove away. When he got home, he had four messages waiting for him, all from Dell. Before he could finish listening to them, Dell called again.

"Mick, you ok? What the hell happened?"

"I'm just fine, Dell. What are you worried about?"

"What am I worried about? Mick, did you forget who you were buying drinks for last night? That sweet young thing was Huey's kid. Does that ring any bells?"

"Oh yeah, Janice. We talked for a while, then she had to get going."

"Damn it. I didn't know what to do last night. Janice, you call her Janice now? I brushed Cookie off, ditched her. Man, she was mad. She slammed the car door and gave me the finger. I packed a bag and drove up here last night thinking I was being followed the whole way."

"What do you mean up here? Are you up at the lake right now?"

"Yeah, I just told you, I didn't know what to think. Hell, I'm sitting up here with a loaded deer rifle just in case Huey Evans, and a car full of goons comes down the road. I only slept about three minutes last night. I've been hearing things, thinking maybe they grabbed you and beat a confession out of you."

"Believe me, Dell, everything's cool. There's no trouble down here. We just ended up together, for a few minutes, is all. Like it was some kind of strange fate to meet again or something. Come on back down to the cities, call Cookie, and tell her you're just stupid."

"You sure there's no trouble, and we don't have Huey on our ass? Because if we do, the best thing that could happen would be we get arrested by the cops, and they lock us up for our own protection."

"Will you calm down? I've got this whole thing under control. Huey Evans is not a problem. How in the hell would he even find out about us? Quit being stupid and just get back down here."

Ten

Huey's blood was boiling and he shouted, "Son of bitch." He slammed down the phone as soon as he heard the voice mail message kick in again. "You can bet my ass she is going to pay back that money, with interest, too. I don't know exactly how, but she's involved. I can feel it. Probably set up the whole damn thing and arranged to have herself kidnapped. Paid a couple of morons to torch my garage with my classic Chevy. If she thinks she can get away with this just by not answering the phone, she's got another thing coming."

He began fingering through his well-worn Rolodex. "It's time I get a little professional help in here. Take a more direct approach and find out exactly what in the hell is going on. We'll see who's not going to take my calls."

He punched in a seven-digit number, waited four rings before he heard the tonal beep, and entered his call back number. He'd used this service before, not without some expense involved, but in situations like this, sometimes it was the only way to deal with the problem. The call was usually returned within the hour, and it had always proven to be money well spent.

Over on the east side of town, Buster Keegan had just finished getting a massage when Huey's number came through on his cellphone. Probably a collection problem that would have to be taken care of in Buster's own highly effective manner. A smile came across his face. Huey always paid well.

He rotated his shoulder, trying to work the last of the kinks out while standing at the locker room payphone with a white towel wrapped around his waist. When Huey answered, Buster gave him the name of a restaurant and the time he would be there, then hung up without waiting for Huey's reply.

As usual he was sitting in a back booth, facing the door, when Huey arrived. Huey had no doubt there was someone else watching, just in case. That wasn't a concern. Huey was here to discuss business, the business of his stepdaughter, Janice, and the hundred grand she wouldn't pay back.

Over coffee, Huey explained the situation. "It's pretty simple. I'm her stepfather, for God's sake. She's as big a pain as her mother was. So, get the money back and let me know who was in on this with her. It's got to be some strange kind of dude," he added, remembering the voice on the phone that had ultimately sent him to Seattle.

"Don't do anything to him. I'll deal with that myself. You just get the money and a name."

"Your daughter? Why don't you just pick up the phone and call her? Or better yet, go over to her place?"

"She's my stepdaughter, and I got my reasons. Look, Buster, with all due respect, that's not really your problem. You just need to get the money from her, not worry about why. She's tight with a nickel that one, just like the old lady was. She's probably got the cash sitting under her bed or in a closet."

"So, how rough do you want me to get?"

"Well, she has to be able to pay, and if she's dead, she can't pay. But, aside from that, feel free to do whatever will get the job done. I can't have people thinking they can hustle me for money. I'd be the laughing stock of this town if anyone got wind of it. And that stunt with my car, burning the garage down. Whoever pulled that little torch job off had inside information and sent me a message. I want to deal with him, personally. I bought into it at first, but the more I think about it, it's just too stupid. A hundred grand? Come on, who could possibly be that dumb?"

✳ ✳ ✳

"How dumb are you, Mick?" It wasn't dangerous enough the way we were working things. Now you decide to sleep with Huey's kid?"

"Dell, will you relax. I told you it was a one-shot deal. She bumped into us by mistake, she doesn't even know who you are. She has no way of getting in touch with me. Shit happens. It's just one of those crazy, spur of the moment things. She couldn't help herself. She just fell for me. You've never ended up in some woman's bed wondering how you got there?"

"Not some woman I kidnapped and held for ransom for God's sake. Not Huey's kid. What if she tries to get in touch with you?"

"I just told you, she can't. We'll just stay away from the War Bonnet for a week or two. I'll give Harlan the word, make sure he doesn't pass out any information on either one of us. You might want to mention something to Cookie, too. We don't need her opening her mouth and saying something stupid to someone." Mickey's cell-phone suddenly rang. "Hello?"

"Oh, hey. Just wanted to see how you were doing, that head feeling any better?" Janice asked.

"Ahh, yeah . . . hi. I'm feeling fine, just fine." Mickey suddenly turned his back to Dell and lowered his voice to almost a whisper." Kinda busy right now. Maybe we could talk a little later."

"It's her, isn't it?" said Dell, standing up, not sure what to do, suddenly looking out the window, up and down the street to see if they were surrounded.

"How 'bout I talk to you a little later?"

"Oh, yeah, sorry to bother you. I was just wondering if maybe you wanted to get together, even later tonight, if that would work for you?"

"Yeah, sounds great. I'll call you in a bit."

"I'll be waiting."

"Oh, that's just great. For not being able to get in touch with you, she seems to have done alright for her-self. What the hell are you thinking? Are you crazy? What if she brings Huey after us? I'm not supposed to mention anything to anyone, but apparently, it's okay for you to hop in the sack with her and have her call you for a second date. Jesus, Mick, this takes the cake. Are there any other surprises you would like to lay on me? You two going to vacation down in Grand Cayman and stay with the Coach's wife, have her cook you up some more spaghetti."

"It wasn't spaghetti. It was linguini, number seven linguini, I always—"

"Cut the crap, Mick. We're not talking about some slap on the wrist offense here. We'll both be dead by the time they decide to let us out. That's if Huey doesn't kill us first. We're looking at federal charges here, federal charges, man. I love you, but you're a class A screw-up. I've always stuck by you, always been there, always gone along, but you seem to have this self destruct gene, and I'm not going down this time. I can't. I won't. So, do whatever in the hell you want here, but until you come to your senses, I'm out of it. You let me know when you start thinking clearly, but I'm not risking everything just because you got the hots for this woman."

"Now, Dell, just hold on."

"Ask yourself this, Mick. What in the hell does she see in you? Christ, look at this joint. You live in a two-bedroom apartment with empty beer cases stacked up for end tables. You got a painting of a naked woman you met in Vegas hanging over your couch, and I'm guessing probably the same sheets on your bed for the last couple of months. You're a goofball, Mick. You don't have a career. You can't hold a job. I know, I know," Dell said, holding up a hand to stop Mickey's protest." You're a no-tary public. Come on man. First of all, that's not a career, okay. And second, you're not. You're not even a notary, Mick. You just bought the stamp."

"Will you calm down, Dell."

"No, not this time. Sometimes I think you tell your-self these lies so often you forget they're lies. All you did was have a guy make you a stamp, and you've been fak-ing the notary gig for years. What's it bring in, about twenty bucks a month? That doesn't buy you drinks for one night. You've never held a job for more than six months. I love you, man, but just think about it. I mean, the woman doesn't have enough headaches in her life. Now she wants to take up with you? Come on Mick, wise up."

"So, does that mean you're not interested in the next little project I've been thinking about?"

"Next project. Are you nuts? Did you hear anything I've been saying?"

"Dell, calm down, old buddy, look at the facts here. Seems to me I've delivered more payola than either one of us has ever seen before. Seems to me that we are both walking around free as a bird. Seems to me that if the cops or the feds were on to us, we would both be locked up by now. Seems to me that so far, both my plans have worked perfectly. Seems to me that—"

"Worked perfectly? Mick, did you listen to anything I just said? You're playing with fire here. How do you know this Janice isn't just setting us up? This is Huey Evans' daughter, for Christ's sake. Forget what he did to us as kids. That doesn't even count. You know what his reputation is."

"I know but—"

"Worked perfectly? The first woman, your new main squeeze, you gave her ten grand, and there's a fifty-fifty chance she's setting you up. The second woman you so carefully chose, we couldn't even get a response from her husband, Coach Buddy. Hell, Mick, she finally had to pay us herself, just to get out of town. That's working perfectly?"

"Are you through, Dell? See, that's the difference between us. You get hung up on the details. You sweat the small shit. I'm more of a big picture guy. I get results. The bottom line is, no matter what you say, we got ourselves two big old contractor bags buried in northern Minnesota, both of them filled with cash. And, I'm going to do it a third time, even if I have to do it alone. So, you in or not?"

"Mick, forget about the last two and how they worked out. I'll give you this, we got the dough. But, the girl, she worries me. In fact, she scares the absolute hell out of me."

"Dell, I know what you mean, but I think she's actually on the level. It would have been easy to give both of us up last night or me toward the end of the night. Instead, she cooks me breakfast and then calls to see if I'm all right. I mean, what's that? I understand you being worried. But I promise you. I'll check it out, be real careful, cover for both of us. I promise I'll check it out, take a real close look, and play it extremely safe. Satisfied?"

They had agreed to get together for dinner, Mickey suggesting that he cook, sounding like a true romantic. All the while, thinking if he was going to check Janice out, what better way to do it than at his duplex, uninterrupted. More importantly, he could feed her for under thirty bucks.

She arrived promptly at seven-thirty, giving him time to clean and dump a lot of junk into the spare bedroom. He'd cleaned the bathroom, dusted a few shiny things, set the table for two, turned off most of the lights, and lit the three Christmas candles on the table. He also set a loaded Luger in a kitchen drawer beneath a dish towel. The Luger had a clip that held nine hollow-point rounds. He fired up the blender just as she rang the doorbell.

"Hi, find the place, okay?" He said as he opened the front door.

"That shirt is great," she said, laughing at the two mermaids dominating his front.

" Come on in. I'm upstairs," he gestured with a hand and followed her up the stairs. She continued talking as they climbed the stairs, then paused her conversation as she stepped into his unit.

"I'm sorry, what did you say?" he asked.

"I said, I love what you've done with the place," she laughed, taking in the beer case end tables, mismatched furniture, and the painting of the naked redhead. "Someone you know?"

"Not anymore," he said, pouring two-thirds of a blender into a glass just slightly smaller than a birdbath and handing it to her. "I thought it might be the perfect night for a margarita."

"Wow, this is a really big glass."

"Yeah, aren't they great? Got 'em down in Mexico."

"Amazing, it holds almost a pitcher's worth," she said.

The air conditioner chugged along, fighting to keep the room at a moderate heat as opposed to slightly cool. Occasionally it kicked in with a power surge that made the lights blink. They ran the gamut of polite conversation. Mickey went into detail how he had just wanted to die after his last bout of Montezuma's Revenge down in Mexico. How he was a businessman of varied interests, dabbling in a variety of different things.

"You mean like kidnapping?"

"You want to hear some great 60s tunes?" he said, ignoring the question. "Pick something out over there." He pointed with his glass at the dusty cassette player sitting on a shelf made of bricks and boards. "I built that, the shelf, painted it, too."

"Where is your computer?"

"I hate using those things. I just have tapes, some pretty good stuff there. Put in any one you like."

"Yeah, I listen to this Bobby Vee one all the time," she said, shaking her head as she looked at the tape.

"Here, you know Ricky Nelson, right? The original teen idol, I mean Poor little Fool? Hello Mary Lou? Garden Party?"

"Where do you even get cassette tapes nowadays?"

He shook his head, slipped Ricky Nelson in, pushed the tape deck closed, and waited for a few seconds of static before Ricky launched into the soft beginning of Lonesome Town, 'There's a place, where lover's go, to cry their troubles away. 'Ricky dropped down an octave, heavy, suddenly close, like the heat outside, and Mickey took her in his arms and started to move.' And they call it lonesome town, where the broken hearts stay.'

He was one hell of a dancer and he softly, gently, directed her. Danced with her, like she'd never, ever been danced with before. Not swirls or spins but slow, close, passionate without ever really touching, just hands and fingers, directing her by the slightest pressures to which she knew instantly, genetically, how to respond. When the song finished, her back was to him. His arms were wrapped around her waist, but not too tight, just perfect, sheltering her from the world. She could feel his breath close to her left ear, exciting her. In just two minutes and nineteen seconds, she'd fallen for Ricky Nelson and Mickey. She wasn't sure if it was the dance or the margaritas.

"Wow," she gasped, turning and looking deep into his eyes.

"Thanks, I had better get that spaghetti going, or we'll never eat," Mickey said, missing every clue and hint, as he walked into the kitchen.

"Anything I can do to help?"

"Yeah, finish that drink. We got wine with dinner. Pasta ala Mickey, tonight."

"Mmm-mmm, sounds like I'll like it."

Over dinner, they both laughed too much, more from the margaritas and the bottom half of their bottle of wine than anything said. Things seemed to be going along nicely for both of them, and so, Mickey figured his timing couldn't be better to ask the question.

"How are things with your father?"

"He is not my father. He's the reason my mother is dead. He killed her a hundred times over. She died of a broken heart. He didn't love her, he despises me, and as far as I'm concerned, he can just go to hell. The sooner, the better."

"More wine?" Mickey asked.

"I told you he calls me a number of times every damn day. He threatens me, trying to get that money back. Thinks I set the whole thing up, burned his stupid car."

"His car? We never did anything to his car."

"Well, someone did. Anyway, you brought it up," she said, then drained her wine glass and thrust it in Mickey's direction." I don't want anything from you. I'm not asking for anything. I was just pumping gas yesterday, saw you go into some lousy dive bar, and got up the courage to sneak in there to look at you. That's all I wanted to do, just look at you. I was just curious, and if I didn't have those beers, we never would have talked. You never would have ended up in my bed, and I wouldn't be here tonight.

"Huey wants you to pay back the money? That doesn't make a lot of sense."

"Gee, really? Tell him that, like it would stop him. But it's not why I talked to you last night. Okay? You were the first guy, oh God. This is how screwed up my life is. You're the first guy I can remember being kind to me. My stepfather's a jerk, my ex is a bigger jerk, and I've had a string of losers you wouldn't believe. Now, I go and run into the guy who kidnapped me and take him into my bed. I'm such a pathetic loser." She suddenly began to cry, head in her hands, pasta sauce splattered on her blouse.

"I think you're being a little too hard on yourself, aren't you? Let's take them one at a time, the easy ones first. Your ex, from what you've said, he's been out of the picture, right?"

She sniffled, nodded, and looked at him through puffy eyes.

"All right, so cross him off the list. You can do better than him. Now those other losers, so what. See that painting, that redhead over the couch? I paid for that, even though she gave it to me as a surprise. Turns out she was doing the damn painter on the side. Amazingly, that's why it took two months to finish the damn thing. She gets copies made and sends them out to LA, so she can become a star. I get the damned painting and a couple of grand worth of credit card bills. She's out in LA, supposedly living the life."

"Is she a star?"

"You don't recognize her, do you? That's because you're looking at her face. She works under a number of different names, usually in a different forty-five-minute video with a different bunch of guys every week or so. That's when she's not winking at cars from some street corner."

"You mean, she's a porn star?"

"I mean, she's in porn, not what you'd call a star, and that's what I got to show for it, that painting. I keep it there to remind me of how stupid I was. Well, and because it actually kinda makes the room, too. I mean, you gotta admit, it ties everything together, the reds, her lipstick, the beer cases and all."

"Yeah, well, my ex and all those losers, that's the easy part, but that still leaves the other problem."

"Huey? He'll dial down, just relax and be patient. Believe me, he'll run out of steam. I've dealt with guys like him all my life. They always run out of steam. Sooner or later, he'll be making someone else's life miserable"

At that exact moment, Buster Keegan happened to be parked outside in front of the house next door. He had followed Janice for the better part of the day as she drove to the grocery store, the Mall of America, a gas station, a dry cleaners, the Grand Ave Liquor store, and back to the grocery store, home and now here. He had watched her park, straighten her top before ringing the doorbell, waiting on the porch, and then entering the house once the guy stepped out and glanced around. The whole process took less than forty-five seconds and was uneventful, until the guy looked up and down the street like a gunfighter, and Buster thought, 'Bingo.'

Only someone who had something to hide looked around that way, too cautious, way too careful. He climbed out of his car and felt the hot, humid air encase him like a plastic dry-cleaning bag.

The place was a duplex, one up, one down. The guy didn't look like he was Charlotte Minx listed as living in unit one, so he must be M. Donnelly in unit two. Buster jotted down the name, took the mail out of the mailbox, and climbed back in his car.

The mail consisted of three pieces; an ad circular, a pizza offer, and a credit card application addressed to Michael Donnelly, or current resident. M equals Michael and Buster had a name. He guessed by the look of Huey's stepdaughter in tight white shorts and a small revealing top that she planned to spend the night, which gave Buster time for a little dinner and research on Michael Donnelly.

"Explain this relationship to me again," Huey said to Buster. They were sitting in Huey's back yard. He had been listening off and on to Buster. Occasionally, he stared behind Buster at the recently poured concrete pad and two courses of freshly laid block that was the foundation for his new garage.

"What'd you say his name was again?"

"Donnelly, Michael Donnelly. Local guy. Did some time a few years back up in Lino Lakes for receiving stolen property. His sentence was about twice what's normal. In fact, he was a first-timer, so it should have been a suspended sentence and probation. This guy gets double the time and serves it all. I figure he's connected—no visible means of support. As I checked him out, I kept getting the sense that it's all just a little too vague. You know, like no one could be that much of a loser on paper unless it's all an act and he's really connected. I couldn't find any employment records for the past twenty years except that he claims to be a notary public. That's like the head of some crime family claiming to grow roses for a living. I think you scratch much below the surface of this guy he's going to be wired to some pretty heavy hitters. Nothing else makes any sense."

"Donnelly, Michael Donnelly. You know," Huey said, scratching his head." It rings a bell back there somewhere, but I just can't place it, not the way you're describing this guy."

"That's why I think you should check him out with some of your contacts, see what's up. But be careful. If this guy is connected the way I think he might be, you don't want to be fooling around. They aren't the type to send warnings. They'll just kill you instead."

"Oh great, he's connected."

"Just ask around. In the meantime, I'll see if I can find out anything else."

"And why doesn't it make sense that he's just some loser?"

"Huey, you know, and I know, no one would be that stupid to try and rip you off for a measly hundred g's unless he had that kind of muscle behind him. No one is that stupid. No one could be that big of a moron."

Eleven

Mickey was in the process of attempting to engage Dell in some polite conversation. At the moment things didn't seem to be going that way.

"Arghh, Jesus Christ, Mick," Dell screamed. "You moron. Relationship. She actually used the word, relationship? Oh, this is just great. It's not bad enough we bump into her at the War Bonnet. It's not bad enough she takes you home to her bed. You get the bright idea to give her your phone number. Then, when she calls, you invite her over to your place for dinner and load the two of you up on margaritas in those great big glasses you have."

"Well, it's not like she was going to be driving."

"So, you take her to bed, at your place. You remember, the place you told me she'd never find, except that you gave her the address and directions. And now you're worried because she has the idea you two are in a relationship. This is just great. You're worried about being in a relationship, and we have better than a fifty-fifty chance of winding up dead before the end of the week."

"Is that it? Are you through?"

"Through? We're both going to be—"

Mickey raised both hands to silence Dell. "I've listened. Somewhere, in that tirade, you may have a point. I mentioned this as just one pal to another, you know, thinking maybe I could look for some support. However, it seems clear to me that in your present state of mind, that's just a little too much to ask for. Okay, if it's one thing I am, it's understanding."

"There are a lot of things you—"

"Let's keep it positive, dude," Mickey said and turned to rummage around in Dell's refrigerator. He pulled out two beers and handed one to Dell." Hey, you're almost out of beer, better start paying attention to what's important in life. Look, I'll be the first to admit it's more than a little weird here. Okay? But, then you've got to admit that just dealing in facts, we're sitting on close to two hundred grand. Come on now, admit it. Just a nod of the head will do."

Dell nodded, ever so slightly.

"Better, much better. Trust me here, man. I got a new idea, and we're going to get you working on that room there, get you focused on thinking positive. You'll be glad to know I've got everything we'll need listed right here," he said, reaching into his back pocket and handing Dell a two-page list of alterations for the basement room.

After handing Dell the list Mickey escaped to the War Bonnet Lounge. That had been almost six hours ago. Now he sat alone on a stool. He'd been drinking coffee for the past hour. At forty-five minutes after closing, he was more sober than not and decided to head home. He hadn't driven more than three blocks, waging an intense internal discussion about the merits of calling Janice at three in the morning when suddenly an SUV appeared directly in front of him. He smashed into the rear while it sat at a complete standstill, waiting for the traffic light to change.

Mickey's tires screeched before he jerked to a stop, slamming his face into the steering wheel, letting him know instantly that his nose was broken. The last thing he needed was a ticket for rear-ending someone, driving while intoxicated, driving without insurance, or all of the above. He thought about throwing it in reverse and heading the other way, then climbed out of his car.

The power window on the SUV slid down, revealing a very, very attractive brunette. She took one look at Mickey holding his nose, bleeding all over his shirt, and said, "Oh my God, are you okay? No, you're not, you're hurt, aren't you, Sweetie?"

"The hell you doin'?" slurred her obviously inebriated companion. "Minding our own damn business, and you plow into us like you own the damn street. Do you have any idea who I am? I could ruin you like this," he said and attempted to snap his fingers two or three times without success.

He seemed older than her by a good generation, possibly two. He wore a starched white shirt, a suit coat, and a loosened tie. His grey hair was close-cropped, though formal, he'd never be accused of being stylish. Oh yeah, and he was drunk. Very drunk. Much more than Mickey.

She had one of those skirts on, more of a belt than a skirt, fishnet hose, and a slinky white top. A granddaughter, maybe? Maybe not.

"Torsten, dear, please shut up," she said, turning to her companion and patting him on the knee." We don't need a scene."

"Maybe you'd like your fat ass thrown in jail. I could do it with one little phone call, throw you right in jail."

Mickey didn't know exactly what to say, and so he just stood there, in the middle of the street, his head titled back, holding the bridge of his nose, bleeding all over the bourbon bottle design on the front of his Hawaiian print shirt.

She smiled sweetly, communicating with Mickey that he should just ignore old Torsten. "Just a minute, we'll be right back," she said and raised the window.

Mickey stood there for a moment before the window was lowered, and she thrust her hand out." I'm sorry for any confusion. Hopefully, this will help compensate you for your time." She smiled sweetly as Torsten sat sullenly next to her in the passenger seat. She pressed something into Mickey's hand before raising the window and driving away.

Mickey watched their tail lights recede down the darkened street. He opened his hand and counted out eight hundred-dollar bills, stared at them as drops of blood splattered on the crumpled currency. He looked up again, could just make out her signaling a left-hand turn at the light a few blocks down, and in seconds, he was driving down the street, speeding with his head tilted back, one hand on the wheel, the other pinching a new curve along the bridge of his nose.

He continued to follow, finally backing off, as they turned left into an underground parking ramp while he coasted to a stop at a traffic light. It was now or never. A quick glance left and right seemed to indicate the coast was clear. He punched it, ran the light, and came along the ramp entrance just in time to get her license number.

"Come on, Mick, knock it off, you're gonna get me in trouble again. You know how I hate doing this shit,"

Terry Hanson whined into the phone. "How come my job with the DMV means you get to find out private information on all our good citizens? Hey, you got a cold? You sound like your nose is plugged."

Mickey ignored the question. "I'm a concerned citizen is all, just trying to help out. I see this SUV driving erratically on the way back from church Sunday morning, and it almost hit some kids. I just want to make sure no one gets hurt, that's all, just looking out for the welfare of children."

"Yeah, touching," Hanson said, sounding unconvinced." It's great you care about the youth of our fair city. And of course, that makes it okay for me to risk losing my job looking up a license number for you."

"What are you risking? Other than the steaks I was planning to drop off. Come on. I'd do it for you. Seems to me when someone needed the right palms greased after your little public urination charge, it was just fine and dandy to call me to get the job done."

"Damn it, Mick," Hanson barked into the phone, then lowered his voice to a whisper." I've asked you before never to mention that."

"And, I never have. Come on, man, it's just between you and me. You know you can trust me."

"Oh, man, why do I even answer the phone when I see it's you calling? Okay, but this is the last time, and I want rib eyes, an inch thick. And get that damn cold checked out. You're liable to give us all bird flu or something."

It was two days before Hanson called Mickey back. "Mick, you okay to talk? Just what the hell are you into here?"

"What's the problem?" Mickey said into his cell phone as he stepped out of his car and brushed cookie crumbs from his shirt.

"The problem is that I didn't buy your stupid tale about an erratic driver Sunday morning for starters. I mean, since when do you go to church?"

"It was the one time I—"

"Never mind. I figured you saw some woman, and she can have the pleasure of telling you to get lost when you call her and explain to her you're the pig who was leering and creeping her out at some stoplight. But then this name came up, and I don't know what kind of scam you're thinking of running, but this is way out of your league."

"So, who is it? The mayor?"

"No, it's not the mayor. It's Torsten Theisen, ring any bells?"

"The governor?"

"He's not the damned governor, you moron. But close, he's Speaker of the House, and he is connected.

Oh, and by the way, he's a real self-righteous type. So I don't know what you're up to, and I don't want to know. But be careful. And remember, you didn't hear any of this from me. Now I expect to see those are one-inch rib eyes very soon."

"Yeah, got it, one inch, thanks," Mickey said and thought, *Torsten, that's what she had called him, interesting.*

"Have you gone completely crazy?" Dell asked, not for the first time." Why would the guy even care if we took her? How do you even plan to find the woman?"

"That's what I'm telling you. I've already got that information," Mickey said. "I know where she lives, and this is clearly a case where we just sell the sizzle, Dell. We let him think we have more information than we do. We make him think she's talked to us. That she let us in on all the secrets they have, showed us a video or something, believe me, he'll jump to all the wrong conclusions."

"What secrets?" asked Dell.

"Well, for starters, I've done a little checking. Seems old Torsten has been the representative from his district for the past twenty-eight years. He's been at the public trough for at least that long."

"So, what does that have to do with anything?" Dell said.

"The point is, he's got a battle ax of a wife and a family up north. He's presented himself as one of those holier than you or me guys, and has those religious types electing him year after year to the legislature. All the while, he's got some hot little gal down here in the steamy old capital city of St. Paul. How do you think that's gonna play up there in Glacial Springs? As a matter of fact, Dell, she's the one who gave me the idea, this woman, yelling at that drunken fool the other night, telling him to shut up or he'd have a public relations nightmare on his hands. I mean, that's what the woman told him. You ain't getting that out of some choir girl down here at a church meeting."

"But you ran into them."

"She wasn't worried about the accident. He could have had me on a silver platter. He could have built this deal into a major whiplash with the right lawyer. Instead, what does she do? She tells him to shut up and hands me eight hundred bucks for the privilege of rear-ending them, then races home. And that tells me two things, first, she's not some one-night stand. Second, he can't be caught publicly with her because there'll be some big scandal. And three, she's got something to lose, too."

"That's what happened to your nose, isn't it? I thought it looked different, but I couldn't quite figure it out, a new curve or something."

"My nose isn't the point. I think what I ran into the other night was one nicely kept little lady and her 'Sugar Daddy,' Torsten Theisen, and he'll pay to get her back if he thinks for even a moment that it might ruin him.

Over the next week, Dell, once again, revamped the room. He had it down to a system, although he thought Mickey's decorating choice of red on red left something to be desired. Mickey had shown up the night before with a Spiderman mask and seemed more than a little miffed when Dell didn't quite share his enthusiasm.

"Jesus, what is it with you, Dell? I mean, you were mad about the paper bag. You didn't like the dog mask. Now, I get Spiderman, and that doesn't turn your crank either. I mean, I'm about to give up here."

"We all deal with the stress a little differently. You buy goofy masks, I worry, there you have it."

"Okay. How about after this woman. Maybe we just take it easy? I think we're both getting stressed on the whole deal," Mickey said, trying to sound conciliatory.

"Stressed? You think? I mean, Mick, neither of the last two events went down anything like the way we planned. To tell you the truth, I don't think I was cut out to be the kidnapping type."

"Don't think of it as kidnapping, Dell. Think of it as sales. You know, selling a product people want. And as far as not going the way we wanted, I don't know. What do we have in those bags buried up at your lake place? I mean, that ain't just peanuts."

"No, it ain't just peanuts, and we're lucky we aren't locked up right now, for the next hundred years. I'm just saying maybe we should give it a rest, that's all."

"Dell, we got more money than we ever dreamed of, and as far as not working the way we planned, it did work. We got the dough. In this line of work, we have to be a little flexible. Maybe that's our real plan, just being flexible."

"Well, Mick, I'm thinking we take a break, maybe forever."

Mickey continued his research, studying up on Torsten Theisen. When he wasn't studying Torsten, cleaning the real estate office, or lapping up bourbon at the War Bonnet, he was hanging around Galtier Plaza, the downtown condo high rise, hoping to catch another glimpse of the brunette.

He learned her name was Nikki Devereaux. Nikki Devereaux, it figured, a woman looking like that had to have a name that matched. Even the act of pronouncing her name had a sexual connotation, repeating it slowly, his bottom lip brushing against his front teeth, almost a sexual suggestion ending in a kiss. Nikki Devereaux. He was smitten.

He had caught a glimpse of her on four separate occasions, but nothing that might suggest a pattern or a work schedule. Meanwhile, he had formulated the beginnings of a plan. Dressed in painter's whites, he had followed cars into the underground ramp, getting the lay of things in the exclusive building. He'd found an unlocked utility closet in the far corner of the parking area and began to fine-tune his plan, much of which was based on dumb luck.

Twelve

Absolute dumb luck was just what arrived at his doorstep late one afternoon, dressed in a small cream-colored top, wide gold belt, extremely short cream-colored skirt, patterned hosiery, and stiletto heels.

The sexy clicking of spiked heels was what first attracted Mickey. He heard them long before he actually saw them. Heard her walking through the condo's underground parking lot, shopping bags in tow, clicking those heels in sexy little steps across the floor, the sound echoing off the white concrete walls.

He was in the process of storing a red, collapsible, two-wheeled dolly, a large empty appliance box, a roll of duct tape, and surgical gloves in the utility closet. Nikki Devereaux was walking toward the elevator, shopping bags in both hands. He glanced up at the sound of her walking, and there she was.

He rolled the dolly with the box in her direction, calling to her to please hold the elevator door for him. A wheel on the dolly squeaked as he approached. A moment later, they were in the elevator together. She had pushed twenty-six, his new lucky number, pushed the number with perfectly manicured Ferrari red nails.

"Floor?" she said.

He pulled a piece of paper from a pocket and pretended to read it. "Twenty-six, please."

"What's that?" she said and nodded in the direction of the large box.

"Stove," he replied, half-surprised at the question since there were pictures of a stove on all four sides of the box beneath the word STOVE." It's taken a lot longer to install than we expected. It happens, you know, what can you do? We're just about finished. Just want to make sure everything is working right before we leave."

"I'm sure they would appreciate that," she said, watching the floor numbers light up over the door, sixteen, seventeen, eighteen . . .

They arrived on the twenty-sixth floor with Mickey enveloped in a heavenly cloud of sexy Nikki Devereaux perfume. Once the door opened, she said," You go ahead, darling, let me hold the door for you."

He rolled the dolly into the hall and turned left, slowly squeaking down the longer length of the hall, thinking there was an unspoken magic between the two of them. She didn't bother to give him a second look but stepped out of the elevator and headed in the opposite direction.

He turned around and followed her, closing the gap with what was going to have to pass as clever conversation. "Gee, I don't know what it is about this side of the building, but I always go the wrong way."

She didn't seem to rush, but he sensed a barely perceptible increase in her pace. He wasn't sure exactly what he was going to do next but knew that whatever it was, he would need his roll of tape. He stood in front of the door next to hers and smiled. He thought maybe he could just dash in before she closed the door, grab her in the privacy of her own unit. Her abduction would become a little private affair, just between the two of them, something they might share laughingly in calmer, quieter times, over a glass of her favorite wine.

She bobbled and dropped her keys, looked up at him at just that moment, and he knew she knew. He saw the change. An animal look in those beautiful brown eyes. She was suddenly fumbling a little too much with her keys, concentrating first on him, then the keys, and that's when she dropped them. He moved toward her, quickly.

He was just reaching, ready to grab sweet, sexy Nikki, spin her around, gently tape those luscious lips so they wouldn't cry out and ruin the moment. He was close enough to smell her perfume again. She would realize there was absolutely no point in fighting her own urges, coyly surrendering to this muscular hero who was—Wham!

With the explosion, Mickey saw stars. Literally. Bright light, jagged, white stars. The left side of his head exploded, leaving him just barely conscious enough to discern her sharp elbow drilling directly into his solar plexus. Bull's Eye! He felt the wind hammered out of his chest cavity in one massive, sledgehammer blow. He was only vaguely aware of the new pain when she grabbed him forcefully by the ears, scraping and digging her manicured Ferrari red nails in deep, digging them into the sides of his neck, then yanking his head down in the direction of her midsection.

His first thought, which turned out to be way off base, was what a strange way to initiate oral sex, only to see her delicious, fantastically firm Nikki thigh bring her cute dimpled little Nikki knee smashing up directly into his nose.

His head bounced up on impact. His scraped and shredded ears were torn from her grip by the sheer force of the blow and rocketed his head backward. He gasped for air as he staggered back against the wall. His hands reflexively grasped his splattered, bleeding nose. He gasped, staggered a step or two, defenseless, beaten, and coughing blood down his chest.

She suddenly dropped her fist from its cocked position and set to deliver the final blow. Only now did she recognize him standing in front of her holding what remained of his nose with both hands. "I know you. You're that moron who rear-ended us. The guy with that dreadful shirt."

It was all the chance he needed, the only chance he had left, and he took it, cold-cocking her with a right hook. He hit her as hard as he could in a final desperate attempt to save his own worthless self. She collapsed on the floor down and out, cold.

"Huh, glass jaw, I knew it," he said, only it came out," Glasth jaw, I knew ith." He quickly grabbed her keys, opened the door, and dragged her inside, where he collapsed in a heap on the floor just as the door closed behind him. He drifted in and out of consciousness, for how long he never knew, coming to only moments before Nikki began to stir. Fear of another beating at her hands propelled him into action. He moved as quickly as the intense pain would allow. Gasping through his mouth, since his splattered nose had been reduced to a mere cosmetic appendage.

He had a throbbing knot on the left side of his head where the eyebrow used to end. His ears felt like they had been twirled in a blender, and his nose, well, his nose was non-functioning and smashed out in the general direction of both cheekbones. He managed to tape her wrists behind her back and tape her ankles together. Then, just to be on the safe side, he wound the tape round and round her like a mummy.

Finally satisfied she couldn't get to him, he got a towel, made an ice pack, and pressed it against his throbbing head.

He sat there in the dark, on the floor, with his back against the wall. He got up three or four times for more ice in an unsuccessful attempt to keep the pain and swelling down. Each time he rose to retrieve more ice, he groaned, using the wall to help him stagger to his feet.

He eventually regained enough strength to go out into the hallway and retrieve the appliance box and dolly.

"Okay," he said, talking with an ice filled, blood-soaked towel held over his nose, and coughing up blood as he worked to get the words out. "Please, believe me. I won't hurt you. But you're going in this box. Now you can do it carefully, or I can hit you over the head and dump you in there. I don't particularly care right now. It's your choice. I'm going to try and move you. Carefully. If I get the idea you're fighting me. I'll drop you."

He set the bloodied ice pack on her white carpet, lowered the box on its side then cautiously wiggled her inside the box. His head throbbed and pounded with every heartbeat as he gasped and grunted. Somehow, he got her into the box, set the box upright, and closed the top. Then he collapsed on the floor, again.

He was out for a bit longer than twenty, and it was well after midnight when he eventually regained enough strength to attempt to wheel Nikki into the elevator, down to the parking level and into his car.

Miraculously, he somehow made it to his car undetected. He popped the lid of the cavernous trunk, grabbed either side of the box, and wrenched it up. The box easily rose until he realized he had never secured the bottom, and he watched as a wrapped and taped Nikki bounced and half-rolled across the floor.

He stood over her, debating for a moment, wondering if it was even worth it, before picking her up and half-rolling, half-dumping her into the trunk. He slammed the trunk closed and quickly drove out of the ramp leaving the box and dolly behind.

During the transportation phase of earlier projects, Mickey had always driven a roundabout route to Dell's. Tonight, he took the most direct route he knew, praying he would remain lucid enough to complete the twenty-five-minute drive without ending up in the ditch.

He eventually made it to Dell's, although there had been two or three times he felt himself losing it and had to press a finger firmly against the knot on the side of his head. The searing pain had refocused his attention, and now he was finally skidding into Dell's driveway, narrowly missing the mailbox, tossing gravel against the wheel wells, while anxiously pressing the automatic garage door opener.

He wasn't quite sure how he had managed to do it, but they had finally arrived, and he unceremoniously dumped his former heartthrob, Nikki Devereaux, onto the bed. He cautiously removed the tape undoing her hands and wrists just before running out of the room and making doubly sure the door was locked behind him.

"Mick, Mickey, hey, you okay? Mickey?" It was an intrusion, a soft familiar voice. "Mick, hey buddy, what the hell happened to you?"

He found himself starring into Dell's bleary eyes and unshaven face, and he was suddenly aware he had trouble breathing.

"Ahh, man," he groaned.

"Take it easy, pal. Man, what happened? Who did this to you? I think you might need a doctor."

"She's downstairs," Mickey whispered and limply pointed in the general direction of the staircase before dropping his head back on the couch and closing his eyes.

Dell turned to the stairs, looked back at Mickey for a nano-second and dashed down the steps." What? No. No, not again. I'm not going through this again." Dell charged back up the stairs a moment later. "What in God's name is the matter with you? Are you crazy?"

Mickey lay on the couch feeling more dead than alive, thinking he just might know the answer to that question.

Thirteen

Torsten Theisen was in the mood to celebrate. His opponents had caved in. He sat in his office, rubbing his hands with pure anticipation, but not for the legislative package he'd just rammed through. Good lord, jobs for two nitwit nephews and the extension of state parkland abutting his lake property all wedged between the lines of an education bill, big deal. Those things were all well and good, but nothing when compared to the personal attention he knew was about to be heaped upon him this very evening by one voter, in particular, Nikki Devereaux.

The best little bit of legislation he had ever engineered had been a year ago getting that little lady a cushy state job updating the Parks Resources Board to the tune of six figures per year. The board had ceased to exist a full year before he created the position so there really was nothing to update. She didn't even have to go to the office, what with the beauty of direct deposit and work from home nowadays. It was all too easy, and Nikki had shown herself to be a very appreciative member of the voting public. Nikki Devereaux a park resource.

He rubbed his hands gleefully, listening on speaker-phone as her phone rang. He stopped when her message kicked in. "Hey, this is Nikki . . ."

It was inadvisable to leave a message. He'd have to call her later, he thought, looking at his desk clock. Right now, he had a press conference to attend.

What a bunch of idiot's Torsten thought to himself, still in a major huff after finding out the press conference would be carried live. He was standing next to the Governor, the two of them behind a wood-grained Formica podium sporting a cardboard state seal, in front of the assembled press corps. He thought he should be telling Nikki what little get-up he wanted her to wear while she was cooking dinner, and instead, he was wasting his time with this collection of buffoons.

"Representative Theisen? The ramifications, sir, of this special session and the package you were able to pass?"

"I heard you," Torsten snapped, removing his hands from the pockets of his brown polyester suit coat, not at all happy about being pulled away from time with Nikki.

"It's a complex issue. But, guided by parents and the dedicated teachers, we'll lay the foundation of what happens in this state long after I'm gone."

"Are you planning to go anywhere, Representative Theisen?" someone shouted from the back row.

"I'm planning to get some much-deserved relaxation." He attempted a smile that he didn't quite accomplish. "After which, I plan to return to my home in Glacial Springs."

"Does that mean you don't relax at home?"

He shot a steely glance in the general direction but couldn't ascertain who had made the comment.

"It means I don't have the time to relax at home. I do god's work, idle hands being the devil's workshop. Something we should all keep in mind before wasting anyone's time."

"Ladies and gentlemen, thank you. I'll be happy to entertain any specific questions you may have for as long as it takes," the press secretary interjected.

"Torsten, take it easy out there, partner," the governor said. They were walking in the direction of the office wing, just a few paces ahead of the Governor's aides. "You would think you had a hot date lined up for tonight."

"I'm not inclined to waste a lot of time on press conference foolishness."

"Live press conferences, Torsten, are never foolish, dangerous maybe, but never foolish. You can't stand the heat, get out of the kitchen."

Meanwhile, in a kitchen up in Glacial Springs, "So, don't have the time to relax at home! We'll just see about that," growled Arliss, Mrs. Torsten Theisen. She slammed the oven door, turned off the kitchen TV, and took a deep breath.

Answer the damn phone, you little ingrate," Torsten muttered, then angrily hit the disconnect button on the speakerphone. It was almost nine in the evening, and Torsten knew, at this stage, the most he could wring out of his schedule was another thirty-six hours before he was due to return to Glacial Springs and joyless, ice-locked, Arliss.

Friends were based on favors in politics, and he wondered if perhaps the entertaining Miss Devereaux had found another market for her engaging favors? He couldn't risk the potential political fallout of storming over and pounding on her door. Those wise-guy city re-porters would love to get hold of a story like that, not to mention what he would have to deal with up in Glacial Springs.

He dialed Nikki's number again, then quickly hung up when her message came on. Nothing riled him more than a citizen not respecting the proper authority of the State. Exactly what was she up to?

Nikki's knee and elbow hurt. Her jaw was awfully sore but didn't appear to be broken. She could move it, although it felt like the whole left side of her molars, top and bottom, didn't quite line up properly. She had gingerly pulled the sticky grey tape off, fortunately, she had worn stockings, so the tape hadn't peeled her skin. That's all she'd need, work on a tan just to have some sex fiend ruin it in one night. The dreadful tape had completely destroyed her outfit, peeled most of the sequins off her belt, and ruined the creamy colored snakeskin on her heels. She examined her hands and counted three broken nails. This was shaping up to be the most dreadful day ever.

He had followed her down the hall, tried to grab her, which was when she recognized him. She hadn't been sure of it until she saw him grabbing his nose in the hallway. It was the way he held it, hands over his face, head tilted back slightly, and bleeding, when it all came back to her. The same fool who had rear ended Torsten's car.

* * *

Mickey was feeling a little bit better after napping past noon, followed by a three-hour visit to urgent care, where they cleaned and bandaged his nose. More importantly, he got a prescription for some very strong pain killers.

"The bottom line is we have to go through with it," he said.

"Damn, damn, damn, damn, damn," Dell whined, pacing back and forth, and shaking his head.

"I heard you the first time," Mickey groaned from the couch. He pressed what remained of his ice pack against the knot on the side of his head.

"No, don't, just don't say another thing, Mick. Does the term 'press our luck 'have any connotations? Here's the good news. If the cops come and arrest us, we're saved from the animals who attacked you. How do you get me into these things? I hate violence. I don't want to wind up looking like you. I mean, look what they did to you, although, I gotta say, it serves you right."

"No guys did this, Dell. That woman downstairs did it all."

"What?"

Mickey squeezed his eyes shut, swallowed, willed himself not to wretch as he half-propped himself up with his elbow. "She did this to me."

"That little girl down there did that to you?"

Mickey signaled Dell the okay sign.

"Oh, that's great. Absolutely beautiful. I oughta give that little thing a medal. Well, you know what? You deserve every bit of it. I'm glad she did it, Mick. Maybe this time you'll learn your lesson. I'm here to tell you, I'm not going to get involved in this one, don't count on me for anything."

By evening Mickey's voice was beginning to improve, not as much of a monotone. The blood collecting in the back of his throat, although not completely stopped, had minimized considerably, and the soup he was cautiously spooning into his mouth was helping to revive him.

"Well, I guess you're right, Mick. I'm just screwed on the deal, aren't I? Just by having her here and feeding the poor little thing, I've become guilty, again, of aiding and abetting you in another idiotic plot."

Mickey blew on his soup spoon.

"I don't know, you tell me, Genius, now what do we do?"

If it were up to Nikki, she would never eat this dreadful concoction. I mean, the carbs alone were killers. And the grease, it was going to attack her complexion by morning. *Clearly*, she thought, looking around, *not even the remotest hope for any facial products.* Things just kept going from bad to worse.

"I mean, like hello, anyone even home?" she wondered out loud, sitting cross-legged on the bed. She stared at the disgusting grease seeping through the pizza delivery box. "Gross, just absolutely gross," she said, then grabbed another piece from the box and ate it.

She could only guess what perverse ideas that creep had in mind for her, and not even a basic cable package in the room. And her nails, three of them broken. Just thinking how long it was going to take them to get back to perfection was enough to bring on a whole negative aura. She would literally have to book a month at a spa, first thing, after getting out of this pathetic little room. Not to mention the major skin work required after a diet of this garbage, she thought, then licked her fingertips and reached for the last slice. A month of non-stop work in a gym to completely detox her system, another two hundred and fifty dollars just to repair the damage to her nails. She was growing more and more depressed.

Torsten couldn't sleep, and just to be spiteful, he thought he'd yank the chain and call Nikki in the middle of the night. He'd called at ten, eleven, midnight, then twelve-thirty, one, one-fifteen, and one-twenty. He was beginning to see a pattern. Apparently, she was out for the night.

Not like her at all, he thought. He tossed and turned for the remainder of the night. He jumped from wanting to spank her out of pure enraged fury to wanting to spank her because he was glad to have her back safe and sound. Then, he was back to the enraged fury point of the argument and so it went, fitfully throughout the night.

He had ceased phoning her somewhere around three in the morning. He couldn't stand to hear the static clip of her voice message one more time and decided to finally get some sleep. Easier said than done, and at six, he finally just rolled out of his disheveled bed, made a cup of instant coffee in a travel mug, and drove to his office.

He'd been there for a few hours, moving stacks of files back and forth, accomplishing little if anything in the way of the people's business. Willing himself not to pick up the phone, place another call and listen to that damn message of hers one more time.

Sometime after midmorning, with the skeleton staff out on yet another coffee break, a sleep deprived, crabbier than usual, Torsten Theisen was forced to answer his own phone.

"Hello?" he half-shouted, then immediately dared to hope it just might be missing Nikki Devereaux, phoning her apologies with a logical explanation followed by some suggestions of exactly how she planned to make it all up to him.

"Representative Theisen, please."

There was something odd about the voice, a nasal quality, as though the caller had a horrible head cold. The pronunciation seemed off. He suspected the caller might be intoxicated and hung up the phone without a second thought.

"I got cut off?" Mickey asked himself, sitting in his steamy car, sweating. The sun glared through the windshield as he stared at the payphone receiver in his hand.

He studied his bandaged reflection in the rearview mirror. Eyes purple, and swollen, a huge lump alongside his left eye, the discoloration seeped along the side of his face in the direction of his ear, the white gauze covering his nose and, of course, those raised abrasions running up his neck and along the backs of his ears.

It was difficult, under the best of circumstances, to keep a low profile with white gauze taped over a major portion of his face. People tended to remember facial bandaging. It was the last thing he needed just now, people making a mental note of seeing him, let alone where.

He had driven north to the far edge of Washington County, where a seldom-used payphone sat in the corner of a rural parking lot. He was the only car in the lot, and he wanted to keep it that way. Just make this call quickly, hope he could be understood between the swelling and the bandaging, and get this whole affair off his plate before something else went horribly wrong.

He waited for a half-hour and dialed again, this time an officious female voice answered.

"Representative Theisen, please," Mickey said, suddenly coming awake.

"Who may I say is calling?"

He was momentarily stumped, and he replied, "George Gates." An alias he had used in the past during a period of failed online dating attempts.

"Let me connect you to Representative Theisen, Mr. Gates."

Suddenly, there he was, smarmy in all his political glory." Hello George, what is it I can do for you?" Torsten oozed over the phone, the upbeat lilt disguising his sour mood.

Mickey was having none of it. He had a throbbing pain running up the back of his head, exploding just behind his closed eyes. As he spoke, he gingerly massaged his forehead with his free hand, cautiously staying away from the bridge of his nose and the left side of his face.

"I'll tell you what you can do for me, Torsten," he visualized the crotchety old drunk attempting to snap his fingers in the car. "We've got something of yours, a little package named Nikki Devereaux. Ring any bells? One hundred grand, cash, tomorrow, call you later." Click, and he was off the line.

Torsten sat in stunned silence. *What in the hell was that? Who in the hell was that? Had he really mentioned Nikki's name?* He dialed Nikki's number again, waiting just long enough to hear the static before her voice message kicked in. *Nikki? Had the voice said a hundred grand or had he said he was hungry? Just what in the hell was going on here?*

Fourteen

ot so much as a peep out of Mickey in the past two days. *What in the hell was going on here?* Janice asked herself. Then, when she finally did get a call, it was her stepfather, Huey— haranguing her for money, like he had a snowball's chance of collecting any.

She was just hanging up after letting Mickey's phone ring for what seemed like hours. She'd even cruised past the War Bonnet Lounge just to see if his car was there. It wasn't. She'd reached the point where she was alternating between never wanting to see him again, ever, and then wanting to see him, just so she could strangle him slowly. The least he could do was face her like a man. Tell her he didn't want to see her. Tell her there was someone else, instead of acting like the worm he really was.

She could call Dell, she supposed, ask him if he'd seen Mickey? Explain to Dell that she was worried about idiot Mickey, maybe get a reading by the way he reacted.

But where those two were concerned, it was anyone's guess what the truth would be.

It had taken about thirty minutes, but the pain killers were finally kicking in, reducing the throbbing in his head to a manageable level. Mickey was writing a script for Nikki to read into a tape recorder. He wasn't going to chance another live phone conversation like the one between Janice and her father, Huey. That had been playing with fire.

The way this whole thing had come down, the last thing he needed was Nikki with a phone in her hands. No, she could just record a message. He'd get that to Torsten, not have to say anything himself, just get the taped message delivered, somehow, get the ransom money and get her out of his life. The sooner, the better.

He finished his script, laid down on the couch to rest, and was just drifting off dreaming he was in a boxing ring. His hands were tied, and Nikki was there. He couldn't tell for sure what she was wearing, something small and revealing, but she had a sledgehammer in each hand and seemed to have no trouble whirling them around effortlessly. He tried to flee, running around the ring as she chased him. The bell sounded and kept ringing, interrupting his dream. He opened his eyes, heard

the phone, and ignored it. Finally, peace and quiet returned.

Dell shaking Mickey's shoulder ten minutes later
ended any hope of rest. "Look at this grocery list," Dell
shouted a Mickey opened his eyes." Mickey, you gotta
back off here, you're eating me out of house and home,
come on." He stared at Mickey on the couch, resplendent
in a screaming yellow shirt, the image of two-dancing
jukeboxes with red music notes emanating out the top on
either side of the front. Had Mickey bothered to roll over,
Dell would see the back of the shirt sported the image of
a large 45 record under the banner,' Rock and roll never
dies!'

Mickey didn't bother to roll over, but he took a deep
breath and gave a loud sigh." It's not me. It's her," he
pointed a thumb in the general direction of the basement
stairs.

"Are you telling me that little thing down there is
responsible for all the food? Who are you trying to kid?"

"Dell, I'm not kidding," Mickey said, slowly sitting
upright. He popped two more pain pills and washed them
down with a glass of water from the coffee table. He
paused to ensure the pills had made the journey.

"Here," he half-tossed a bird mask from a shopping
bag on the floor, along with a pocket tape recorder and
the script he had carefully written out.

"What the hell is this?" Dell asked, thinking the mask looked familiar but not quite able to get a handle on it.

"Tweety Bird," Mickey said.

"I hated Tweety Bird. The cartoons just sucked. I always liked the cat, Sylvester. But, I'm not going in that room with her, so it doesn't matter. I mean, look what she did to you."

"She blindsided me. Just a couple of lucky shots stunned me for a moment, that's all."

"Yeah, well, I don't plan on getting blindsided. She probably hates Tweety Bird as much as I do," he said and tossed the mask onto the coffee table.

"Then I guess we're just stuck with her, aren't we? Because if I go in there, I can guarantee you there are going to be problems. Besides, if we just let her know we're not going to hurt her, let her know that this is the way to get her ass out of here. You'll have her eating out of your hand in no time. Besides, you whined and told me you didn't like the Spiderman mask, so there you go."

Nikki Devereaux polished off the last of her grilled cheese sandwich. It was cold, but that wasn't really the issue. She still felt absolutely ravenous. When she was nervous, she got stressed, and when she was stressed, she ate. Eating tended to make her more stressed, which in turn caused her to eat more. In very short order, it became a vicious cycle. Eating to relieve stress, stressing because she ate so much. Right now, she could really go for a slice of last night's greasy pizza.

She had always been this way, as far back as when she was plain old Alice Bronkowski from Northfield, Minnesota. It was the same when she dyed her hair red and danced under the stage name Ember. From Ember, she had reinvented herself as Monique Ménage. She bid a quick adieu to Monique after the solicitation charge, which had caused her to stress and balloon. Ultimately, after a boatload of jazzercise and Lean Cuisines, she had reinvented herself as Nikki Devereaux, and it was as Nikki that she had felt most at home.

She had found her true calling as a personal lobbyist for just one key client, namely herself. Handling one key account, Torsten Theisen. At least, until the night when that disgustingly dreadful moron rear-ended them. Now, here she was in this gross little room, pigging out on gross food, putting on about ten pounds a day, and if she didn't get out of here soon, she was going to explode.

The sound of the door opening startled her. She stared wide-eyed as a man wearing a mask approached her cautiously, half-a-step at a time. He held sheets of yellow legal paper and some kind of device out in front of him.

Her first thought was, *The device might be a taser or some shock control thingy*, but relaxed when she saw it was just a small tape recorder. He stopped just short of the foot of the bed, and it suddenly dawned on her what the mask was supposed to be.

"I have to tell you. I hated Tweety Bird as a kid."

The mask nodded, not saying a thing.

"Here," she replied to the nod, handing him the empty plate. "I'm finished. When's dinner?"

He extended the paper to her, which she grabbed, and began to read quietly. It took her a few moments to go through the directions, nodding her head, seeming to agree.

"Hey, Tweety, you had better be kidding here. A hundred grand. That's all you think I'm worth? A lousy hundred grand. This is insulting. I'll be a laughing stock," she shouted and shook the sheets of legal paper in Dell's face.

She was suddenly off the edge of the bed. She backed Dell up in the direction of the door, thrust a pointed finger toward him like a dagger with a broken Ferrari-red tip, accentuating every other word.

"A hundred grand! What kind of a bad joke is this? Do you have any idea who you're dealing with? I'm worth at least ten times this! I've got shoes that are more expensive than this. Arghh!" she screamed, tossed the papers up in the air, then stomped back toward the bed as the sheets of yellow paper drifted back and forth before quietly settling on the floor.

Dell stood stone still, not wanting to further excite her with any movement. It was a little like finding yourself in the cage of a lion, hoping if maybe you just remained still, the thing might not notice you.

Nikki seemed to smell his fear, and slowly, like a cat appraising a mouse, she turned her head in Dell's direction. "So, you're going to ransom me? That's what this is all about?" A smile came across her lips, eyes glaring, examining Dell." You're not that moron who ran into me the other night, are you?"

Dell shifted his weight, cautiously moving an inch or two toward the door as he shook his head no.

"Well, if you see that idiot, you can tell him from me, I'm not finished. Not by a long shot. Now, give me that," she indicated the papers scattered on the floor.

Dell was about to reach for them when an image of Mickey, beaten, swollen and bloody on the couch, more dead than alive, flooded his brain. He silently pointed to the bed, moving his hand to indicate he wanted her to sit on the bed before he picked up the papers.

"Oh, for God's sake. I don't believe this," she said, scooping up the papers." You're almost as stupid as that other idiot. Get out of here before I change my mind."

Dell nodded and hurried to the door. Mickey, who had been listening and watching through the peephole, opened the door to let him out.

"Hey, Tweety, honey, get me something else to wear, okay. I've been in this outfit too long, and I'm way past dewy. Besides, that other fool ruined my shoes and belt," she said and pointed at her shoes lying on the floor.

Dell nodded again, stood staring at her for a second or two as she sat cross-legged on the bed reading the script.

"Come on!" Mickey whispered, finally pulling him out the door.

"Oh, and some ice cream might be nice, too," she called.

"See what I mean? Do you see what I mean? She's an absolute nut case," Mickey said as he pulled Dell out the door.

"Oh, I don't know, Mick. I mean, she hates your guts. She can't be all bad."

Mickey put his eye up to the peephole again and watched her reading the script. Her lips moved as she worked her way thru the lines he'd written. She put the script down, picked up the small recorder, pushed a couple of buttons, and said, "Test, test."

"Hey, where do you think you're going?" Mickey called to Dell, heading out the door.

"I'm going to get her some clothes, like she told me, and maybe some ice cream, too."

"Are you kidding me? She doesn't—"

Dell hurried up the stairs, cutting Mickey off in mid-sentence.

Great, thought Mickey, looking back through the peephole. Now Dell was leaving the world of the sane. He watched Nikki rehearse her lines, practice her inflections. She shook her head in disgust, rolled her eyes in exasperation, and started over again.

"You got her a black bustier with red lace and a grey sweatsuit? I don't see the logic. How does this help the situation we're in right now? Besides, this bustier is probably too small," Mickey shook the garment at Dell.

"Yeah, I know, but the sweatsuit is one size fits all, so hopefully, she can be comfortable and feel pretty at the same time. You know how important they say that is to women."

"I don't know anything of the sort. Well, go ahead. You might as well toss them in there. I'm certainly not going to risk it. She doesn't seem to have the best reaction to me. And what the hell is that?" he asked, referring to a box under Dell's arm.

"Snicker's ice cream cones, just to, you know, keep her happy."

"Happy? I told you before. The woman is nuts. Don't let her looks fool you, Dell. You're thinking with the wrong head."

"Yeah, well, like I said before, she hates you, so she can't be all bad." Dell pulled on the Tweety Bird mask, knocked on the door then nodded at Mickey to pull it open.

"Oh, hey, Tweety. What, for me?" She nodded at the pile of folded clothing he carried, thinking, *what in God's name is that disgusting black thing with the red lace.*

"Say, I was able to give you a couple of different versions of what you wrote down. I've got a sad, sadder, and saddest version, whichever one you want to use, no additional charge. That was a joke," she added, not really able to detect any reaction from behind the mask. "I still think you're way too low with the money thing, but then again, you're the professionals. Anyway, I'm sure you don't need me telling you how to run your business. Okay, thanks," she said, taking the clothing and handing Dell the recorder, dismissing him, taking a closer look at the black garment with the red lace.

Dell lingered for a moment, hoping she'd move the top and uncover the Snickers ice cream cone he'd hidden.

"Mmm-mm, I love it," she said, suddenly spotting the ice cream.

"Can you believe it?" Dell said once he was out of the room. "She made versions. Christ, we'll have her out of here in no time."

Mickey smiled for the first time in almost two days, then winced at the sudden pain it caused.

He chose the version he thought would have the best effect, Nikki's saddest, then drove to the state capitol, pulling into a White Castle parking lot, almost kitty-corner from the capitol grounds, and waited.

It didn't take too long for the perfect targets to show, two kids, no more than eleven, skateboarding down the sidewalk.

"Hey, guys, can you give me a hand here?" he called, holding a manila envelope addressed to Torsten Theisen, Room 211, Capitol Building. "You see that building over there?"

"You mean that big one?" the shorter of the two said, then pointed at the Capitol just across the street and giggled.

No, the other one, you little brat, Mickey thought. "Yeah, that one, you're very smart, son. Look, I'll give each of you guys five dollars," he held out two fives with the envelope." All you have to do is deliver this little package to the address written here on the front."

"You play the piano, mister? My uncle, he plays."

"Huh?"

"Your shirt. It looks like a piano there," the kid pointed to Mickey's shirt, a broad keyboard running the length of the front from the top of the collar down to the hem, a pale pink on pink background pattern of swirling champagne glasses.

"Oh, no, I don't play," Mickey half-stuttered." Think you guys can deliver this?"

"Why are you wearing plastic gloves," the shorter one said.

"I injured my hands, and I have to wear gloves. Hey, I can ask two other guys. Maybe they'd like to make five bucks."

"Why don't you do it?" asked the taller of the two. Both kids hung back a few feet, just out of reach, and more than a little streetwise.

"Why don't I do what?"

"Why don't you deliver the package?"

"Good question, son. As two smart kids like you can see, I was in a horrible accident, and I don't have the strength to make it all the way over there. So, I thought maybe you guys could help me. Okay? Five bucks."

"Why don't you just drive?"

"Because I thought maybe you two would be able to use five dollars. Well, what do you think, fellas?" He rubbed the bills back and forth slightly, letting them hear the sound of currency.

They looked at one another and communicated, somehow, two inner-city entrepreneurs." Ten bucks . . . each."

"Ten bucks. Are you, are you sure you can get it there for me? Because it's very important that the man gets this package."

"Sheesh," the taller one snorted." We'll get it there. Just show us the ten bucks first, man. Else, we got other things we gotta do." His shorter companion didn't say anything but nodded in agreement.

Mickey was sure they'd learned the street haggling trade from exposure to their mother's chosen profession but found himself trapped. He pocketed the fives and pulled out two tens. "The name and office number are right here. Thanks for your help," he said, then watched as they skateboarded off against traffic before he fled the scene.

"Children aren't allowed in here. Get out," Torsten Theisen yelled at the two young boys entering his outer office carrying skateboards.

"We got us a delivery," one of them said.

"What do you mean a delivery?"

"Man give us this package, said we was to bring it here to the address what's on the front. Then this here Mr. Torsten, he gonna give us ten dollars, each," the shorter of the two lied.

"Look, I don't know what the two of you think you're trying to pull. Hmm-mmm, a package, you say?" he said, focusing on the manila envelope they carried, suddenly interested.

"Yes, sir. Man told us to bring it right up here. Give it to this man here," he pointed to Torsten's name penned on the front of the envelope." Soon as we get ten dollars."

"Ten dollars?" Torsten exclaimed.

"Each," the taller boy added, moving back a step.

"Okay, son, here's for you," he fished the last two bills from his wallet, thanking God they were tens and quickly snatched the envelope. "Now, run along."

Twenty minutes later, he turned the recorder off after listening over and over again to the heart-breaking plea from Nikki Devereaux. Obviously, she was just holding on by a thread. He reread the written instructions demanding one hundred thousand dollars in twenties.

How had this happened? How had they found her? How had they been linked together, Torsten and Nikki? God, it couldn't be his fault, could it? Not for the first time, he shook his head and cursed the den of iniquity the capital city had become.

On the other hand, if he could get this mess off his plate, keep the whole thing quiet, keep his seat in the house, keep his unrelenting wife, Arliss, at bay, all for just a hundred grand, it was a bargain. The good Lord was watching over Torsten, that was for damn sure. A hundred grand? Goodness, he had that in campaign contribution cash stuffed in a safe up at the lake. Not in twenties, maybe, but that was a small matter, and if he left now, he could be back before morning.

Fifteen

Mickey paced back and forth across Dell's kitchen. "I'm barely back, things are just starting to finally go our way, and you drop this on me. Why the hell did you even answer the damn thing?" He was waving the beer Dell had handed to him the moment he opened the door.

"Hey, last time I checked, it was my house. I mean, the phone rings, I answer the thing. It's a novel concept, I know," Dell said.

"Well, you're nuts. Janice is coming out here? Did you tell her anything else besides I would be back later? God save me, I had it all covered. I was going to tell her we decided to go up walleye fishing in Canada. Of course now, you've managed to screw that plan up royally."

"Mick, you gotta be kidding, that's your plan? Walleye aren't even biting this time of year. It's too damn hot."

"Knock it off," Mickey said and stormed out of the kitchen.

Dell remained leaning against the kitchen counter, sipping his beer, figuring he would just let Mickey calm down for a while. It was three maybe four sips later that he heard the first loud crash and he ran outside.

"What in the hell are you doing?" Dell shouted as Mickey hoisted another concrete block over his head and threw it onto the hood of his car. "Mick, stop it, stop it."

"Well, thanks to you answering the phone, just because it rings, Janice is going to take one look at me and wonder what the hell happened?" he hoisted another concrete block over his head and launched it onto the hood. "Where do you keep the baseball bats?"

"What the . . ."

"I'm going to tell her I was involved in an accident. Her next question is going to be . . ." Mickey picked up a four-foot length of fence post, swung it into the right headlight, then moved to the side, forcing Dell to jump back and out of the way as he swung into the windshield. Dell winced at the sound of the impact and saw a crystal web that radiated out perhaps eighteen inches in all directions.

"Her next question will be, what does my car look like? Well, thanks to certain people who feel they have to answer the phone, now my car has had an accident.

Happy?" Mickey had a slight smile on his face that, combined with his nose, made him look not quite sane.

"I was thinking you could tell her you fell off a ladder or something. You know, like maybe we were working on the roof, and you slipped. I never told her you had a car accident. I just said an accident." Dell punctuated the last statement with a long pull on his beer can.

Mickey stopped, stood quite still, then dropped the fence post. He accessed the damage he had done to his car, the hood, both front quarter panels, the windshield, the right headlight. "You never told her a car accident? Thanks for sharing," he said and calmly walked back into the house.

"Let me just share a little something with you, Mickey," Janice said as she paced back and forth across Dell's living room." I was worried. Okay? I know I'm stupid, but I was worried about you. Not that you give a damn. God only knows why I even bother, because you don't care about anyone except your own self. I called and called and called. All the while wondering where you were. Were you dead in a ditch? Did you drown? Had you been hit by lightning? And, when I wasn't calling, I was crying, my heart was literally breaking."

She'd been going on for the better part of thirty minutes, pacing, yelling, crying, screaming, and Mickey was eyeing the vial of pain pills longingly, thinking he had heard all of this somewhere before. He had, three times before, as a matter of fact, all within the past half-hour.

After the phone call, Janice had hung up and raced to Dell's. She pounded on the front door and began to unload the moment she saw Mickey pretending to be semi-conscious on the couch. He barely had enough time to set the stage, damage his car, wrap gauze around his head, and get the ice packs out. He'd collected every prescription container he could find, filling them with breath mints he found in a drawer, lining them up on the coffee table, so it looked like he was on a ton of medication. He was just getting a robe out when he spotted her car raising dust as she roared up the driveway. He'd barely had enough time to slip the robe on over his piano shirt, toss his jeans behind the couch, and pretend to be napping when she burst through the door. Dell, the worthless coward, was suddenly nowhere to be found.

"What?" he groaned.

"I said, have you bothered to listen to even one damn thing I've been saying? Or, are you off in some ridiculous fantasy world again, where you seem more comfortable living your life instead of making any commitment to a responsible, worthwhile endeavor…"

'Commitment.' Now he did need those pain pills. *Had he heard that right? The word 'commitment 'shot across the bow.*

She paused, "Here, let me help you. How many?" opening up the vial of pain killers.

Mickey signaled with two fingers, not wanting to look her in the eye, choosing instead to appear more injured and completely miserable, which, under the circumstances, wasn't all that difficult.

"Okay, I'll stop for now. We'll continue this some other time. When you're feeling better."

I can hardly wait, he thought.

"Look, I'd kiss you, but you're so banged up I don't know where." She kissed her finger and gently touched the gauze he had wrapped around the top of his head.

"Be good, get some rest. I'm still mad at you but call me when you're able. I'll check up on you tomorrow," She slung her purse over her shoulder, and softly closed the door behind her.

Mickey nodded from the couch, pretending to drift off to sleep, then watched, peeking from the corner of the window to make sure she left.

"Man, that was one pissed off lady," Dell said, suddenly appearing from nowhere. He stood behind Mickey, the two of them watching as her car reached the county road and roared off. "Look at her go. She must have that thing floored."

"Yeah, thanks for all your help. Where the hell did you go?" Mickey turned away from the window and began unwrapping the gauze from around the top of his head.

"I hid under my bed," Dell replied matter of factly. "What the hell is all prescription bottles out here, and what's with the head?"

"Are you kidding? You heard her. This is probably the only reason I'm still alive. There were a couple of times when she was pacing back and forth, I thought for sure she was going to run into the kitchen and grab a knife. Man, I tell you."

"Yeah, she was pretty pissed off."

"I've got to get moving so we can unload that witch downstairs."

"Nikki?"

"No, the other witch. Don't even start," Mickey said, gently touching the outer edges of his nose. The swelling was gradually receding, giving way to a variety of different hues, all in the purple family. "I just want to bring this whole chapter to a close and go back to living my simple life. I've got to get into the office tonight, burn some instructions for our pal, Torsten, and hopefully, within the next forty-eight hours, we'll be another hundred grand ahead of the game."

"What office?"

"The real estate office, where I clean?"

"Oh yeah, your office. I guess I just forgot."

* * *

"Mmm-mmm, I'm sure this is the right address. Anyway, it's the one on the corner, the door actually faces the side street, but it's really easy to find, Tweety," Nikki said, then stuffed the last of the ice cream cone into her mouth.

Dell had just handed her a written request for Torsten Theisen's address, the unit he stayed in when he was doing the people's business, except for those nights when he was doing Nikki. He had sweetened the request with two Snickers ice cream cones.

Nikki was sitting cross-legged on the bed, wearing a robe and gray sweat pants. She licked her fingers and anxiously tore open the second cone. "No point in letting this melt," she said and took a large bite. "Mmm-mmm, just remember, the doorbell doesn't work. Hasn't all session. Really gets Torsten mad, but the landlord doesn't seem to give a damn. So, anyway, you have to knock," she said, then took another large bite of the ice-cream cone.

Dell cautiously took the piece of paper she handed him and quickly exited the room.

"When's dinner?" she called after him.

✳ ✳ ✳

On his way home from cleaning the office, Mickey drove past Torsten's address, finding it just as Nikki had described, a corner unit, set behind a thick hedge and two large elm trees. One of a half-dozen, two-story brick townhouses. Each front door was inset slightly, affording a bit of privacy to residents and providing Mickey the opportunity, at 3:00 in the morning, to quietly slither up to the door and leave his payoff instructions.

He hadn't planned on ringing the doorbell or even knocking, for that matter. That was the nice thing about leaving items on a doorstep in the middle of the night. You never ran into anyone. He just left the instructions along with an empty cardboard box for Torsten's payment on the front stoop, hoping Torsten had the good sense to exit out the front door when he left in the morning.

He was back in his car in just a few seconds. A minute or two later, he was making a left-hand turn onto a busier street. At this hour, there was only one other vehicle he had to wait for. Wouldn't you know, no blinker and a left-hand turn right in front of him, forcing Mickey to slam on the breaks to avoid hitting the fool. What were the odds?

                              * * *

His trip should have taken a lot longer, and Torsten was amazed he was already back in town, hours ahead of what he thought it would take to get up to his cabin and back. He would have been happy if it weren't for the dreadful circumstances. Still, all in all, he was relieved to have the cash, although it would entail months of hard-core fundraising to get the old slush fund coffers built up to where they had been. Up to the lake and back, no real traffic either way and wouldn't that just be his luck, almost broadsided by some fool in a wreck of a car turning off of his street at this hour. All those miles round trip, ahead of schedule, and just when you think things might be going your way, you run into a moron. The car was missing a headlight, had a damaged windshield, and the hood was all banged up. It might just be an idea for a bit of proper legislation next session, keep folks like that off the road and away from law-abiding citizens like himself.

After parking in front, he waited in his car for a few moments, lights off. He checked the street for a long minute before he pulled out the bag of campaign contribution cash. He carried it from the front seat up to his door, where he saw the box and envelope Mickey had left only a few short moments before.

Torsten slept like the dead on his living room couch, never even bothered to get out of his clothes. The phone ringing woke him from his dream of Nikki. There was only one call he was interested in today, and it wasn't supposed to come through until eleven fifteen. Torsten rolled over, closed his eyes, fighting to regain his sleep, and ignored the phone.

The instructions seemed relatively clear and straightforward. He would be told where to drive, leave the box they had provided him with the cash inside, then return home and wait for Nikki. Under the circumstances, Torsten had no choice but to trust them.

Didn't that just give one pause for thought, Arliss reflected after hanging up the phone. And just where was Mr. Relaxation at seven in the morning? There was bound to be some ridiculous explanation, and Arliss decided that it just might be best to confront Torsten down in the capital and get to the bottom of all this completely childish behavior. The sooner, the better. If she left now, she could be there later this morning.

"Look, I call the guy at eleven fifteen this morning. He won't be able to trace a payphone call that's going to last less than thirty seconds. I'll use an accent and a cloth over the phone." Mickey said. He held a thick breakfast sausage in his hand, waved it in Dell's direction to emphasize his point, then stuffed it into his mouth. He licked his fingertips, and talked as he chewed. "Mmm, I figure by mid-afternoon we'll be in a higher rent district of 'Easy Street.' I'll hand the stuff to you like we planned, you drive up north, bury the stuff, and hightail it back down here. Then, I'll defuse Janice and get that mess quieted down."

At ten after eleven, Mickey placed his call to Torsten Theisen. It hadn't been the easiest of mornings, Dell, as Tweety Bird, delivered a sheet of written instructions to Nikki, who had put up a hell of a fuss about the grey sweatsuit she had to wear.

"Maybe some other color would be better for her?" Dell had offered, after emerging from the room in the midst of her tirade.

"This isn't about style, Dell. This is about not getting caught. She is not calling the shots here. We are. Now, get her taped up, put this pillowcase over her head before we start to fall behind schedule. Either she cooperates, or I'll pick out her outfit, and we both know she'll be a lot less happy with whatever I choose. Get back in there and tell her that."

The threat of Mickey choosing her clothes had seemed to be a bit more pressure than even Nikki could stand. After a hasty midmorning snack of a king-sized Butterfinger candy bar, she allowed Dell, or rather Tweety Bird, to tape her wrists, place the pillowcase over her head and guide her into the trunk of Mickey's car.

Dell had placed a pillow in the trunk for her head, carefully taping her feet once she was in the trunk and tossing another Butterfinger in with her for a quick snack once she was released.

Mickey drove off, not as concerned about the exchange as he was relieved to return her to her rightful place next to Torsten, where they could conspire to make someone else miserable. Now, it only remained to set the final act in motion, and Mickey did just that, dialing Torsten Theisen at his townhouse.

Torsten followed his instructions explicitly, wanting to complete the exchange with as little trouble as possible. He had all the cash in the box this gang of cutthroats had provided. He waited at his dining room table and jumped to answer the phone, barely halfway through the first ring.

"Yes?"

"Ready?" a voice said.

My God thought Torsten, *I'll be lucky if they don't deliver her in pieces.* "Yes, yes, I'm ready. Let's just get this whole business completed."

"Change of plans," the voice snickered. Place the box in the southeast corner of the top floor of the River Ramp, you know it, this ramp, Señor?"

Señor? Thought Torsten, *international kidnappers.* "Yes, yes, I know the ramp. I can be there shortly," he said. It was just a few blocks from his townhouse, and he drove past it daily.

"Just leave the box on the top floor, southeast corner, and drive back home. Clear?"

"Yes, yes perfectly."

Mickey hung up the phone, walked across the street to his car already parked in the ramp. This was where things could get a little dicey, innocently waiting in the ramp, simply minding his own business, a woman bound up in his trunk wearing a grey sweatsuit with a pillowcase over her head. Not the easiest set of circumstances to explain your way out of.

Torsten would never be called a drinking man. He was more of a teetotaler. But just now, despite the morning hour, he needed some fortification, and he poured himself a swallow, possibly two, of aquavit, for medicinal purposes only. He swallowed it down, let it burn, then picked up his box and left on his appointed delivery.

Mickey waited on the first floor of the parking ramp. Every minute seemed to drag for what seemed like an hour. Adrenaline coursed through his veins. His pulse pounded in his head and throbbed through his smashed nose. Finally, he saw Torsten drive to the upper level, then exit the ramp two or three minutes later.

Mickey slumped down almost below the dash and prayed fervently that no one would spot him. Prayed that all four of his possible exits weren't blocked by the police, that snipers weren't stationed on the surrounding rooftops, or a helicopter wasn't hovering overhead.

He eventually climbed out of his car and walked up to the deserted top level. He grabbed the box and hurried back to his car. Thinking as he walked that, *If it was filled with cut newspaper, he was probably nailed anyway and if it was full of cash, he had a pretty good chance of pulling the whole thing off.* Either way, the dye was cast.

He gingerly helped Nikki Devereaux out of his trunk, cringing with the memory of his previous close encounter with her. He half-hoisted, half-pulled her out of the trunk, thinking she hadn't seemed this heavy just three days ago. He loosened her wrists just enough so she could eventually free herself but giving him a generous three or four minutes to drive out of the ramp.

He thought about saying something clever, thought about maybe kicking her for beating him up. In the end, he just said, "Mademoiselle," in his best Canadian hockey accent, "count to one hundred very, very slowly."

He jumped behind the wheel and drove off as quickly as prudently possible, desperately searching for squad cars and laughing out loud when he didn't see any.

It took Nikki no more than two minutes to unwrap the tape, pull the pillowcase off her head and start walking. She got her bearings immediately, realizing she was just a couple of blocks from Torsten's townhouse, feeling ridiculous in heels and a grey sweatsuit but taking comfort in the large Butterfinger candy bar.

What she wanted right now was a shower, a decent outfit, and a couple of weeks at a spa.

Torsten hadn't been home for two minutes and was wondering what he should do now. Did he wait? Go to his office? Drive as quickly as possible up to Glacial Springs? He couldn't decide what to do and was deep in thought, pondering, when an intense pounding on his front door answered all his questions.

Amazing, Nikki was back that fast. "It worked, it worked," he half-shouted, hurried to the door, and tore it open. "Darling."

"Don't you darling me. I'm in no mood for any of your fiddle faddle, Torsten," Arliss barked and brushed past him into the living room. She turned and waved a finger in his face."I'm in absolutely no mood for any 'business of the people' nonsense. I've a good mind to just—" She stopped in mid-sentence, spying the bottle of aquavit next to the empty glass on the dining room table. She walked over, examined the glass, and immediately detected Torsten's earlier use. She checked her watch to confirm the morning hour before slowly straightening herself. A black patent leather purse hung from a meaty forearm. Her arms were crossed, and her grey hair was permed tightly against her skull.

"Perhaps, you would care to explain yourself," she said, a demand rather than a question posed to the cornered Torsten.

She took a step closer, realized his clothes were wrinkled that he was in need of a shave, bleary-eyed and yes, smelled of aquavit.

"Torsten, what on earth could you possibly be thinking, carrying on this way? Disgraceful, that's what this is, positively disgraceful and disreputable." She pointed to the bottle of aquavit sitting on the dining room table. If this is your idea of relaxation, I find it completely unacceptable. You will cease this behavior immediately, do you hear me? Immediately. You're carrying on like a stumblebum, and that behavior will not last one moment longer. Is that clear? When I think of all that I have— What was that?" she asked, interrupting herself.

"Huh?" Torsten barely managed to grunt out, completely stupefied. He was still in the process of recovering from the shock of Arliss pounding on his front door in the middle of possibly the most important and desperate transaction of his life.

"Don't you huh me. I thought I heard something out in the kitchen," she said, turning on her heel and gaining speed as she burst through the swinging kitchen door.

Nikki had found the key under the flower pot where Torsten always left it for her. They had the understanding that it would be best if she quietly entered from the back door, no point in getting the neighbors talking about her comings and goings. Just now, she was focused on a very long, very hot bath before climbing into some different clothes and calling Torsten at his office to come pick her up and take her home. She was not in the best of moods after being forced to traipse four blocks along a busy commercial street dressed in this ridiculous outfit like some common tramp. Hair an absolute mess, three broken nails, ruined heels and jiggling what felt like twenty or thirty extra pounds. Add to all that the fact that she had been ransomed at a bargain basement discount price of a hundred thousand dollars. If word of this ever got out, she would be an absolute laughing stock.

She thought she heard something, then thought, hmm-mmm, not like Torsten to watch TV, let alone leave it on, and she started for the living room to investigate. They met in mid-door swing, Arliss bursting through the door, catching Nikki not quite fully on the chin. The blow was enough to momentarily stun, sending Nikki reeling backward. She didn't fall, unfortunately, for if she had, it might have provided her the moment or two needed to collect her senses. Instead, she reverted to her hallway battle with Mickey just a few nights earlier, thinking I'll be damned if he gets away with this again. She kicked out blindly, finding her intended target. She kicked again and followed up with a smashing blow to the back of the neck that sent the permed hair object of her aggression crashing to the floor. She was ready to deliver more, but there were a couple of things not quite right. The first was the grey-haired woman with the five-dollar perm lying on the floor, and then there was Torsten, screaming incoherently.

"Ahh-hhh, stop it, stop it. My God, stop it, are you crazy?"

Nikki had just about had it with the whole sordid mess. Her nails, her food cravings, the added weight, this stupid, unattractive outfit, grey was one of the worst colors on her, for God's sake. Now, following the complete mortification of being ransomed at a discount, Torsten was screaming because his mother had attacked her. Well, that was just about enough.

"Oh, just bite me, Torsten," she shouted back and stormed into the dining room, poured an extremely healthy amount of aquavit into the glass, and drank it down. "I need a ride home, now," she said in a raspy voice. Then shuddered as the burning liquid seared its way through her chest.

Sixteen

O ver the course of the next couple of weeks, Mickey's nose healed. Along with giving him a new look, it gave Janice an incentive to suggest to him the benefits of reconstructive surgery. "Even if it was a hit and run, shouldn't your insurance policy pick up the cost to get that repaired. I mean, honey, did you contact them about it?"

It was Saturday night, and Janice had told him in no uncertain terms he was taking her out to dinner and that no, they were not going to sit in the War Bonnet Lounge all night and drink. So, they were sitting in a booth at Potty's, a trendy place with a trendier name. Janice was on her third twelve-dollar cosmopolitan, and Mickey was trying to figure out why it was different if you got drunk on twelve-dollar drinks here instead of the two-dollar drinks at the War Bonnet?

She had been going on for the past fifteen minutes about calling an attorney to sue his insurance company and getting his nose reconstructed. "You could pick one out, a nose, I mean, maybe one like a movie star, Tom Cruise, or someone like that."

"Maybe Sammy Davis Junior," he interjected.

"No, not his, but they have all these pictures, so you can choose one, I mean, it's not like you'd be losing anything, and it still looks like it really hurts. Now, what you need to do…"

What he needed to do, thought Mickey *was get on with another project*. The past few weeks had put some distance between the Nikki Devereaux deal and his current idea. Actually, it had been something Janice had said, early on, harping about a lawyer, and that got Mickey thinking that the last time he had used a lawyer was when Jack Kelley had charged him cash in advance to be sentenced to sixteen months in Lino Lakes on the receiving stolen property charge.

Getting a hundred grand from Jack Kelley would be a nice little payback after having to cool his heels locked up with criminals for sixteen months. He shook his head just thinking about it.

"What do you mean no, Mickey? Are you even listening to anything I've said?"

"Yeah, Janice, I heard it all." He didn't add, before.

"Well, I was just saying that it would seem to me you would want to avail yourself of the services of a good attorney. I mean, a jury would take one look at you and award you whatever it took to get that nose fixed. And, did I mention they have these books, and you can pick out a nose from the book, or one from a movie star, say like Tom Cruise? Now Tom Cruise…”

Yeah, Jack Kelley.

"Can you imagine the two of us," Mickey had said, putting his arm around Dell." Sitting on that kind of dough? All those working stiffs with their regular pain-in-the-ass jobs, pensions, and fancy little vacations. We by-passed all of em, just using the old noggin'."

"And this is perfect, Jack Kelley, he's a shyster. Exactly the type of guy who won't go to the cops because he's always doing something crooked. Like the time he nicked me for seventy-five hundred dollars, so I could sit on my ass up in Lino lakes, looking out at the world, locked up with real criminals for a year and a half."

Mickey found, during the course of his late-night office research, that Jack Kelley had since moved on to fleecing elderly clients and mismanaging trust accounts. At least that's what he had been doing up to the time of his disbarment. Kelley had two properties listed in his portfolio and didn't owe a dime on either of them. A home in St. Paul and a lake place up north, both of them completely free and clear. To Mickey's way of thinking, that made things pretty easy, *snatch the wife, stick with the hundred-grand game plan and let things take their natural course.*

He'd gotten Kelley's address off the internet and had been following his wife, Bunny, off and on for the past week. A little blonde with a very surly attitude. Apparently, her favorite weapon was her tongue, which she apparently kept honed to a razor's edge.

It served old Jack right, thought Mickey. She had a frown etched on her face that two facelifts had been unable to erase. It might be more of a payback if he didn't grab her, just leave her out there, making every day miserable for Kelley.

She was nothing if not routine, leaving the house every day around nine in the morning for a workout. Tuesday and Friday were her hair days, blonde, blonde, and more blonde. Then shopping every day before a late lunch where the little darling pounded down brandy manhattans like they were going out of style, home usually by four o'clock. They never seemed to go out at night, and she made a run to the liquor store every other day.

Actually, he had never seen Kelley but figured he was either up and out early or left later while Mickey was following Bunny around town. Probably just as well he didn't see him, why run the risk of being recognized. Jack might be a disbarred old scammer, but he wasn't stupid, and the prisons were full of guys who had underestimated someone. Mickey knew that for a fact.

After reviewing a number of different options, he settled on quietly grabbing Bunny from the house when she came home in the afternoon. She was a little thing, but then so was Nikki and she had nearly killed him. He was thinking he would toss something over her, a sheet or a coat, wrap her up, throw her over his shoulder and dump her in the back seat. Hopefully, she'd be tired from a combination of shopping and brandy manhattans and wouldn't give him any trouble. He just had to figure out a few of the finer details, like getting into her house, grabbing her, getting her into his car, not being spotted by neighbors, and oh yeah, avoiding arrest.

A walk around her backyard one sunny afternoon convinced him he could slip in the house through a large basement window conveniently covered by one of those fancy bushes that turned red in the fall. Sneak in, wait patiently, grab her from behind, and carry her out in a drop cloth.

He wore a painting outfit for the occasion. New white pants with the loops for brushes, a paint-splattered t-shirt from an ill-fated attempt to paint Janice's living room, a baseball cap, and sunglasses.

The day was cloudy, slate grey with a light but continuous rain, almost a mist but not quite. The clouds made his sunglasses appear silly, but he wore them in case some nosey neighbor spotted him.

The basement window he had chosen was hidden behind a large bush, which turned out to be rather thorny, more like ornamental razor wire than a leafy thing. He was able to quickly undo the window, pushing it in and popping it, unfortunately, a little too quickly. The window dropped out of the frame. Mickey bobbled it for a second before it crashed to the floor, sending shards of broken glass in every direction. He stared at the empty opening for a moment, tossed a drop cloth down onto the floor, and wiggled as quickly as possible into the basement.

He stood there, breathing heavily in some kind of laundry room, just barely able to make out a furnace and water heater in a dark corner. He listened for any sound resembling life on the floor above, waited a minute or two, then gathered up his drop cloth and made his way upstairs.

Once upstairs, he quickly checked around for the most likely spot to grab her. He was thinking about that, weighing his options in the kitchen when the decision was made for him. Bunny suddenly stepped out of the garage, key in hand, and walked toward the back door. Had he paid attention, he would have noticed her stagger, but he was consumed with the idea of hiding. He quickly stepped into the small bathroom, just off the rear hall next to the back door.

She snapped the lock open, and he froze, afraid to even breathe, remaining as still as a statue. Sweat rolled down his back, soaked through his paint-splattered t-shirt, and darkened the brim of his baseball cap.

Bunny Kelley brushed her hair back and steadied herself in the back entryway. She left her set of keys in the lock and slammed the door behind her. What she needed right now was a little afternoon drink, just to help her nap.

Mickey remained in the tiny bathroom. His drop cloth was somewhere in the hallway, and he feared she might see it when he heard her stumble and fall.

"What the hell," she mumbled on her way down, her voice slurred. She let out a grunt as she hit the floor and remained there.

The moment wasn't lost on Mickey, and he leaped out of the bathroom and quickly rolled her up in the drop cloth.

Bunny made a gagging sound and attempted to kick her legs a bit, but that was the extent of her resistance.

Mickey rolled her over in the drop cloth a few times. She was tightly secured, and other than some silly sound and a few halfhearted kicks, she offered no resistance. He tossed her over his shoulder, just like he had planned, and carried her out the back door to his car parked in the alley. She made a grunt when he dumped her on the floor of the back seat, but other than that, she was quiet for the entire drive out to Dell's.

He drove right into the tuck-under garage, grabbed the drop cloth and Bunny's ankles, threw her over his shoulder, and bounced her, more gently than not, onto the bed.

Dell had applied a blue theme to the room. The floor was a garish, unforgettable, navy blue peel and stick tile he had found on sale. The walls, done in what could only be described as a Blessed Virgin blue, reminded Mickey of grade school classrooms while spending his formative years standing in the hall.

He kept an eye pressed to the peephole and watched as Bunny's feet and ankles slowly began to move. She gradually unwrapped, unrolled, and finally pulled herself from inside the large canvas drop cloth.

She must have fallen asleep wrapped up in that thing, he thought. She pulled the last of the drop cloth over her head, looked around bleary-eyed, and then threw up on herself. She made no attempt to move, run to the bathroom, pull her hair out of the way, or clean herself off. She sat on the bed, casting a bleary eye slowly around the room before throwing up a second time.

If Dell was unhappy to arrive home and learn he was in violation of a number of federal and state laws again, he was even less thrilled wearing the Lassie mask when delivering dinner and a clean robe to Bunny.

"What's with the dog thing, Mick? You couldn't find something else? I don't want to wear it."

"Well, if you're that unhappy, we could return to the paper bag. But oh, wait, you didn't like that either, now did you?"

Dell's reaction was nothing compared to the tantrum Bunny Kelley had. Dell walked into the room, wearing the Lassie mask, carrying a clean robe and some hot pizza. The small room was stuffy, pungent and Dell actually recoiled, pausing by the doorway for a moment to fill his lungs and hold his breath. The blue walls and floors did nothing to help.

Bunny suddenly bolted upright on the bed. "Where the hell am I?" she asked, wiping the back of her hand across her lips, oblivious to his Lassie mask. "Aren't we supposed to have the intervention first? That's the way he's always done it before. Jesus, and he says I've got the problem."

She laughed and said, "You ought to see him lap up his drinks on any given day. But I know damn well you're not going do anything about him, now, are you? No," she hissed, bounding off the bed, bloodshot eyes boring in on Dell.

"You won't touch him. He's got all of you locked up in his pocket anyway. Doesn't he? Well, doesn't he?"

She moved toward Dell, a large, smelly cat stalking her prey. Her killer instinct detected Dell's fear as he began to back up in the direction of the door. He was afraid if he took his eyes off her, she might attack, rip his throat out or go for the crotch.

"You're afraid of him, aren't you?" she hissed, and poked a finger at Dell.

Dell tossed the robe in her direction, dropped the pizza box on the floor along with the note Mickey had written, and hurriedly fled the room.

"Hey, wait a minute. I know you, dog boy. You're Lassie, aren't you? When are you going to confront me? Tell me a couple of drinks are too much for me to handle. Call me a drunk, again. You tell Jack Kelley he can screw himself, you hear me?" Dell jumped outside the room, slamming the door behind him. "He can screw himself," Bunny screamed at the door as she kicked it. "Screw himself."

"Mick, we got an absolute wacko on our hands," Dell said and pulled off the mask. "You grabbed a certifiable lunatic. Did you see that? She was thinking of attacking me. Tell me again, who the hell is she?"

"Screw yourself, Jack. I wish we never met," she screamed and kicked the door again.

Mickey stood wide-eyed, a stunned, shocked look on his face, suggesting he had completely lost whatever semblance of a plan he had. "I've been watching her for a week. I had no idea, man, now what?"

"Mick, who would pay money to get that back in their life?"

That was exactly Mickey's fear.

The kitchen table was littered with a half-dozen beer cans and various pages from the newspaper's sports section. It had been a very quiet thirty-five minutes of stewing and picking over half-nibbled, luke-warm pizza before Mickey finally broke the silence.

"Another beer?" he asked, getting up and pulling a can from the almost empty twelve pack sitting on the counter. "Okay, we can't just take her back. I mean, we can, but why? Let's at least try. Send him the damn note. I'm gonna write it tonight, slip it under his front door, call him about four in the morning, catch him off guard. We'll get this nailed down. Dell, I promise."

He tore a handful of cheese and sausage off a piece of pizza and stuffed it into his mouth. "Umm-mmm, this is why we set the amount at a hundred grand. It's do-able for these jerks. He'll pay," Mickey nodded, sounding like he was trying to convince himself. "I know how this guy operates. He'll pay up."

"Know how he operates? Mick, how he operates is he got you sent to jail for sixteen months and charged you for the privilege. If you know how he operates and you wanted to get back at the guy, you should have left that Bunny woman at his house. Why deny the guy the pleasure of putting up with that dreadful creature every day?"

It was just a little after four in the morning when Mickey called Jack Kelley's home from a payphone downtown. The phone was just outside a darkened filling station. The street was completely deserted at this hour. He wasn't too worried about disguising the sound of his voice, although he planned to use a French accent, just in case. He sat in his car in the dark, and dialed the number for the third time, then waited as his call rolled over to voice mail.

Bunny's voice, sweet but business-like, repeated for the third time," We're unavailable but please," Blah, blah, blah. It was hard to equate this professional sounding charming woman with the lunatic in the blue room at Dell's.

The house had been completely dark over an hour ago when Mickey tiptoed up to the front door and dropped his note down the mail slot. The plan had been to just wake old Jack Kelley up with the call, tell him to get his ass downstairs and read the damn note, then wait for further instructions. But now what?

"How'd it go?" Dell asked, standing at the stove and scrambling eggs for breakfast as Mickey dragged himself up the stairs to the kitchen. The room had that morning smell of coffee, frying bacon, and toast.

"I never talked to the jerk on the phone," he said, shaking his head as he stepped into the kitchen. "What are you doing up?"

"Mick, come on, this is going from bad to worse. We got—"

"Shhhh." Mickey had his finger to his lips." Don't let her hear you."

"Mick. We got a certifiable nut case down there, and we can't even get ahold of her old man to let him know we got her. Jesus, if I were him, I'd be out celebrating. Did you ever consider we may have done this guy a favor? I thought you were supposed to be the guy who had this all figured out."

Mickey ignored him. "Maybe he's got the phone off the hook, or he wears hearing aids or something. Look, take it easy. I'll try the house in a few hours again. If that doesn't work, then I'll call his office. Relax, I've got this all under control."

Mickey's call to the Kelley house three hours later, got the same result, rolling right into Bunny's upbeat little message. "Damn it," he said, hanging up as soon as he heard her cheery voice. His call to Jack Kelley's office was even worse. The number was no longer in service. When he called directory assistance for a new listing, the closest they could come was the Kelley Plumbing and Heating Company.

"What do you mean, where is he?" Bunny screamed at the door after kicking it and crumpling the note Mickey had just slipped into the room. "You idiot, he lives in Florida. Didn't he tell you that when he had you pick me up and bring me to this godforsaken dump? This is the worst treatment facility I've ever been in. And, by the way, the food here stinks. You want me to recover. You can start by cooking something edible instead of the garbage you've…"

Mickey trudged wearily back upstairs into the kitchen to write her another note. She didn't stop screaming, and he could still hear the noise. Fortunately, he was far enough away and unable to discern specific words. He was losing patience, not at all sure what to do next, except move her clothes, the slacks, sweater, and her underwear from the washer to the dryer. He had to gain control of this whole situation before they had a real disaster on their hands.

His new note was simple, 'Trade you a nice big manhattan for a phone number to call your husband. 'He wrapped the note around a pen, tiptoed back to her room, quickly opened the door, tossed in the note with the pen, and closed the door, not unlike throwing a steak to a lion.

"My God," she moaned." This is without a doubt the strangest rehab facility I've ever been in. Here's his cell phone number. He's at his condo down in Naples. That's Naples, Florida. Go easy on the Vermouth, very little ice and no damn cherry. Here," she said, shoving the note under the door." Hey, the pen won't fit. Did you hear me?

I gave you his number. Now you keep your half of the bargain. Hello? Hello, is anyone there?"

Mickey didn't want to take the time to drive across town to a payphone, but he knew this was exactly the way guys screwed up. Not following the plan just because a little heat was on. Not only did he drive across town, but he drove at the posted speed limit, determined not to attract any attention.

Jack Kelley answered on the third ring, "Hello." A jovial inflection, not quite a shout, more of a 'this is your lucky day, 'kind of greeting, nothing like the lawyer Mickey remembered.

"Hello?"

"Kelley, we've got your wife, Bunny. She won't be harmed as long as you do as you're told. We'll return her, once you've followed our instructions and complied."

"Return her?" snorted Jack Kelley." Is this some kind of joke? How'd you get this number anyway? I think you've made a mistake here, and if this isn't a wrong number, you've made an even bigger mistake. A very big mistake."

It was the way Kelley said it, the inflection in his voice. Mickey wondered why the guy couldn't have pushed that hard in the courtroom where he was supposed to defend Mickey instead of rolling over and playing lapdog to that hanging judge.

"Oh, Jack, did I happen to mention she told us."

"Told you what?" snorted Kelley, sounding full of bluster, but Mickey sensed he was suddenly annoyed and still on the line.

"You think you've had problems up till now? You know exactly what I mean. And if it gets out, you'll never see the light of day, not in your lifetime."

"That drunken old bitty doesn't know what she's talking about, and I don't know what you're talking about. But you had better understand one thing. I don't respond to anonymous phone calls or threats, so you had better just rethink whatever—"

" Let me tell you what you had better do, Jack. You had better get your ass back up here and pick up our instructions from your mailbox. I expect you back in town by tomorrow evening." Mickey said and hung up the phone. He stared at the receiver for a long time, wondering what was next. Thinking again, there was something not quite right about Kelley's response. Then wondering what it was Bunny knew, that had gotten a rise out of him.

Mickey clung desperately to the hope that he had Kelley. But, it was beginning to feel more and more like a wild hope, a desperate shot. He didn't notice the sun was shining, didn't hear the bird singing outside as he pulled Bunny's clothes out of the dryer. His mood was grim. He was preoccupied. There was just something there that he couldn't quite put his finger on.

He delivered the clothes along with another manhattan, cautiously peeking through the door first. She lay curled up across the bed, in a semi-fetal position, arms between her legs. She didn't seem asleep, more just lethargic than anything else, laying there, staring at the wall.

He quickly opened the door, set the drink just inside, and hurriedly tossed her clean clothes in the general direction of her bed. He closed the door before she had the chance to roll over, let alone attack.

She slowly looked up from the bed, glanced at the clothes on the floor then spotted the manhattan. She jumped off the bed, grabbed the glass, sniffed the contents for a half-second before draining a good third, then carefully held the glass as she picked up her clothes.

"Is this some kind of a joke?" she said, looking at the wrinkled slacks, still warm from the dryer. "Jesus, you've ruined these. And look at this," she shouted and held up her shrunken sweater, now barely large enough for a small infant. "What kind of nuthouse is this? You can't even do the damned laundry right. Get me out of here!" she screamed and threw the clothes at the door. "You tell, Jack, he had better get me out of here, and fast, because I have had it."

* * *

Jack Kelley sat in a chair in the living room of his Naples condo. It had all been too good to be true. He'd known from the moment he told Bunny that he would regret sharing his secret with her. Just had to show off, he thought, just had to try and impress her. He knew he would have to do a number of things, the first of which was to get back up to Minnesota, so he could find out who was behind this and deal with them. Then, he planned to deal with poor Bunny. Sorry, but it was long overdue. He reached for the phone.

The following afternoon Jack Kelley reread the note as he stood in the foyer of Bunny's house. Was this for real? Did he travel all the way from Florida for this? Maybe he was overreacting. This was so stupid, it had to be a joke or something Bunny cooked up herself. Then again, maybe whoever phoned him yesterday was so shrewd that they knew exactly what they were doing. Well, anyway, shrewd enough to think they knew, which to his way of thinking made them really stupid if they thought they could screw with him.

"Everything's clear, Mr. Kelley. There's a broken basement window. I've got someone coming in to repair it shortly." The man speaking nodded toward a large individual climbing the stairs to the second floor." Carl will be stationed upstairs. I'll be answering the door and the phone. I'd also like to have people in the front and back, just to play it safe. Mr. Kelley?"

Kelley reread the note a final time. "What? I'm sorry, Pauly, I was just thinking. What was it?"

There's something about large men who still go by the name Pauly that makes you not want to ask too many questions about their line of work. This Pauly, in black slacks, a golf shirt, and sport coat with a 9mm Glock tucked into his waistband, gave you that feeling.

"I said I'd like to put some people in front and back, just to play it safe, in case someone comes around again." Guys like Pauly always had people.

"Mmm-mmm, no, no one outside. I don't think this requires that kind of attention just now. Let's see how things develop, and I'll answer the phone."

With that, Kelley climbed the staircase up to the den so he could think. He poured himself a bourbon before sitting behind his desk and looking at the note again.

One hundred grand? Had they dropped a zero? No, the hundred grand had to be their way of telling him they knew far more than they were letting on. Yeah, a hundred grand, it wasn't a coincidence. They were sending him a message, plain and simple. Somehow, she had talked, and they were going to hang him out to dry. He knew it wouldn't stop with whatever sum they ultimately demanded.

He sat there sipping and rereading, wondering what he should do, weighing the odds, knowing he had already made his decision. He made it months ago, in fact, he just hadn't acted on it until now. Once he reviewed the thought clearly, it wasn't a leap to make the phone call. He just picked up the phone and calmly dialed.

"You got a problem?" was how the phone was answered.

"Yeah," Kelley said. "I want to get it taken care of as quickly as possible. There might be an additional complication, but nothing we can't handle. I'll give you details as soon as I know more."

Seventeen

Mickey could only hope Jack Kelley would answer the phone. He didn't want to contemplate the guy not caring enough to come back and pay a ransom for his wife. He could feel himself stressing out, hadn't felt this stressed in a long, long time, so he was having a cigarette, just one, just to calm down, if that was possible. There was still something that just wasn't making sense here.

He dialed Kelley's home number from yet another payphone. He held a balloon in his lap, inhaling a lung full of helium on the first ring. Kelley picked up on the third.

"Kelley, thanks for coming back," Mickey said, sounding more like a demented munchkin with a high squeaky voice than anything threatening.

Kelley was momentarily caught off guard by the voice, it took a lot for him not to have a response ready, right there on the tip of his tongue, but for once he was actually speechless. Maybe he had underestimated these guys.

"Kelley?" squeaked Mickey.

"Yeah, go ahead, I'm listening."

"Good, see that you do," said Mickey, his voice suddenly changing on the last words, dropping to a more natural octave. He quickly tucked the receiver against his shoulder and inhaled another lungful of helium.

Kelley listened during the unnatural pause. Another message? Something wasn't right, he'd done a bit of this in his younger days, and this was not how it was supposed to work.

"Do you have the hundred thousand dollars?" Mickey said.

"No. I only just got in from the airport," Kelley lied, gambling they weren't watching him. Waiting for them to get to the real point, positive the hundred grand was just a signal that said they knew all about the payoffs and contracts. Knowing they had him, for the moment. If he just bided his time, he could solve this problem and a few others in the process.

"You are to follow our directions carefully," Mickey said, glancing at his watch. It was already after four. "You'll be phoned tomorrow morning, have the money and be," Mickey's voice began to drop again, "prepared to act." He thought he better inhale another lungful of helium, and he brought the balloon up to his mouth, cradling the receiver against his shoulder. The receiver, the balloon, the cigarette in his hand… Boom! "Ahhh, hell!" he screamed, dropping the receiver, fumbling with it before hurriedly hanging up.

"Hello, hello, hello!" Kelley shouted into the phone after hearing the gunshot. Jesus, he thought, animals. Damned animals. Maybe he had underestimated? What sort of organization was he up against? Did they just shoot Bunny? It would save him the time but also demonstrated a ruthlessness that caused more than a little concern.

Three hours later, Mickey's ear was still ringing as he sat in the restaurant booth deep in thought. He turned the situation over and examined it from a number of different angles. Something just wasn't right, hanging there just out of his reach.

He had told Dell to mix a large pitcher of manhattans and feed one to Bunny every thirty minutes. It was time to get back to Dell's and figure out their next step provided Kelley came up with the cash. If he didn't, Mickey was ready to throw a blindfold over Bunny and just take her back.

He watched Janice moving from table to table pouring coffee. This was the part he liked. She would come up to him, put her hand on his shoulder, and whisper the meal was on the house. He would leave a generous tip, and everyone would be happy.

"Will there be anything else, sir?" The same thing she always said, not quite as playful as usual, but maybe she was a little busy. She always said it in bed after they'd romped around for an hour or two and were finally exhausted. This afternoon she sounded more like a waitress than a lover, and she actually left the bill before walking into the kitchen where he couldn't follow. God, it just doesn't end.

A half-hour later, he was pulling into Dell's driveway, trying to remember if he had left a tip or not, wondering what new disaster awaited him inside. It didn't take long to find out. As soon as he opened the door, he saw Dell sitting on the steps, listening to Bunny howling. Dell wide-eyed, a little pale with his hair standing on end and the Lassie mask at his feet.

"Man, where in the hell have you been? I ran out of Manhattan's an hour ago, been listening to that for the past forty minutes. She's been screaming and throwing things, howling like a damn dog."

"Lassie, you son-of-a-bitch, my glass is empty! You hear me? Lassie, woof, woof, woof! Lassie, come, sit, heel, roll over. Lassie, I need another drinkie."

"She drank the whole pitcher?" Mickey asked, look-ing at the empty pitcher next to the mask at Dell's feet. "You didn't have any?"

"Have any? Are you kidding? She would have killed me if she thought I took some," he shifted on the stairs, seemed to push himself a bit further away from Bunny's room. "Mick, she just went through that pitcher like it was water. I've never seen anything like it. She got a little meaner every time I came in to pour her another. The last glass was about half-full, and she damn near took my head off. I'm sure she would have thrown the glass at me if it had been empty. I would have mixed some more but kept thinking you were going to be home soon. That was over an hour ago."

"Man, she can really pound 'em down," Mickey said, scratching his head, wondering what to do next.

"Well, I can tell you this, that is one mean little woman in there. I don't know if that lawyer Kelley is gonna be in any hurry to pay money to get her back. I sure as hell wouldn't."

"He should have our money tomorrow morning, and we can be finished with this. By the time he got back from his place in Naples, it was too late to get to the bank and set it up for today," Mickey said.

"Naples, like in Florida?"

That was the second time Mickey had run into that implication, and it reverberated somewhere in the back of his mind. "Yeah, Naples, Florida. Why, do you know another Naples where people have condos?"

"Well, no, it's just that you said they had two places, a house in town and a cabin up north. I don't remember you mentioning anything about a condo down in Naples. That would make it three places, unless they ditched the cabin for the condo, right?"

"That's probably exactly what they did," Mickey said, thinking this is part of what had been bothering him. The real estate files had never mentioned a condo in Florida. *They must be out of date*, he thought, knowing in the same instant that was rather unlikely.

"All right, I'll have to get a few things arranged before tomorrow, so we can get paid and get this creature off our hands. But before I go, let me mix up another round, double strength, for our guest so we can all get some peace and quiet tonight."

"No," Jack Kelley said to the voice on the other end of the line. A voice he'd dealt with in the past but never actually met. "I don't think it would be wise to use local talent for this particular problem. These people are far more shrewd than they appear on the surface. They seem to know exactly what they're doing, telling me just a hundred grand, and then firing the pistol. Christ, I don't know how, but they know all about it."

"So, you're sure she talked?" the voice asked. Kelley knew he was on the hot seat right now.

"Yeah, I'm not just sure, I'm positive. She told them everything she knows, but she didn't know that much. I mean, she knows we got the contracts, but in all honesty, that's never been hidden. It's a matter of public record. Hell, the trucks have been out there with our name on them pouring four lanes of concrete every day for the past eighteen months."

"But your involvement, it's not common knowledge, if it was, the deal never would have gone through, the—"

"The deal was set to fall apart until I had that pesky reporter whacked, set it up to look like he was mugged. I paid a hundred grand, cash, to have him eliminated. We got the deal, and now it all comes back to haunt me twenty-four months later. Obviously, Bunny didn't know about that part, and I'm not blaming you. But, you had better check and see if you got a leak somewhere, or maybe someone doing business on the side, yanking our chain."

Kelley was on thin ice, skating out at the edge, but he'd had a point to make, and now he had made it. "I think it best we get some outside talent up here, only because I'm not sure how far this goes. These guys I'm dealing with will contact me tomorrow and tell me what they really want."

"I thought you said they told you?"

"Nah. They said they wanted a hundred grand. Come on, what's that? They're just sending a message that they know about the reporter we had taken out, that stiff named Tarbox."

"Yeah, that was the guy. Remember? He had all those dogs with him, Dalmented's, the ones with them spots. And they didn't do shit. Didn't bark, or bite, nothing, the dumb things just sat there. That the way it went down?"

It was always Timmy White's favorite story, and Kelley had long ago given up telling him he'd already told him. He just launched into the tale, pictured the aging thug getting comfortable in a favorite chair, listening to him as if it was the first time he had ever heard the story.

"Yeah, okay, so there were two dogs, Dalmatians. You were right. They're the ones with the spots. We just walked up and shot the guy. He was standing at the ATM, the dogs sitting next to him. He was getting twenty bucks, that's it, just twenty. You know anything you can do for twenty bucks these days? And when we shot him, the dogs just sat there and looked at him, and then looked at us."

Kelley looked at his watch, wanting this conversation to be over, but knew he had to finish the story about how the dogs just sat there. "They didn't do a thing, no barking, nothing, just looked up at us, then at him on the ground. Rather well behaved, actually."

On the other end of the line, White erupted in laughter. "Oh, that's the best part, hot shot reporter, and the mutts don't even bark." His laughter erupted into a coughing jag that lasted ten or fifteen seconds, coughing into the phone and Kelley's ear until he finally cleared the phlegm.

"Anyway, look," Kelley said, trying to get back on subject, once the coughing stopped. "We need to get this contained and nailed down. Preferably sooner, rather than later, before we have a real mess on our hands. All you'll have to do is sit back, keep counting your money while I make sure there aren't any other problems for either one of us. But like I said at the beginning, I want you to be aware of exactly what's going on, so there aren't any surprises. I'll continue to keep you informed."

"Yeah, okay, keep me informed, Jack." White cleared his throat a couple of times, rumbling more phlegm." You're the guy on the scene. Let me know if you have any problems. You know I don't like problems."

"I'll keep you apprised of the situation and talk to
you in a few days." With that, he hung up and gave himself a small pat on the back. That hadn't gone too badly.

"Apprised of the situation," White mumbled to himself. "Throw all those big college words at me. Tell your
old lady about our business deal. I need this like I need a
hole in the head. Apprised of the situation, I'll apprise
you of the situation you just got yourself into. You'll
wish you had some of them Dalmented's to just sit and
watch. Twenty bucks from an ATM, you ain't gonna be
worth even that by the time I'm finished with you."
Timmy White started laughing, which started another
coughing jag.

Once Bunny had finally passed out, Dell began to
calm down. Mickey promised him she would be gone in
the next twenty-four hours. Then he drove over to
Janice's to see what her problem had been. There were
times he felt like he was the only sane person in the
whole world, and this was one of them. He stood pleading his case out on her front porch.

"Look, Janice, I already said, the only reason I didn't leave a tip is I only had ten bucks. Would it have made you feel any better if I left seventy-five cents? Cause that's all I had, seventy-five cents, that would have pissed you off even more. I've already explained on the phone. I've been working on a project, that's why I wasn't home when you stopped by. That's why I haven't answered your phone calls. And, that's why I haven't been over to see you until tonight."

He could hear her on the other side of the front door. "Well, anyway, I just wanted to let you know that. I have to get to the office now," he said, checking his watch, seeing it was already after midnight. "I know you have to get up early, but I wanted to just stop by and tell you."

The porch light suddenly came on, the lock clicked, and the door slowly opened no more than an inch. "Oh, hi Mickey," Janice's daughter Ashley said." Mom isn't here right now. I'll tell her you stopped by," she said and closed the door before he had a chance to reply.

"I'm telling you for the last time. I had absolutely nothing to do with anything that happened, okay. Don't you understand? Don't you get it?" Janice pleaded to her father as she leaned against his kitchen counter." Do you really think I would kidnap myself, burn down your damn garage with your precious car in it while Ashley was here, make you pay the ransom, and then come to this house tonight? Jesus Christ, you have a more warped viewpoint of life than I ever thought possible. Bulletin to you," she said, tears welling in her eyes, making her furious at herself for crying in front of him.

"I'm not like you, at all. I'm like mommy, good and kind, and I might make mistakes, but that's all they are, just mistakes. It's never intentional, like you. I don't try to hurt people. So, you are just going to have to accept the fact that I knew nothing about this. Just let me get on with my life and leave me alone. If I never, ever heard from you again, it would be too soon."

"Shit," said Huey, shaking his head, thinking of pouring himself another drink, but wanting to get his next dig in first. Watch her run out of the house, discovered, caught, guilty and owing him a hundred grand. He was leaning against the pale green Formica counter, his back to the kitchen sink and the window. The soft light above the window added to the orange cast bouncing off the old varnished cabinets. The light was just barely enough to catch a peek of the newly framed garage standing just beyond his back door.

"So, you didn't set this up? You know nothing about it?"

"Why don't you believe me?" she sniffled.

"Okay, goody two shoes, so if you had nothing to do with it, then just who the hell is this Michael Donnelly jerk?"

"I don't know any Michael Don . . . wait, Mickey?" She stopped suddenly in mid-sentence and stood a little straighter with genuine surprise on her face. "You mean Mickey? I'm kind of seeing a Mickey Donnelly, but I've never heard him called Michael before, by anyone. In fact, I never really had a conversation with him until weeks after this whole thing happened."

Her reaction was not the one Huey had expected, and it caught him off guard. When she mentioned the name Mickey, a very dim bulb went off in the dark recesses of his mind. It rang a bell, but he couldn't put it together. The same thing had happened when Buster Keegan had first given him the name. "How old is this jerk, Donnelly?"

"I don't know, maybe my age, a year or two older, I never asked him?" she lied.

It wasn't adding up to Huey. Some guy her age that connected, and Huey didn't know him? It didn't make sense. Buster had given him some bullshit information that seemed clear. And, he was half-convinced this idiot of a stepdaughter was telling him the truth. She didn't have anything to do with the kidnapping.

"I'm going to find out what the hell is going on here, then I'll deal with it," he paused, letting the silence hang in the night air for a long moment. "In the meantime, just get out," he said.

She left without saying another word, trying her best to storm out, looking hurt and wounded.

"You got a big problem, Buster," Huey shouted into the phone.

Buster Keegan, on the receiving end of Huey's rant, gave a long, silent sigh.

"That information you gave me just ain't right. For one thing, how can a guy my stepdaughter's age be connected the way you figure he is? Pup's still wet behind the ears, for God's sake. Second of all, this guy Donnelly, you said Michael, she said Mickey. What the hell? Which one is it? Either way, I can't place him. About all I can come up with is maybe some punk might have worked for me way back when. I don't know, the name rings a bell, but I got no idea why. So, what you need to do is find out more about this idiot for me. Find out if he's really connected cause I don't think he is. This whole thing just ain't adding up. So, find out for me and fast!" Huey screamed.

Buster sat starring at his phone for a long moment and sighed, another day ruined. He reviewed the information he had passed on to Huey. And there it was, right in front of him, the guy he had watched doing the gunslinger routine, cautiously stepping onto the porch, looking up and down the street, that guy was easily fifty, more like Huey's age. Huey had referred to Donnelly as his stepdaughter's age, late twenties, maybe early thirties. No way they were talking about the same person. He thought about calling Huey back, then thought it might be better to let him calm down while Buster rechecked his own facts.

After cleaning the office, Mickey checked and rechecked the lender's file on Jack Kelley. There was no mention of a condo in Naples. Nor for that matter, mention of a wife named Bunny.

According to the records Jack Kelley's wife had been saddled with the name Petronella at birth by otherwise loving parents. The nickname Bunny had probably been given to her during her high school years.

It all made perfect sense to Mickey, thinking her friends called her Bunny because she probably liked carrots. But the Naples thing still bothered him, the real estate files were updated regularly, and even if it was a transaction not handled by this branch office, it would have be listed under his net worth, his assets. The problem was, it wasn't.

It was well after four in the morning when he finally parked in front of his house and sat behind the wheel, thinking. He wearily climbed the front porch steps and saw a hand-written note from Janice taped to the front door, call her when he got home.

God, he thought, I don't have the energy, and I'm sure she didn't want a call at four in the morning. I need some sleep and one way or the other, paid or not, I'm getting rid of Bunny Kelley today, and then we'll just give this whole thing a rest.

He drifted off after setting his alarm to give himself three hours of much-needed sleep, wondering if anyone else had the kind of problems that always seemed to find their way to his doorstep.

It wasn't that he was groggy from lack of sleep, he was, in fact, but that was only part of his problem. Mickey saw his current effort, operation Bunny, going right down the proverbial toilet. That headache and the fact that he was stumbling around his own kitchen trying to find where Janice had reorganized everything did nothing for his overall attitude.

Right now, all he wanted was a spoon to shovel sugar into one of the new matching coffee mugs she had insisted he buy. After opening up the third drawer and finding more matching towels and no silverware, he gave up, reached for the sugar bowl, and shook it into his mug. He let out a long sigh, took a tentative sip of coffee, and wondered how things had ever gotten so complicated.

His eyes settled on the note he had found taped to his door barely three hours before; ***Call me when you get in, Janice.***

"Oh, hi," was how she answered. "Work late last night?"

He bristled at her tone but decided to sweet talk his way around the question. "Yeah, major plumbing back up. So, once I got things unclogged, I had to steam clean carpets, then do the normal work. I didn't get home until a little after four, and I figured that might not be the best time to call. Everything okay?"

"Well, no, not exactly. I could come over if you were going to be home for a while."

If it had been any other morning, he might have agreed, but on this particular morning, he had to get out to Dell's. He had to make sure Bunny hadn't killed Dell or driven him crazy and escaped. Then he had to call Jack Kelley, get the ransom going. He didn't see how he could fit Janice into the morning lineup." I'm a little pressed for time this morning. How about in a couple of days?"

It was the wrong thing to say, and the icy silence on the other end left no doubt.

"Hello?"

"It's pretty important, and I promise not to take up more than one minute of your apparently valuable time. But I think we had better talk."

"I'm sorry, you're right, yeah, please, come on over. I do have to be somewhere, but it can wait."

"I'm on my way," she said, sounding a lot happier as she hung up.

"Damn it!" he yelled.

He was buttoning his shirt, a silky, shiny black shirt with a red Ford on the back and white dice on the collar, one of his favorites. He casually glanced out the bedroom window to see Janice pulling up to the curb in front of his house.

It took him a minute or two to come down the staircase and let her in. He cautiously peered around the corner from his second-floor landing, watching her from the top of the stairs as she waited at the door. She looked anxious, fidgety, and he watched her for any telltale sign that might suggest she had a gun. He watched her long enough that she had to ring the doorbell a second time. He moved a bit slower than normal down the staircase, never taking his eyes off her, right hand at the small of his back, ready to pull the Luger and fire a couple of rounds just to back her off. Let her know he wasn't a pushover and then remind her she'd netted a cool ten grand cash in the deal.

"Hey," she said, brushing past him as he opened the door, running up the stairs before he had a chance to respond." Sorry, I've got about ten pots of coffee in me, and I need to use your bathroom, fast," she yelled over her shoulder and disappeared into his apartment.

Mickey looked up and down the deserted street before closing the door and slowly climbing the stairs after her.

"Oh, God, that feels better," she said, coming out of the bathroom. She paused to inspect him top to bottom. "That outfit is particularly dreadful, not your colors at all."

"You rushed over here to be my fashion coordinator?"

"No, not that you don't need one. There's a bit of a problem that's developed."

"What kind of problem? I had a vasectomy, so it can't be—"

"That's not it, you idiot. It's my stepfather, that other idiot," she blurted out before sobbing uncontrollably, moving slightly forward so Mickey could wrap his arms around her.

He stood there, wishing the painting of Ginger, the naked redhead from Vegas, was still hanging on the wall. He listened to Janice cry and thought, *I hate this shit.*

Eighteen

K elley was waiting patiently, watching the phone on his desk, willing the damn thing to ring. "You need anything, Mr. Kelley?" It was Carl lumbering down the hallway, poking his large head into the study, making sure everything was in order.

"No, Carl, thank you, everything is just fine," he said, dismissing the large man, thinking, *Isn't it strange, all this protection and I'm waiting on a phone call. Who are these people?*

Almost noon and no call, but the longer they waited, the better the odds grew in Kelley's favor. His special help was flying up from Chicago on a private jet. He had used their talents effectively before. They brought their own equipment, worked efficiently, ruthlessly, and were capable of cleaning up a mess like this in twenty-four hours, then quietly flying out of town without leaving a trace.

This operation would be a little different than the past. Not only were they going to terminate the instigators, he wanted them to eliminate Bunny, too. She was out of control, and frankly, he couldn't stand the sight of her. Now that she had apparently opened her big, fat, drunken mouth and told them about murdering the reporter, Tarbox, well, that was the last straw. She was a loose end he could no longer afford, and she had ceased being any kind of pleasure long ago. That led to the third task he would require of them, dispose of the bodies.

The last time he had used their talents, he had wanted a message sent loud and clear. And it had worked. Three rounds between the eyes while you're standing at an ATM machine with two dogs had delivered a very effective message to all parties concerned. At least, until Bunny had opened her big mouth and he found himself in this mess. Now, he just wanted her and whoever was involved with her to quietly disappear, and he could go back to simply collecting payments.

Right now, Mickey's life seemed to be stuck on 'Loser Lane' just a block off of 'Horse Shit Highway.' He was driving about five miles below the speed limit on the way out to Dell's, feeling depressed. Janice had given him the little day brightener that her psychopathic step-father, Huey, was about to find everything out and come gunning for him. Not for the last time in the past hour, he cursed himself for thinking with the wrong head, concluding, as traffic zipped around him and a carload of kids gave him the finger, that it wasn't all his fault.

Now, he was wondering exactly how he was going to break the news to Dell. Tell his lifelong pal their worst fear had come true. Huey Evans was on to them. Normal pals just went fishing. Why in hell did they get involved with something that resulted in federal charges and death by Huey?

All too soon, he found himself in Dell's driveway, slowly creeping toward the house, past Dell's van and into the tuck-under garage. Maybe he could convince Dell they should move out of state or, better yet, out of the country.

"So, how's she doing down there?" Mickey asked, climbing the basement steps into the kitchen.

"She drank almost all of that second pitcher, then all of a sudden dropped like a rock to the floor. Hasn't moved since, and to tell the truth, I was too scared to go in there in case something happened."

"In case something happened? You mean like she's dead?"

"No, not dead, that would be too easy. I mean, she's so damn mean she might attack me or something. Mick, you heard her, she was in there howling, she may be a little thing, but neither one of us wants to tangle with her. She's still passed out on that old drop cloth of yours snoring away."

"Well, we're going to finish this up as soon as possible, today, hopefully. If not, we'll just give her back if we have to, just leave her somewhere. What do you say about us taking a little trip, maybe down to the Grand Cayman Islands?"

"Just give her back? After all we've been through? Mick, for once in our worthless lives, things are finally starting to go our way. Yeah, she's a pain in the ass, but what's the rush? We get the money, we lay low, relax, take it easy. You want some warm weather, we can go to Texas, Florida, or somewhere. I mean, what's the rush?"

"No rush, it's just—"

"Oh, shit, what are you leaving out, Mickey?"

"Jesus, Dell. What is it with you that I have to be leaving something out? Can't I just have a good idea I'd like to share with you? Share some good fortune with my pal. Why do you naturally assume something is going to go wrong?"

"What? The cops are on to us, right? I knew it. I knew it was all getting just too cute, I knew—"

"Will you relax. The cops aren't on to us, for God's sake. See, there you go pushing the old panic button, flipping out over nothing."

"Well, then what is it? If it's not the cops because I can tell by the way you always start dancing around that— Oh God, it's Huey, isn't it? It's Huey Evans. You got involved with this Janice, and she told him, didn't she?"

"No, that's not exactly what—"

"I knew it. It's my own damn fault. I shouldn't even blame you, Mick. Hell, I know you're a moron. No, I've got no one to blame, but myself for getting involved with you. You know what?" He laughed, not quite sanely. "That just makes me a bigger moron. I know it's been hard, but somehow, I've managed to find someone dumber than you, namely me. And, now I'm going to die."

"Will you just slow down for a minute. Just stop and look at the opportunity we have here."

"Opportunity, opportunity for what? To pay in advance at O'Halloran's funeral home? Opportunity? What, the opportunity to have Huey finish what he started when we were kids and finally kill us? Are you nuts? You mean like the choice we now have is to let the feds lock us up for life or let Huey just gun us down? That opportunity? Oh, great, this is just wonderful, old pal. This—"

Mickey grabbed Dell by the shoulders and shook him." See? This is why I'm the idea guy, and I admit this was all my idea. It was my idea that we each get more cash than we've ever had. It was my idea that we get another hundred grand to split for that little thing passed out downstairs on the floor, I admit that. And you're right. It was my idea that we go somewhere nice and enjoy the rest of our lives sipping drinks on the beach and staring at women wearing practically nothing at all. You're right, Dell, it was all my idea."

"Mick, we can't just leave. I mean, Jesus, how are we going to live? Where are we going to—"

"We can, Dell, because I have ideas. We can do it because we'll have cash just waiting for more opportunity. Now, look, I've got to call that shyster lawyer, Kelley, make sure he's got the next installment for our retirement account ready to be delivered, and then I'll be back, maybe forty minutes."

"What about . . ." Dell looked to the door leading downstairs.

"Her? Just leave her, as long as she's asleep and quiet, why wake her? Neither one of us needs the hassle right now. Why don't you get ready to drive up north. We'll have to grab the cash from your lake place."

"Do you think I should pack anything?"

"Pack, hell no, don't pack. Dell, anything we need, we can buy, pay cash for it. All our troubles are finally over."

$$* * *$$

"They're downstairs, Mr. Kelley," Pauly said. His large frame in the doorway blocked most of the light from the hall.

"Show them up, please."

Less than a minute later, Pauly opened the door again and stepped into the room. He nodded to Kelley, still seated behind his desk. Pauly was followed by two men, unique in appearance, only from the standpoint that there was absolutely nothing unique about them. Not their clothes, their height, their hair, nor their faces. They were the sort of men you might meet, shake hands with, and immediately forget their names.

They entered the room, and Kelley stood, nodded to two chairs opposite his desk." Jack Kelley, good to see you guys again, gentlemen," he said, in his best regular guy voice, and held out his hand.

Neither of the two acknowledged his effort. They glanced quickly around the room then settled into the leather chairs.

"Yes, well, I want to thank you both for coming up on such short notice. Can I offer you gentlemen anything?"

Both men shook their heads, neither making an effort at a verbal reply.

"Thanks, Pauly. I think that will be all we need right now."

Pauly nodded and left the room, softly closing the door behind him.

Kelley could just catch the shadow of Pauly's feet planted on the opposite side of the door, ready to burst back into the room should any assistance be required.

After a brief moment, Kelley felt the silence had already lasted too long. The air in the room had seemed to suddenly grow heavy, and he wondered for a quick moment if maybe the thermostat had gone haywire. His mouth all the way to the back of his throat felt suddenly parched, and he wished he had asked Pauly to bring a pitcher of water when he had the chance. He thought about calling him on the other side of the door, then just as quickly decided against it.

As he fidgeted with some papers on his desk, he noticed a bit of difference between the two, facially mostly, the one with a longer nose, ice-blue eyes, pale skin, possibly German or Polish. The man stared at Kelley, trancelike, expressionless. The other, a bit more tone to the skin, but not much, hair slightly darker, blonde verging on brown, examined his fingernails casually, paying no attention. They seemed to blend into the chairs. Certainly not large men like Pauly or Carl, but not small either. They appeared compact, tight, and hard. Kelley couldn't quite put a finger on it, certainly not the sort you would slap on the back and tell a joke to. In fact, they looked like they wouldn't know any jokes, at least not any good ones.

"Yes, well," Kelley said. He cleared his dried throat and pulled his large desk chair up against the ornate desk." As I said earlier, thank you for coming on such short notice. Now, did Mr. White bring you up to date on the little difficulty we seem to have up here?"

He waited for a long couple of moments, thinking perhaps they had somehow not heard him. Just as he was about to repeat the question, the fellow with the long nose exhaled and began to speak.

"We know someone, an individual, or individuals, has your wife. They requested payment to get her back. You would like for us to eliminate whoever is involved."

"And also, the woman, your wife," his partner added.

"We'll dispose of any incriminating evidence," Long Nose said.

"I thought they were going to contact me this morning, but I haven't heard a damn thing. Probably just as well. Now that you're here, I expect that the demand they mentioned yesterday will change. That hundred-grand had to be an initial figure. I'm sure they got information they shouldn't have from Bunny, and now they'll want more money. A lot more money."

                                 * * *

Mickey had just pulled alongside a payphone at a
Seven-Eleven. He had Kelley's number scrawled across
a bar napkin from the War Bonnet Lounge and taped to
the dashboard. He reached out his window and pushed
the buttons on the payphone. A moment later, it began to
ring.

Kelley sat at his desk and stared at the phone, finally
answering after the fourth ring, playing it cool.

"Yes."

"Kelley, do you have the money?" Mickey asked in
almost a whisper.

"How much are we talking about?" Kelley asked and
wondered about the voice disguise. Sharp, very sharp.
They weren't missing a trick. He glanced up and looked
into the cold, lifeless eyes of Long Nose, staring back at
him.

"Like I told you yesterday, one hundred thousand
dollars, that's the magic number."

There it is, thought Kelley, the guy really yanking
his chain, sending a message. They're good, very good.

"And, is that all you're going to want?" Kelley asked,
feeling as though he had just leaned out over the edge of
a tall cliff by asking the question.

Mickey wondered if Kelley had gotten the police involved, and they were tracing the call right now. He immediately hung up the phone, calmly drove out of the Seven-Eleven lot, heart pounding. He took the first right, then the next left, before checking his mirror to see if he was being followed.

Kelley drummed his fingers on the desk, wondering what to do. He did know one thing. He had just about had it with his guests and their silent routine. "Gentlemen, it would appear this may take a while. Would you be so kind as to leave me a number where I might contact you? As soon as we have something you can act on, I'll let you know. Otherwise, I'm afraid I'll just be wasting your time."

"I think we'll just stay here."

Kelley looked at both of them." Suit yourself. Pauly," he called.

The door swung open immediately, and Pauly filled the doorway." Yes sir, Mr. Kelley?"

"Pauly, get me something to drink."

"A water?"

"No, I'll take a bourbon, no ice. Gentlemen?"

Long Nose blinked, barely shook his head once, indicating no, his partner gave no response at all.

"Just the bourbon, Pauly, and no ice."

* * *

Mickey felt he could hear his traveling music just a little louder after that brief exchange with Kelley. The prudent thing to do at this point would be for Mickey and Dell to quietly leave town, maybe for the rest of their lives. It had been quite a day. He had learned that mad man Huey Evans was on their tail, Dell was whining, Bunny was passed out, Kelley screwed up a simple ransom payment and probably brought the cops in, and Janice wasn't talking to him except to let him know her stepfather intended to kill him.

As he drove back to his place, he thought, *It wasn't that he didn't appreciate the matching dishes, the new coordinated furniture, two end tables, the nice throw rug, all the things she picked out. Yeah it was fine, great. He even liked some of the clothes she had gotten for him. He would never be the khaki slacks sort of chump, but that aside he could say his life did seem a bit more organized, and that was good.*

Of course, now he had the kind of place where guys would never feel comfortable coming over and playing poker. And she was always on that color pallet jag, telling him his clothes weren't right. Her old man is out there somewhere looking to gun him down, and Janice is giving him a fashion once over.

What he did was pack about a half-dozen shirts, a pair of shorts, his shaving kit, and a bottle opener. He was back out the door in under five minutes, with everything stuffed into an old gym bag. He didn't even bother to close the door tightly behind him, just pulled it halfway closed, and walked calmly down the staircase, never looking back. He pulled the old Luger out of his belt, laid it on the front seat, and drove off around the corner.

If they had been ten seconds earlier, Buster Keegan and Huey Evans probably would have collided with Mickey's car. But that didn't happen because Huey had insisted on two things. First, he was going with Buster to check out Mickey's place, and second, he was bringing his shotgun. That ate up a good ten minutes. The two of them arguing back and forth while Huey uncased a smart looking, side by side double barrel with silver mounts. He loaded it, stuffed additional shells in his pocket then stormed out to Buster's Mercedes. He tossed the shotgun in the back, climbed into the front seat, and waited with his arms crossed.

"I'm not driving you across town with a loaded shotgun in my back seat," Buster said, starting the car. Then he pulled away from the curb and did exactly that.

They drove in silence. Huey back to turning over the names Michael and Mickey Donnelly in his mind, thinking they were familiar yet still unable to recall exactly why. He thought of all the people he'd screwed over the past thirty years, trying his best to find a link. In the meantime, Buster drove across town, *thinking this was exactly why he enjoyed working alone.*

So, ten seconds after Mickey had turned the corner, Buster pulled up in front of the duplex, stopping in the parking spot still warm from Mickey's car.

"This dump?" Huey said. He looked at Buster, not quite believing the peeling frame structure they were parked in front of. Somehow, he had envisioned a place on a grander scale.

"Well, you said he only hit you for a hundred grand. Apparently he likes to think small. Leave that damn shotgun here, will you? He may not be the right guy, for all we know," Buster said.

"He's the right guy. Didn't you tell me she spent the night here? Think about it. This guy gets the inside dope on me. He knows to torch my garage with my gorgeous Chevy in there, and it's not the right guy? If this jerk is home, I'm getting paid!" he yelled, then pulled the shotgun off the back seat and calmly walked up the front steps.

"Jesus," Buster said to no one. He looked up and down the street to make sure there wasn't a squad car or a nosey neighbor watching before he followed Huey up the steps.

On the porch, Buster pointed to the mailbox labeled 2, and pulled out a handful of advertising circulars, most addressed to resident. He thumbed through the stack, stopping at one addressed to Michael J Donnelly or current resident. He showed it to Huey, who couldn't seem to care less.

Huey got a disgusted frown on his face, took a step back, and kicked the old door squarely just alongside the doorknob. The door flew open, and Huey grunted at Buster." You can stay here and read the mail if you want. I'll see if anyone's home." He hurried up the creaking staircase and waited for Buster at the top.

The door to the second-floor unit was open an inch or two. Buster cautioned Huey by holding his finger to his lips. He carefully pushed the door open to get a peek into the room. After a moment, he pushed it open a little more to get a better view.

"Screw this," Huey said and shouldered the door, bouncing it off the wall. He charged past Buster, shotgun first, into the room. In a matter of a minute or two, they had gone through the entire unit, even checking closets and under the bed to determine if Mickey was hiding somewhere.

"Jesus Christ," groaned Huey looking around." Who decorated this dump? Dried flowers on the wall, and check these candles out," he sniffed." Smells like Christmas in a whore house. Furniture reminds me of some old lady's place. The kind of joint where they don't let you sit on anything."

"That's it," said Buster, walking into the kitchen, opening cabinets, looking inside, then turning around and opening the refrigerator, staring at the bottles of beer filling the better part of two shelves. An empty pizza delivery box sat on top of the beer bottles.

"What do you mean, that's it? This ain't no whore house, least wise not like one I've ever been in."

"No," Buster said looking around, nodding. "The mail, or the lack of anything pertinent in the mail. The furniture, you're right, no one has used this place. Look at this refrigerator," he said, stepping back so Huey could see in and view the beer bottles. "No one in their right mind could live like this, nothing of a personal nature here, no food. This is some sort of safe house."

"Huh?"

"It's a front, Huey. He just used this place for a while and then left it. I'm sure if we checked, we'd find the rent has been paid for five or six months in advance. Whoever was here, I'll bet they stayed for a few days, maybe a week tops. Look around. You see a computer, any food, a shaving razor, or even a toothbrush anywhere? The night I saw your daughter here, the guy moved like a pro, checking up and down the street, making sure it was safe. Everywhere he goes, he's like that, cautious, careful, like a cat, hell this guy is a real pro."

"Oh, bullshit, just cause the guy likes beer and bought some new furniture, get off it," Huey said, not sounding at all convinced. "What about that name, Donnelly. My daughter picked up on it when I mentioned it. And those clothes in the closet and those shoes."

"Well, maybe the guy used that name with her. As for those clothes, you check them out? They're off the rack from Good Will if you look at them closely. Shoes too, it's all just window dressing, stage props. Go check it out. My guess is you'll find stuff you could wear to paint a house and maybe a dress-up shirt, but nothing in-between."

"Are you telling me—"

"I'm telling you this guy is a pro. He's connected. Come on, think about it, Huey! No one lives like this and then pulls off what you say they did? This guy is most likely long gone. This has the mark of a real pro, someone not taking any chances."

Nineteen

Mickey hated to take any more chances, but he felt trapped. He had to figure out if Kelley really had the cops with him. What could they do? Trace him to a different county in ninety seconds and then arrest him? Not very likely. He redialed Kelley's number.

Kelley sat at his desk wanting another bourbon so bad he could scream, but he didn't dare, have the bourbon that is. He jumped when the phone finally rang, figuring to hell with playing it cool or sounding too eager." Hello, this is Jack Kelley."

Mickey lowered his voice to a whisper. "Kelley, we spoke about one hundred thousand dollars. I want it in twenties, non-sequential numbers, unmarked, no damn dye pack. Place it in a cardboard box, tape the box closed, and wait for my next call. By the way, we had a nice chat with your wife. When she gets a couple of drinks in her, she talks an awful lot. We know what you did," Mickey said, adding that last bit from a movie.

Long Nose watched as Kelley's face went from crimson red to pale white. The life actually seemed to drain from the man.

He hung up the phone, collected himself for a moment before looking at the two men seated across from him. "They're sticking to a hundred grand, at least for now. I expect that'll change. I'm going to need the two of you to make sure this whole thing is very quietly contained. Right now, I've got to make a couple of calls to get that cash. I'll have Pauly and Carl accompany me. In the event I'm being watched, I would prefer that these people know absolutely nothing about you two."

He got a nod from Long Nose and looked over to the partner, who amazingly looked up and smiled at Kelley.

"Pauly, get the car!"

Against Buster's better judgment, Huey had torn the place apart twice. Looking under furniture, overturning the couch after slitting the cushions open. He sliced the mattress and box spring. He took everything out of the closet and threw it on the floor. In short, he ransacked the place and still came up empty-handed.

"Huey, we're on borrowed time here. I'll lay you odds that not only are we never, ever, going to find anything, but now your fingerprints are most likely the only ones in this place. So, whatever these guys pulled off, now there's a good chance that you could get hung for it. So, please, can we just get the hell out of here?"

Huey looked around at the mess he'd created. His initial anger more or less spent. "Grab the beer out of the refrigerator, and let's get out of this dump. I can feel it. I know I'm close to whatever it is. I can't quite put my finger on it yet, but I will damn it. I will."He brushed past Buster, shotgun trailing in his right hand. "Make sure you open one of those beers up unless you've got an opener in that fancy car you drive." Huey began sipping his beer as Buster pulled into rush hour traffic. "I'm thinking the best place to be right now is on Janice's ass. Why not just see if she leads us to this guy?"

"Think she still knows where he is? That place looked like it had been a while since anyone was there. Who in the hell would stay there for any length of time? No one I know," Buster said.

"Oh, she knows, all right. I'll bet she knows where he is right now."

"God, where in the hell have you been, Mick? I was worried. I've been expecting to see Huey race up the driveway any minute, ready to pound my head in, just for old times' sake," Dell said.

"Huey ain't gonna be bothering us, and he certainly ain't gonna be pounding anyone's head in. At least not yours or mine. Everything's going like clockwork. Kelley's off to get our cash. I'll call him in a bit. We'll be rid of little Miss Manhattan downstairs in short order, then off to a little warm weather vacation."

Dell smiled weakly.

"Hey, come on, we've been through way too much to get hosed up now. I'll take care of it, don't worry, I've got a plan."

"Yeah, that's what worries me, Mick, another one of your plans."

"Everything's on schedule. I just need you to head up to the lake and grab that cash. In the meantime, I'm going to set up the drop off with Kelley for tomorrow morning."

"Tomorrow?"

"Once we get Kelley's payment, we need to leave town fast. You head up to the lake, get our bankroll, and come on back. I'll deal with everything down here. Now, not another word, I've got to get moving," Mickey said.

As he drove toward the payphone, he could feel the stress gradually ebbing away now that things were finally in motion. Dell would return after midnight with their cash. They would dump Bunny in the morning, get Kelley's money. Then, while Huey checked whatever he wanted to check, Mickey and Del would leisurely drive to Florida. From there, they could grab a flight to Grand Cayman, maybe LA, or just stay in Florida.

Kelley glared at the phone, letting it ring twice before he answered. "Yes," he said in a no-nonsense tone. Whoever this was on the other end, they were going to get an unscheduled appointment with Long Nose and his friend.

"Kelley?" Mickey said, still having trouble associating the booming baritone with the shyster lawyer who charged him for the privilege of serving time in Lino Lakes.

"Expecting someone else?"

"Kelley?" Mickey asked again.

"Yes, this is me, Jack Kelley," the voice unable to disguise his irritation.

"I'll call you in the morning," Mickey said and hung up. He wasn't sure what Kelley was up to, but he had a strong feeling something wasn't right.

"No, wait, wait," Kelley shouted just as the line went dead. They know, he thought. I don't know how, but they know. He managed a weak smile at Long Nose staring at him from across the desk.

It was well after midnight before Dell returned with the trash bags stuffed with twenty-dollar bills.

"I have a bad feeling," Mickey said. So we're going to play things super cautious. We don't need problems with Kelley, and I don't need Huey breathing down our neck. I've got a plan."

"Yeah, I know you've got a plan, Mick. The only problem is every time I ask you about your plan, you don't come up with any details. You just change the subject and tell me not to worry, and that really makes me worry. Right now, I'm worried big time. In fact, I'm scared to death."

"Just relax. This will all be over tomorrow morning. We'll be laughing about the whole thing, heading south without a care in the world."

"See, see? You're not telling me a damn thing, Mick. My ass is on the line right along with yours, so let's be honest. You don't have any idea what we're going to do with Bunny down there, do you? Let's just drop her off at her house tonight and be done with the whole deal. There, that's my plan. Then all we have to worry about is Huey trying to kill us."

For a moment, Mickey looked like he was actually considering Dell's idea.

"That's not a bad thought. But that's not what we're going to do. So just pack a suitcase, toss in some suntan lotion, and don't worry. We'll go over everything in the morning, I've just got a couple of minor details to work out, and then I'll fill you in. Okay?"

"Minor details, you're sure?"

"Yeah, just some little things I'm thinking through. We'll talk over breakfast. Get me up at seven. We got a busy day ahead of us."

"You sure?"

"Seven o'clock," Mickey said, as he rolled onto the couch. As he grabbing the TV remote, he wondered *just what in the hell he was going to do?*

In between pacing, reassuring her daughter that nothing was wrong, and hanging up the phone every time Mickey's answering machine kicked in, Janice was a basket case. It was his usual routine, no contact, no calls, no email, not even so much as a text message. She had no idea if he was alive, dead, or hanging by his thumbs somewhere.

God, he could be so attentive when they were together and such a jerk the rest of the time. She would love to string him up herself, and it wouldn't be by the thumbs. Why didn't he call?

She had paced herself into a frenzy going back and forth in her bedroom, and she simply wasn't going to take it anymore. She tossed her jacket over her pink flannel nightgown and hurried out to her car. The fluffy faux feathers along her hem barely skimmed the sidewalk. She had to scrunch her toes to keep her fuzzy slippers from falling off. She didn't care what she looked like.

She just wanted Mickey to see how upset he had made her.

She slammed a fuzzy slipper down on the accelerator and raced off into the night. If she had to wait all night for him to come home, she didn't care.

"Man, she looks really pissed off," Buster said, not at all sure he wanted to follow her right now.

Huey shook his head. "Just like her mother. I saw that woman pissed off like this thousands of times. This is exactly what we've been waiting for, come on, don't lose her."

Janice made the fifteen-minute drive to Mickey's in just under eight minutes, then sat steaming behind the wheel, parked in front of the darkened duplex. She didn't see his El Dorado anywhere on the street.

"That bastard. Three in the morning, and he's not home yet. Out running around town, making a fool out of me, and I'm sitting here hoping he'll come home so we can have a talk. I'm such a pathetic loser."

She rummaged around her glove compartment and found a Milky Way candy bar she had saved for just such an emergency. The bar had melted and reformed more than once. The chocolate, now partially white, cracked and crumbled as she inhaled the thing in four large bites. There, she thought, spiraling down into an even deeper depression. Now, I'll be a fat loser.

"What do you think she's doing? It looks like she's just sitting there," Buster said.

"Yup. She's sitting there just getting more and more pissed off."

"What?"

"Believe me. She's just like her mother. She'll work herself into a lather over something and blow whatever the problem is out of all proportion. So much for your idiotic idea about this place being a halfway house," Huey said.

"I didn't say halfway house. I said safe house. A place where they come and go, use it for a job, and then walk away. She might think the guy actually lives there, but he's already long gone. I can't believe he came back and cleaned up the mess you left. My guess is he hasn't contacted her, and this is the only place she can think of. We're in for a very long, very dull night."

"She'll sit there and get all worked up until she can't even think straight. Then, she's gonna storm into that place and ream the guy out. Believe me. She's thinking about the same one or two things, over and over again, working herself up into a crazy state. If he's in there, I almost feel sorry for the poor bastard. There won't be much left for us. If he's not there, she'll head to wherever she thinks she might find him. I was on the receiving end of this enough times with her mother."

"The one difference is her mother used to choke down about a pound of chocolate and drink a gallon of malted milkshakes. After she reamed me out, I had to suffer through a month of her dieting to lose ten pounds.

No thanks, I'll just watch from a distance for a while. Sooner or later, she'll go in, and we can follow. There'll be enough fireworks no one will hear us coming."

"Well, since you know all about it, you can wake me when the fireworks start," Buster said. He slouched down in his seat and closed his eyes for some much needed sleep. As he drifted off, he reminded himself to never, ever get involved with Huey again.

Mickey woke to the smell of bacon frying. The sun was just coming up and he stumbled off the couch and into the kitchen to get a mug of coffee. "You doing okay?"

"Yeah, I suppose," Dell said.

After breakfast, they both went downstairs and attempted to wake Bunny. Dell was in the room wearing the Lassie mask. He was shaking Bunny, who had just crawled under the covers down to the foot of the bed where she had begun to growl. He held a bottle of aspirin and a glass of water in the hope they could get her to a point where she could be moved.

Mickey stood in the doorway, hoping he wouldn't have to get involved, although it was beginning to look like that was exactly what he was going to have to do.

"Come on, Bunny, how about some aspirin and a nice pitcher of manhattans once we get you going this morning?" Dell said. After a few more minutes with no result, he reached beneath the blanket, grabbed what he hoped were her ankles, and pulled her out from under the covers.

She squirmed for a moment but didn't put up much of a struggle. Her eyes gradually opened, and she appeared almost cognizant. He quickly taped her ankles, and she presented her wrists, which he bound, then pulled a pillowcase over her head.

"Once we get in the car, you can go right back to sleep, Bunny," Mickey said from the doorway. "We'll have you back with that shyster lawyer husband before noon. We won't hurt you. Believe me we don't even want to touch you, so thanks for cooperating."

Before he knew what to do, she had reached up, pulled the pillowcase off her head, and faced him. "Shyster lawyer husband? Are you kidding me? Jack's a lot of things, but he's not a damn lawyer. Good lord he's a real estate developer."

"Oh, yeah? Well, I knew him years ago, before he was disbarred," Mickey said, holding his hands in front of his face.

"Disbarred?" Bunny said, shaking her head. "Jack's never practiced law in his life. Believe me, you can accuse him of a lot of things, but being a lawyer isn't one of them. A lawyer? Jack Kelley? Now, that's really funny."

"Are you telling me your husband isn't a balding, pudgy guy about this high?" Mickey said and held his hand up at about chin level.

Bunny shook her head no.

"And that he wasn't disbarred eight, maybe ten years ago? For trust fund abuse? Hell, Bunny, it was in all the papers. I read the article online recently. That's probably how the two of you got that cabin up north, stealing dough from some poor old ladies' pension fund."

"Mister, you're crazy. First of all, the Jack Kelley I've been married to for thirty-seven and a half years is six feet two inches tall. He has a full head of hair, although it's salt and pepper now. He's never been a lawyer, never been disbarred, never been in charge of a trust fund. We've never had a cabin up north, although we do have a condo down in Naples."

"You're sure he's not a lawyer?"

Bunny shook her head and cackled. "I think you two morons made a very big mistake. And when you see who you're dealing with, you're going to be very unhappy. Oh, Jesus, this is just too funny for words."

Mickey stood there with a stunned look on his face as Dell shifted into panic mode. "Mick?"

"Shh-shh, I'm thinking."

"Listen, boys, having the wrong Jack Kelley is the least of your problems. My husband Jack is a lot of things, including a complete bastard. But he's not the kind to take something like this lightly, and he certainly would have gotten some expert help, if you catch my drift."

"Why do you think I drink? You think I like what I've become? It might look like the good life, but Jack will run over anyone for a nickel. And you were planning to just take money from him? Just like that? Sorry, boys."

"You sure he wasn't—"

"Why would I lie about that? No, Jack was never a lawyer, never disbarred, he's tall and all the other stuff I said. Sounds to me like you two screwed with the wrong Jack Kelley."

"Is your given name Petronella?" Mickey said, grasping at straws.

"Petronella? Damn, I wish. Good Lord, no, it's Chasity. Believe me, if I could have traded Petronella for Chasity as a teenager, I would have jumped at the chance."

Dell shuffled out of the room, shaking his head as he pulled off the Lassie mask.

"Hey, Dell, hold up. Umm-mmm, be back in a minute, Bunny," Mickey called over his shoulder as he hurried after Dell.

"Great plan, Mick. You're so in touch with this one you grabbed the wrong wife from the wrong guy. Terrific. I just knew this was screwed up. And, once again, I've got no one to blame but myself."

"Knock it off, Dell. I knew this all along."

"Bullshit, Mick, you just—"

"Shut up and listen, Dell. This doesn't change a thing. In fact, it's better, breaks the pattern we were in. Yeah, my thinking on this was definitely screwed up. That's why I wanted to involve someone that we conceivably have no earthly connection to. All these jerks, Huey, Coach Buddy, even that legislator, they all had a tie to us. But this one, our last score, we'll just pull it off and walk away with the cash. Just the way we planned."

"Just the way we—Come on, Mick. For Christ's sake, you didn't know about this. You didn't have the slightest idea this had happened. Hell, you were just in there arguing with Bunny, trying to convince her she was someone else. Arguing that the great Mickey Donnelly couldn't possibly be guilty of a screw up of this magnitude. Damn it, Mick."

"Well, Dell, I don't know what else to tell you. We can drop her off somewhere, just head out of town, hope no one comes looking for us. Live frugally, count our pennies for the rest of our lives, eat macaroni and cheese every night. Or, maybe we can pull it off one more time, live like the free spirits we should be. Not a care in the world, drink from a crystal glass, live life to the fullest, taking the—"

"Okay, Mick, okay. I get it. Yeah, let's do it, we'll do all that shit. Sure, but just for once, be honest with me. I figure after all these years of being your wingman I've earned it."

"Are you telling me you think I'm . . ." Mickey stopped and looked at Dell. "Yeah, okay. You've more than earned it, so here it is. I don't have much of a plan other than making this guy drive all over town. Eventually, with a little luck, I'll get him to leave that box of cash somewhere that I think feels safe enough to let me grab it without getting caught. It's what's worked for me, for us, in the past."

Dell gave a long sigh.

"Simple? Mick, it sounds idiotic. Here, you wear this damn mask and get Bunny into the car. Then we'll figure something out."

Janice woke with an aching back and leg cramps from a fitful few hours waiting in her car for Mickey to come home. She was still mad, but her rage was tempered by exhaustion, not to mention a slightly desperate need to use a bathroom. She decided to ring the doorbell in the off chance his car was in the shop, or at the very least, to eliminate the opportunity of him insisting he had been home and didn't know she was parked out front.

Before she was even on the front porch, she noticed the door was ajar. She entered, quickly climbed the stairs only to find his apartment wide open and, to put it mildly, completely trashed. She could only hope there was still toilet paper.

Buster and Huey had been sleeping in shifts. Just now, Buster was watching Janice as she climbed out of her car, up to the front porch, and in the front door. He figured he'd give her five minutes before he woke Huey. She was back out the door in little more than three, looking frantic and hurrying to her car. Huey woke just as Buster started the car and made a U-turn in the middle of the road, following her at a distance.

"They together?" Huey asked, rubbing his eyes.

"No."

"You got any coffee? God, I feel like a piece of plumbing, all bent up."

"What do you think this is, a diner? No, Huey, I don't have any coffee."

"Whoa, you wake up on the wrong side of the bed? Where's she going anyway?"

"I don't have any idea where in the hell she's going, Huey. That's why I thought we might want to follow her."

They followed Janice all the way out to Dell's. Watched at a distance as she pounded on the front door then entered the house by way of a tuck-under garage. She ran out a minute later, jumped back in her car, and raced back toward town.

"God, this is crazy. I don't know who or what she's looking for, but my guess is she hasn't found it yet," Buster said.

"Way to get a handle on the obvious. She's so much like her mother it's actually frightening. Going around half-cocked, not knowing who or what she's looking for. This has been a complete waste of my time," Huey said.

"Yeah? Well, just for the record, I warned you. I told you not to come. But you were the one who insisted. You were the one who argued with me. Told me—"

"Whatever. Jesus Christ, I thought for sure she was going to lead us to wherever this guy was. Just like her mother, even that gets screwed up."

"I'm guessing right now she has no idea what to do. Probably feels about as ripped off as we do," Buster said.

"That does nothing in the way of bringing me any damn comfort. It was my money, she's the ticket, and I want it back."

Buster thought, *all he wanted right now was a hot shower and some sleep. God strike him dead if he got involved with Huey ever again.*

Twenty

ell glanced around and said, "Don't worry. There's a pay phone you can use about two blocks from the site. We'll be able to see them coming in any direction. We'll take Bunny up a few floors, have them send the dough up in the elevator. We grab the dough and send Bunny down. There's four different ways off every floor and out of the building. Even if this guy does have help, he'll never be able to catch us."

Mickey glanced into the back seat where Bunny was softly snoring. "Great plan except for one thing, aren't we going to attract attention bringing her up to the top floor?"

Dell had a slight grin on his face. "Oh, did I forget to mention, the entire construction site is shut down? No crews are there for another week. We'll have the place to ourselves. Of course, it's all locked up, but then again, I've got the keys, so that won't really be a problem for us." He fumbled in his pocket then dangled shiny keys for Mickey to see.

* * *

As far as Jack Kelley could tell, his two guests never left the chairs they were sitting in, never even slept. He felt bad about Bunny, but she would have to go. He couldn't risk having her around, causing more problems. He was just about to ask his guests if they'd like more coffee when his phone rang. He answered halfway through the initial ring.

"Yes."

"Kelley," Mickey whispered. "You've got the money? A hundred grand?"

"Oh, brother," Bunny said from the back seat.

"I want you to head downtown. Corner of Sixth and Saint Peter, there's a construction site. Place the funds in the construction elevator in the lobby and send them up to the top floor. We've got a number of us posted around the building so, please, don't waste our time trying to pull a fast one. It won't work. I expect to see you within the hour."

Mickey hung up the payphone and said, "Okay, let's get over there. I just hope you know what you're doing, Dell. We got everything riding on this, the last thing we need is a surprise."

Mickey waited for the traffic to clear so he could complete his illegal left-hand turn. Eventually, he just accelerated, ignoring the horn blast from the UPS truck, and jumped across the oncoming traffic.

"You got a death wish this morning?"

Mickey shrugged and drove through the empty ramp to the far side. Dell directed him to a secluded parking spot just off the back alley, in the event they needed to make a fast getaway.

Mickey was climbing up the stairwell, heading toward the fourteenth floor with quite a few floors to go. He had just paused to catch his breath when Dell popped his head out from the door on the ninth floor.

"Mick, hey . . . Mick," he whispered.

"God, Dell, you just about gave me a heart attack. What the hell are you doing, and where is Bunny?"

"Part of the beauty of this place, come on up, I'll show you," Dell said and ducked back into the hallway.

Mickey quickly huffed up the remaining flights and followed Dell, or at least where he thought Dell had gone. He stood and looked out on a vast empty room, virtually the entire floor.

"Dell, damn it, this isn't the time to be screwing around. Where in the hell are you?"

"Hey, Mick," Dell called from behind, causing Micky to jump.

"Jesus Christ, are you—"

"Isn't it great? A little break room we had set up here. You can nap or whatever, and the foreman will never find you. Looks like the entire floor is completely empty. We can grab the cash, send Bunny down, and just wait Kelley out if we have to. He'll never find us if we duck in here."

Mickey poked his head in the small room. Bunny was sitting on the floor with her back against the wall and the pillowcase still over her head. "Dell, I gotta say, this is genius, pure genius. We better keep an eye peeled for Kelley. He should be here in the next thirty minutes."

"If I ever get my hands on Mickey, I'll strangle him," Janice sniffled. "That complete jerk, that crumb, that bum, that total, absolute loser, that moron. Here I am, driving around downtown, in the middle of the morning wearing a pink nightgown and fuzzy slippers. I'll kill him for doing this to me. I swear to God."

It was then that she thought she recognized the El Dorado making an illegal left-hand turn. It was the horn blast from a UPS truck that initially caught her attention. The silhouette of 'Mickey's big fat head' and his banged up, dented car set her temper off again.

"Now, where in the hell is she going?" Buster asked, just wanting the whole awful experience to be over.

"Who the hell knows? I need some coffee and get me back to my office. I'm ready to go home. She's crazier than her mother ever was."

"No, wait a minute, either she spotted us, which I doubt, or she's on to something." She hasn't picked up on us for the past seven hours. I don't know why she would now."

"Look, I'm telling you she's nuts, just like her mother. So, get me back to my office."

"Huey, you wanted to come along, have all the fun. Well, this is how it's done."

Five minutes later, Buster was standing in the lower parking level, next to Janice's burgundy Olds 88, scanning the vast, empty parking area. He was tired and kept his voice low as he stated the obvious.

"Well, this is her car, but your guess is as good as mine as to where the hell she went. She can't be more than a minute or two ahead of us. I don't know, dressed the way she is, maybe you're right, the whole thing is crazy."

Huey pulled his shotgun out of the back seat, then slammed the car door.

"Keep it down, damn it, she's liable to hear us," Buster said.

"Ahh, bullshit. I tell you what, Buster. You've been pussy-footing around all night. Waiting, following, waiting, following. The only thing I got out of this is an aching back. I used to think you were pretty sharp, but you're an idiot. So, just get the hell out of here. Knowing Janice, she's probably in the bathroom, for Christ's sake. I'm through fooling around. I'm gonna do what I should have done in the beginning, only do it my way and get the information I need to get my money back."

Buster looked at Huey across the roof of his car. The tirades, the complaining, the bitching, he had half a mind to leave Huey here and let him think about how he planned to get home carrying a shotgun.

"Go on, damn it, get the hell out of here," Huey shouted, then leveled the shotgun in Buster's general direction.

"You know," Buster said, then thought better of giving Huey any cautionary warning. "Okay, Huey, have it your way. You know how to reach me once you decide to calm down."

"Just get the hell out of here," Huey said as Buster climbed back into the car. "And you can forget about getting paid for any of this, you hear, forget about it," he screamed as Buster's car retreated up the ramp.

"Idiot." Now where in the hell had Janice gone? It was time to get his money back.

Huey stepped into the cavernous space that would ultimately serve as the main floor. Where, exactly, would a young nutcase woman, wearing a pink nightgown and fuzzy slippers, wander off to at a construction site?

He carried his shotgun leisurely over his shoulder, quietly humming, of all things, the Wedding March,

'Here Comes the Bride.' He was humming it like a funeral dirge. He looked over the vast expanse of open floor with row after row of metal studs sectioning off future hallways and offices. Where in the hell would she go?

"It's that building back there," Kelley said as they drove past the large construction site. Bunny must have known a lot more than he would have guessed. The cost overruns on this project had served as a nice profit center for both he and Timmy White up until the entire project was shut down. Some bean counter, somewhere, pulling the plug until they sorted out the financial irregularities. But he had no idea Bunny knew of his involvement. Why else would the kidnappers have chosen this location except to let him know? They might have been a pain in the rear, but Kelley was suddenly glad he had Long Nose and his friend along.

"I'll drop you off at the end of the next block."

"We need ten minutes before you come into the building," Long Nose said. He pronounced it 'Build-ink'. Kelley stared at him in the rearview mirror. "Ho-kay?"

Kelley glanced at the digital clock on the dashboard. "That's cutting it kind of close, don't you think. Okay, ten minutes, I'll do it."

Up on the ninth floor, Dell signaled Mickey. "A car just drove into the parking area."

"That'll be Kelley, right on time," Mickey said.

Two stories underground, Kelley got out of his car and placed his hand on the hood of the rust spotted, burgundy olds 88. *What a gas-guzzling beast*, he thought, making note of the still warm hood. Typical of the way they'd operated, a step ahead of him until now. Obviously, the nondescript vehicle was stashed down here to spirit them off once they had the money. *The money* he thought and quickly got back in his car and drove up to the main parking level.

He carried the box into the eerily vacant first floor. He walked past long tables covered with blueprints and miscellaneous bits of nonsense to the bright red construction elevator. He placed the box on the elevator, then, as instructed, cupped his hands and called, "Olly, Olly in free. Olly, Olly in free." Yelling it like a kid playing a game. He waited for what seemed like an eternity before the elevator lurched upward, the high pitched, whining engine bringing the elevator to the floors above.

Dell heard Kelley yelling and looked at Mickey.

"My own little idea," Mickey said, then looked down the open shaft as the elevator slowly rose towards them.

The effort of climbing five stories on a staircase had begun to calm Janice down. All that changed the moment she heard Kelley yelling. "I'll strangle him, I swear to god, and throw him out the window." She watched as the elevator rose past the fifth floor. She ran to the open shaft and began to count the floors, thinking wherever it stopped would be the floor she had a better than even chance of getting her hands around Mickey's neck.

Down on the third floor, Huey listened to Kelley yelling then watched as the elevator rose past him. Spray painted graffiti scrawled in green on the elevator wall read 'You Suck!' and seemed to be directed specifically at Huey.

That did it, Huey thought, and counted the floors as the elevator continued to rise. Somewhere up there, Janice was waiting, mocking him, laughing, and all of this her idea of some kind of joke. "We'll see who's laughing after this," Huey said.

At first, Long Nose and his friend thought they might have some real trouble on their hands, since the building open and completely vacant. Their approach could be covered from any number of uncountable hiding places and sniper stations. They'd never have the opportunity to fire a shot before they were both dead. That was before they heard Kelley yelling.

The fool, they thought, then watched as the elevator rose. They counted the floors as it continued to climb, up, and up. Wherever it stopped, they would find their elusive quarry, deal with him, then deal with Kelley, plus the added bonus of killing his wife.

* * *

Dell brought the elevator up to the ninth floor. He stared for a long moment at the box sitting in the corner. Mickey stood beside him doing the same thing. Only his mouth was hanging open.

"Well, it's not going to get off there by itself," Dell said.

"Huh?"

"Let's check it out. Here, just in case there's a dye pack," Dell said, handing Mickey a handful of newspaper.

"If there's a dye pack, that isn't going to be of much use. Let's just make sure there's cash in there. We can count it later. I'd just as soon get Bunny off our hands and get the hell out of here," Mickey said.

"No argument from me." Dell stepped onto the elevator and gingerly slid the box across the floor using his foot.

"Will you relax. What could possibly go wrong at this stage?"

"You disgusting, idiotic, two-faced, moron," Janice screamed from behind. She was red-faced after running up the stairs to the ninth floor.

"I knew it. I just knew you two fools would be up to something. Oh, gee, I'm sorry, maybe you didn't think a phone call might be in order. You know? So, I don't wig out the way I'm doing now after not hearing a word from you and seeing your place ransacked. This is the meanest, cruelest, worst thing you've ever done to me, Mickey. You absolute idiot."

Tears ran down her flushed cheeks, which made her even more irate at not being able to control herself.

"Man, that is really scary," Dell said under his breath.

The two of them remained riveted in place as she marched toward them in her pink nightgown and fuzzy slippers, with her face flushed and fists clenched. The pink faux feathers along the hem of the nightgown had turned grey after traipsing through nine flights of construction dust.

"Oh, Jesus," Mickey groaned.

Huey wasn't just breathing heavily. He was wheezing, gasping for air on the seventh floor. He paused for a brief moment just to catch his breath, or he would be worthless by the time he climbed up to the ninth floor. As soon as he heard Janice screaming from above, he stumbled on, carrying his shotgun, sweat pouring down his face and running down his back.

Long Nose and his pal moved cautiously up the stairwell. One providing cover for the other as they leapfrogged their way up, half a flight at a time. They paused to check out each floor, so no one had the opportunity to surprise them from behind.

They could hear one, possibly two people on the stairs above them making quite a bit of noise, maybe even stumbling. It suggested there could well be multiple individuals to eliminate before they could turn their attention to Kelley and his wife.

"Ahh, umm, hi . . . honey. What brings you here?" Mickey said. He attempted to signal with his hands in an effort to get Janice to calm down.

"Mick? We really don't have time for this bullshit right now. Bummer, Mickey, real bummer," Dell half-whispered, still riveted to the floor.

"Okay, okay, relax. I got everything under control, man." Mickey said, turning toward Dell, although his eyes said otherwise.

"Oh? So now you think you can control me. Is that it? And don't you honey me," Janice shouted as Mickey approached cautiously.

"Now, Janice, honey, let's calm down. You have to admit, this whole picture here, it's just a little unexpected, baby, that's all. Calm down, now, honey."

"Don't baby me, you moron. And I don't intend to calm down. You have one hell of a lot of explaining to do, and you had better get started. Whatever made you think you could just—"

"You can all stay right where you are. Nobody moves," Huey gasped, as he leaned against the door frame.

"Oh, God. Thanks, Janice, you brought your father. Thanks a lot for including us in the old family reunion," Mickey said.

"Shit, that's Huey Evans," Dell said.

"Do I know you two idiots from somewhere?" Huey said and started towards them with his shotgun leveled at the group.

"You, nut case in her nightgown, move over here, and you two fools do the same," Huey said, directing them with his shotgun.

"You know what? I have had it up to here with all your bullying. Do you hear me? I have had it," Janice shouted.

"All you've had, spoiled little girl, is your own way. So, you, shut the hell up and move over there with Laurel and Hardy." He motioned again with his shotgun.

Janice stood staring wide-eyed, her feet apparently nailed to the floor.

"I'm not going to tell you again, move those fuzzy little slippers over there, now. And you, fat ass, you that Donnelly jerk I've been looking for? Where do I know you from? Did you work for me once? More importantly, where in the hell is the money you took from me?"

A sudden icy chill seemed to descend over the small group. No one made an attempt to answer.

"Hey. All of you, move your ass over there, further, go on, keep moving." Huey motioned again with the shotgun, then focused on the cardboard box Dell had pushed off the elevator and onto the concrete floor.

"Well, what do we have here?" He slid the box over a foot or two, then reached down to open it up.

"Hmmm, don't tell me you were nice enough to have my cash all packaged up for me, so I can just walk out of here, paid in full. Call us even once I leave you with a little reminder not to ever try and jack me around again."

Twenty-one

Long Nose signaled to his partner that he could count at least four people. He wasn't sure why the woman was in a costume, but it must have something to do with the next phase of their plan. It didn't really matter now. What they had to do was to get everyone to drop their weapons.

He whispered into his partner's ear. They would go in on either side of the door, one low, one high. First man goes in low and to the right, taking the area 12-6. The second goes in high and covers 6-12. They'd done it countless times, practiced it until it was automatic, lined up, one behind the other, and moving on the count of three. Long Nose signaled with his fingers, one, two…

Both Dell and Janice thought they might have caught an imperceptible something in the stairwell, movement, glitter, a light, or maybe a shadow. Neither one was really sure, but they both glanced over Huey's shoulder toward the doorway. A reaction not lost on Huey.

He spun around just as Long Nose made his move through the doorway, coming in low and to the right. The blast from both barrels of Huey's shotgun caught Long Nose at about chin level, picking him up and slamming him back and over the stairwell railing. He crashed a half flight below. That seemed to calm any reaction his partner may have had, and he ran back down the staircase, pausing just long enough to look at what was left of Long Nose before continuing down the stairs racing toward the ground floor.

"What in the hell was that?" Huey said, looking shocked and peering through acrid smoke toward the now empty doorway.

Dell and Mickey stood riveted to the floor, their mouths open, ears still ringing from the sound of the blast. They could smell the cordite as they stared through the smoke at the empty doorway. An echo of fading footsteps bounced up from the stairwell.

Janice was already on the move before Huey could react. She wrenched the shotgun from his hands then hit him in the stomach, hard, full force with the butt of the weapon. As he doubled up, she cracked him across the back of the head with both barrels.

"God, I've wanted to do that for years," she said as Huey landed on the floor. "Okay, boys, he's not dead, but he's going to wish he was when he wakes up. Is there another way out of this place?" she asked and stepped over Huey.

"She's right, Mick. Come on, let's get going. We can take the back staircase it's on the other side," Dell said.

Mickey ran to the small area where Bunny sat on the floor. He left the pillowcase on her head as he spoke to her. "I'm undoing your hands. When you get all the tape off, you're free to go. We will never, ever bother you again. I promise, in fact, all of us promise."

He freed her hands then hurried across the vast, empty floor catching up to Janice and Dell on the back staircase. Mickey and Dell slowed and calmly walked out the back entrance carrying their box to the El Dorado. Janice made her way down two more levels, climbed in her car, and drove home.

Kelley waited a long time after he saw Long Nose's partner run down the stairs and out the door. He thought he might have heard some noise from another part of the building a few minutes later, but he couldn't be sure. He cautiously climbed the steps up to the ninth floor, past Long Nose's body lying in the stairwell. He guessed, more or less accurately, what had happened, at least as far as Long Nose was concerned, dead before he went over the railing.

He found Huey Evans sprawled out on the floor, groggy, confused, and more than willing to remain where he was. Of course, the double-barreled shotgun Kelley pointed at his head served as a powerful incentive until the police arrived.

Following Bunny's mistaken identification of Huey as one of her kidnappers, he was charged, tried, and convicted on kidnapping and murder charges. He had attempted an insanity plea, claiming of all things that his stepdaughter had been there to pick up the ransom money in a pink nightgown. He further claimed that she had scammed him out of a hundred thousand dollars, but his defense never really got off the ground, and the trial concluded in just three days.

Huey was sentenced to twenty-five years, without parole, at his age effectively a life sentence. He is currently serving his sentence in Stillwater prison.

The trial publicity and her stepfather's claims proved too much for Janice. She ultimately quit her waitress job and left town with her daughter, Ashley.

Long Nose's partner left town, but not before he tied up one loose end, namely Jack Kelley. He commandeered Kelley's car and drove back to Chicago. Along the way, he tossed a piece of Kelley out the window every thirty miles, just as regular as clockwork.

Prologue

Dell creaked open the lid to their cooler. Across the back of his t-shirt was the image of a sailfish jumping over an inept fisherman in a rowboat.

"You want another?" he asked with his back to Mickey, grabbing two beers and not waiting for an answer. He passed the chilled can over his shoulder.

Mickey, wearing a straw Panama hat and a neon blue shirt festooned with sailboats, handed his fishing rod to the attractive blonde coed at his side. "I'm telling you, this is the best place to fish. Look around at everyone here. Do you really think we'd be fishing here if it was lousy? Come on, give me a little credit." He popped open his can and licked the beer spray off his tanned hand. He hoped she didn't actually catch a fish. He hated dealing with the damn things.

Her top was knotted above her midsection, revealing a tanned, flat stomach. She'd gone from gangly to gorgeous over the course of a couple of years, and now, at eighteen, she was a drop-dead beauty. Wholesome, solid, in that kind of cornsilk Midwestern way, just like her mother. She looked to be the kind of woman you could count on to watch your back.

She'd done a lot of growing up over the past three years, a lot of maturing, and had her own job waiting tables at her mother's restaurant when she wasn't attending classes.

She liked Mickey, was fond of him for becoming the father she never had. And, being just like her mom, she wasn't beyond speaking her mind.

"The only reason you two and all these other guys fish here is because that store at the end of the pier sells beer. And right next to the beer store is the fish market. How many people do you know catch fish and then bring the fillet's home wrapped in white paper? And since when can you catch walleye in the Pacific? Come on, Mickey, admit it, you're full of it."

"Yeah, well maybe, Ashley, but don't tell your mom."

"She already knows, you moron."

The End

Thank you for taking the time to read *Reduced Ransom!* the first book in the Hotshots series. Reviews are a big help. If you enjoyed the read, I would really appreciate a review. Even if it's just a sentence or two it really, really helps.
All the best,
Mike

Check out the sample of the next book in the *Finders Keepers*, the second book in the Hotshot series.

FINDERS KEEPERS

Second Edition

MIKE FARICY

One

It was unusual for any traffic to be on the rural Minnesota road this close to the Canadian border, let alone this late at night. That the vehicle was a red, steel-plated armored van carrying shrink-wrapped kilos of cocaine should have been a once-in-a-lifetime occurrence. For Cecil and his crew, Carlo DaLuca, Izzie Erdman, Skoog and Jimmy, it was just another weekly run.

Carlo DaLuca's bulk oozed out of the passenger seat. His triple chins jiggled in time to the gravel road. His loud snoring helped to keep Cecil awake, who was more concerned about hitting a moose than running into any law-enforcement types. They had been working the route successfully for the better part of two months. There were no rivals looking to rip them off. No pesky undercover stings to worry about, no informers, and no turf wars. They just drove north. Izzie Erdman and Skoog would motor out to the middle of the lake and exchange the kilos for cash, which kept everyone happy. What could possibly go wrong?

Meanwhile, earlier that day, Austin Boothe crammed the final White Castle burger into his mouth and washed it down with a Leinenkugel beer. He was average-sized and just on the verge of developing a beer belly. His thinning, unkempt brown hair was maybe two years away from a comb-over. His skin was pale from far too many hours in front of the TV.

"I hope you don't plan on leaving little white boxes all over the floor again, Austin. Like I don't have enough to do already." Celeste stood three feet behind him with her arms extended. She grasped red, eight-ounce weights, turning left to right at the waist in time to music pounding from her earphones. "Five, six, seven, eight."

"Where'd you hide the damn remote, baby doll?"

"I'm dancing three till close tonight. Five, six, seven, eight. Need you to pick up some things from my mom's. Five, six, seven, eight. And clean all this up, will ya?" She dropped the weights next to the recliner, a cream-colored faux-leather affair with a strip of grey duct tape at the end of each arm.

"I mean it, Austin. I need you to get that stuff for me." She walked down her trailer's narrow hall, pulling the t-shirt over her head.

"No can do, baby. I got a meeting. I'm planning some shit," he called to her.

"I already told you, I'm dancing tonight. Hope you're not seeing that worthless brother of yours again. Are you? Please tell me that's not who you're meeting."

"How can you be busy? Who goes to watch strippers at three in the afternoon?"

"Big tippers is who, the rich business types, all the corporate executives."

"Big tippers, right. I'd like to—"

"Just pick up the stuff at my mom's. Will ya?" she said, then slammed the bathroom door to make her point.

Later that afternoon and over the course of three beers and multiple dishes of popcorn, Austin and his brother Andre reviewed their simple plan. Every Friday, Ladies' Night, the club where Celeste danced, had a large amount of cash. The cash was picked up by an armored van service, Knox Security, and then transported to the Miners National Bank for deposit.

Two additional pieces of information tied all of this together. The bank's IT manager, heavy tipping Rodney Debbens, was a regular admirer of Celeste's. The other night he whispered to her during a lap dance. "I'm working on this damn security upgrade over the entire weekend. So I won't be in. But, if you're interested, maybe you'd like to come down sometime. Get a private tour of how all the new software works."

Celeste giggled, steamed his bifocals, took the parasol from his drink, and placed it in her cleavage.

"Now, Rodney, why would I want to see anything soft?" She retold the tale to Austin, making the point that Rodney had stuffed a nice, crisp, twenty-dollar bill in her thong.

The second piece of information was from Chester Penfield, night watchman at Knox Security. Seventy-eight-year-old Chester had worked security for the past two months. He was armed with a flashlight, a cell phone, and a panic button mounted on the desk where he sat when he wasn't making his three-minute rounds of the concrete-block building. As a man in uniform, he was burdened with a good deal of responsibility and needed the daily stress release of a boiler-maker. Austin overheard him one recent afternoon at the bar.

"I ain't gonna tell ya where a certain large deposit is from, boys. But let me just say, them gals make an awful lot of money flashing around their bare behinds."

Since there wasn't a proctology practice in town, the Boothe brothers put two and two together over beers, and suddenly a plan was born.

"I, I just don't know," Andre said, shaking his head as he worked his way through another beer.

He was a younger version of Austin, physically unremarkable, thin, with unkempt brown hair. He'd been attempting to grow a mustache for the past five or six weeks, not that anyone had really noticed.

"You getting cold feet on me? Now?" Austin asked.

"No, no, nothing like that. It just seems so simple, and if it's so simple, why hasn't—"

"Simple? Hell, that's the beauty of this. It is simple. All that bullshit about split-second timing, secret combinations, and hanging from tall buildings? Leave that to Hollywood and that pissant, Tom Cruise."

"Yeah, but this sounds so easy that something—"

"It sounds easy because we've planned everything. That security building is in the middle of a damn forest, one road in and the same road out. We go in the back way, through the woods, no one sees us. We'll be waiting when that armored van drives up to the loading dock. They unload the thing, won't be more than a little old bank bag. We're hiding and come out from under the dock. 'Hands up, boys. Everyone back in the van.' We chain the damn door shut, and we're out of there. Forty-five seconds, tops."

"The guards?"

"Guards? You mean like old Chester? What's he gonna do? Shine a flashlight on us? The Gleeson brothers driving the damn van? Those two together have to come in at close to seven hundred pounds. The only problem is there won't be room for Chester with those two fatties stuffed in the back."

"But they can push an alarm."

"We're counting on that. It'll take the cops at least ten minutes to get out there. Course, that's if they're in the car, ready to go. They'll be coming down that dark road. It'll take 'em at least another five, maybe ten minutes to cut the locks we put on the armored van. Call it twenty minutes. Hell, we're hot-footing it over on County 12. Just two guys heading to the cabin for a little weekend fishing. We got this one in the bag, man. All we gotta do is relax and get ready for our stroll down Easy Street."

TWO

What was now the Knox Security building had, at different stages in its life, been a contractor's warehouse, a propane gas company, and a short-lived pottery factory that went bust way back in 2005. After that, the building stood vacant for a number of years. For Chicago brothers Salvatore and Massimo Saventinni, the setting was perfect. The building was virtually isolated in the wilderness of Northern Minnesota. It sat in relative proximity to the Canadian border. Most importantly, there was no one within miles who gave a damn.

They converted the walk-in, propane-fired kiln from the pottery factory into a makeshift vault that was still capable of incinerating anything inside at 2350F. For a dollar above minimum wage, the brothers hired Chester as a night watchman and the Gleeson boys, two otherwise unemployable locals, to provide the perception of a legal enterprise.

The concept had been the brainchild of Massimo, at seventy, the younger brother by eight years. They hired the locals on a part-time basis. Filter a few thousand dollars through the town bank to make things look legitimate, all the while hauling kilos up to Canada and funneling cash back down to Chicago.

It worked like the proverbial charm. In fact, business had grown to such an extent that the armored van was now making a regular weekend run through the pristine wilderness to the Canadian border in order to meet the increased demand for product.

It was this regular weekend run that had given the Gleeson brothers and Chester every Friday night off, with pay. They were replaced with a crew of street-smart Chicago wise-guys. The wise-guys continued to keep up appearances, making the Ladies' Night deposit every Friday at the Miners National Bank. Except for this Friday, when the cash would be held in the Knox security vault until heavy-tipping bank IT manager Rodney Debbens phoned to say the security system at the bank was back online.

Austin and Andre Boothe, attired in black sweatshirts, black jeans, dark brown cotton garden gloves, and clown masks, huddled beneath the loading dock, crouched up against the building's damp concrete block wall. They were armed with the twelve-gauge shotguns they used every fall for duck hunting. They had no intention of using the shotguns, secure in the knowledge that both fat Gleeson brothers and seventy-eight-year-old Chester would take one look and freak.

The armored van, stuffed with three million-plus in illicit drug money plus the thirty-five-hundred-dollar Ladies' Night deposit, backed into the Knox loading dock. Shrill beeping and flashing taillights warned that the seven-ton, armor-plated vehicle was moving in reverse.

Overhead, the garage door opened. A heavy cart rolled across the wooden planks of the loading dock. Austin figured it must be seventy-eight-year-old night watchman Chester. Andre flashed his brother a questioning look, but Austin shook his head, signaling there was nothing to worry about. Once the van was turned off, both the passenger and driver's doors flew open.

Austin and Andre instinctively pressed back against the concrete-block wall, concentrating on the footsteps overhead. Since they ignored the exiting driver and passenger, it failed to register with either of them that the three-hundred-and-fifty-pound Gleeson brothers would not be wearing handmade Italian shoes nor tailored Armani trousers.

Austin couldn't quite make sense of the footsteps overhead. It sounded like half a dozen people up there, but then again, the Gleeson boys were awfully big. The rubber clown mask pulled over his head severely limited his ability to discern what was being said, and so he signaled Andre with a poke from his twelve-gauge to begin cautiously crawling out. They planned to slip out from under the loading dock, one on either side of the massive armored van, point the twelve-gauge shotguns, not say a word, grab the money, and run. Easy as one, two, three.

The plan began to go wrong almost immediately. Austin, ready to jump out from beneath the dock, gave a final glance in Andre's direction. Andre signaled that he was caught on a nail. Austin watched and waited while his heart pounded out a warning to anyone standing directly overhead. Andre laid down his shotgun and worked to free himself. After what seemed like an hour, he signaled a thumbs-up. For just a half-moment, Austin thought about shooting Andre but then nodded, and as planned, they jumped out in unison.

Who was more surprised? Austin and Andre, expecting to find the fat Gleeson's and geriatric Chester, or the five broad-shouldered, muscled, Chicago wise-guys glaring like a pack of wolves at two trembling shotguns held by fools wearing clown masks? Someone, maybe everyone, exclaimed, "Shit," just under their breath, and then the smallest of the huddled group flashed some sort of weapon out from behind his back and squirted what sounded like a thousand rounds in Austin's general direction.

Austin's shotgun discharged as he ducked, exploding an overhead light on the loading dock. Andre fired his shotgun, racked another shell, and fired again in sheer panic. The wise-guys moved as one inside the block building, quickly pointing weapons back out the door and firing wildly.

Two steps into his retreat, Austin spotted the keys still in the ignition. He jumped into the driver's seat of the van, fired up the engine, and floored it. He picked up Andre, sprinting for the tree line halfway across the parking lot.

"Get in! Get in! Come on, damn it."

"Oh my God!" Andre screamed, hopping onto the running board and dropping his shotgun in the process.

The large sideview mirror suddenly shattered on the driver's side. Then two spider webs appeared across the laminated driver's window, rounds accurately aimed at Austin's head. A number of metallic pings struck the welded steel side of the van as they raced out of the parking lot and down the dark road.

"Oh my God!" Andre screamed and started to pray.

A minute later, Austin swung a hard right onto a logging trail. As he turned, the still open rear doors slammed against the side of the van. He drove up over a slight rise, cut the lights, and crept cautiously through the forest, guided only by moonlight. No sooner had he cleared the slight rise when the trail behind was momentarily illuminated by two cars racing past in hot pursuit.

"Who the hell are those guys?" Andre screamed.

"I don't know, but we're getting our asses out of here. You okay?"

"No! I think I wet my pants."

"We can get new pants. Right now, let's just get to my pickup and as far away from here as possible."

They continued a mile or two further until Austin felt the heavy vehicle slowly begin to slide off the muddy logging trail. He braked, shifted, spun the wheels, shifted some more, and became hopelessly mired in mud. They climbed out of the cab and stared at all four massive wheels buried clear up to the axles.

"Oh, this is just great. Now what do we do?" groaned Andre.

They slopped and slid their way to the rear of the van. Their feet were caked with heavy mud as they peered inside. There wasn't a bank bag anywhere. There were, however, what looked like six large nylon shoulder bags, complete with shoulder straps, secured to a two-wheeled dolly.

"Are you kidding me? After all that, all we get is lousy laptops?" Andre said.

"I don't think these are from Ladies' Night," Austin said as he stepped onto the massive bumper. He crouched and scurried toward the front of the cargo area. The two-wheeled dolly was clamped to the front wall. The nylon bags were held firmly in place by elastic cords. He pulled the top bag off the stack and unzipped it.

"Jesus!" he exclaimed after a very long pause.

"Now what?" Andre asked.

"Man alive."

"What's wrong?"

"More damn money than I've ever seen in my life," Austin said then hurriedly slid the bag across the chromed-steel floor. He tore the next bag off the stack and unzipped it.

"Oh, man."

He unzipped the third, glanced quickly inside, and slid it across the floor. He slung the next bag across his shoulder, grabbed the final two in his hands, and exited.

"You mean to tell me those gals make this kind of dough stripping? Oh, sorry, didn't mean Celeste or nothing. I just meant that—"

"This ain't Ladies' Night money, not this much. I don't know where it's from, but I think it'd be a good idea if we got the hell out of here as fast as possible. Pick up those bags, and let's go."

"Where?" Andre asked, looking around the dense, dark forest.

"Well, not back the way we came, that's for damn sure. We gotta get over to my pickup on County 12."

They left the armored van and began walking as fast as possible toward where they thought the pickup might be. With luck, they had maybe four or possibly five miles to travel.

The estimate in travel distance would have been correct if the logging road had continued. Unfortunately, it came to an end about fifty yards further, on the shore of Lake Willis, still within sight of the armored van. Using dead reckoning, they continued around the lake, through the dense forest, and in a general westerly direction, praying they would stumble onto pavement, sooner rather than later.

Three

The tires on his Mercedes screeched to a stop at the 'T' in the road. "What in the hell," Cecil roared as he pounded the steering wheel. "Which way? Which way?" He stepped on the gas, fishtailed left, not waiting for a response.

"Right, right, go right!" Jimmy screamed, too late.

The blue BMW behind them skidded around the corner to the right and raced off in the opposite direction.

Cecil scanned the road ahead for any sign of the armored van as he raced over the top of a hill. Nothing. He exhaled and regained control. Heavy hands sporting scarred knuckles gripped the wheel. His muscled arms eventually relaxed. *Deep cleansing breath,* he reminded himself. His chiseled face sported a half-dozen puckers from the shotgun pellets he had yet to notice.

He accelerated to the top of the next hill and lurched to a stop. He jumped out the driver's door and stood on the doorframe, looking off into the distance. He couldn't see taillights or the glow from headlights. Although the road ran straight for miles, he saw nothing but darkness.

He watched, held his breath for an interminable period and hoped, but there was nothing out there except forest stillness.

"Come on! Come on. Let's go!" Jimmy rasped from the passenger seat.

"Too late, damn it. Either they pulled off, or they didn't come this way. Don't make a damn bit of difference. We lost 'em. Maybe the other guys had better luck."

"You can't be givin' up? Just like that?"

"No, just not wasting our time is all." He rubbed his face, felt a few pellets just under his skin, and gradually became aware of a few more in his muscled right arm. A direct blast, at that distance, would have taken off half his head. Cool, very cool. Whoever it was, they must have had awfully good information to pull off something like this, just two of them. They had to be pros, real pros.

He drove back toward the Knox Security building, deep in thought. He was compiling a short laundry list of professionals that may have been able to pull this off. He had already arrived at the conclusion that whoever had stolen the armored van had to have had a fair amount of inside information. Where did that come from? He was running through his shortlist again when something caught his eye, and he suddenly slammed on the brakes.

"What? What is it?" Jimmy asked. He gripped a MAC-10, eyes wide, looking furtively into the dark forest.

Cecil backed across the road and pulled alongside some sort of trail. It was the logging road, although neither he nor Jimmy had ever heard of such a thing. He stepped out of the car and looked at the heavy tire tracks in the mud. "Shit!"

"What the hell?" Jimmy asked.

"Call those other guys. Get 'em back here. The bastards turned off here. Christ, and we raced right past them, damn it. Cool, very cool."

"I can't get any damn service," Jimmy yelled, looking at his cell phone.

"What?"

"No phone service. Cecil, look around. Man, we're in the middle of fricking nowhere. It's the damned wilderness."

Cecil quickly climbed in, backed up a few feet, turned onto the logging road, and followed the muddy ruts. Brush and weeds pinged along the low undercarriage of his Mercedes.

"You gotta be kidding me. We're probably heading right into an ambush if some bear or wolf don't eat us alive first," Jimmy said.

Cecil followed the ruts deeper into the forest then stopped on a short rise. "See if you can call those guys from here."

"I told ya, it comes up no service."

"Humor me anyway. See if you can get 'em."

"Cecil, we're just wasting our…" The phone suddenly kicked in. "Hey, hey! Where are you guys? Find anything? No, no, we headed back to the building, but now we're off on some wild bear path or something. Cecil found some tracks." Jimmy paused, listening for a moment. "No, I'm not kidding. Yeah, tracks, like I said. Look, get back to that road, 'bout a half-mile down," he said, nodding at Cecil. "Half-mile down, on the left-hand side. You can see the damned tracks in the mud. We'll be waiting for you." Jimmy nodded then glanced hopefully over at Cecil, who shook his head no. "No, I guess we won't be waiting. Just hurry up and get here fast, man. We need backup."

The Mercedes rolled down the far side of the rise, not really accelerating, continuing to follow the rutted trail. Five minutes later, they could see the red roof of the armored van in the moonlight.

"You think that's it?" Jimmy asked.

"How many shiny, red, armored vans do you think are out here?" Cecil said as he opened the door and looked around. A slight breeze rustled leaves, a crow called in the distance, a thin sliver of gray on the horizon signaled the approach of sunrise.

"What if they're still there?" Jimmy asked.

"Still there? Would you be?"

"I'm thinking maybe we should wait for the other guys. They'll be here in a minute. They didn't sound that far away." Jimmy's eyes darted around the surrounding dark forest.

"These guys are already gone. Probably had a helicopter or something pick them up or a couple of those all-terrain bike things. You know, with the big wheels?"

"Mmm-mmm." Jimmy nodded but had no idea what Cecil was talking about.

Cecil walked around the armored van. Whoever it was, they were long gone. Of course, they hadn't left before making sure the massive vehicle effectively blocked any attempt to follow. He grudgingly had to admit, if he wasn't sure before, he was sure now, they were professional all the way. A helicopter was certainly an option. Maybe they had a boat on the lake to take them across to some road on the far side. Probably another vehicle was waiting for them there. Very well planned out, and, unfortunately, the information to make those plans had to have come from within Cecil's own tight little group. The big question now was, who?

* * *

The only question in Austin and Andre's mind was, *how much farther?* By their own best guess, they had fought and clawed their way through six or seven miles of dense forest. In truth, it was closer to two miles, and for all intents and purposes, they still remained in the middle of a vast wilderness. The nylon bags, three apiece, had felt weightless when they first gazed on the contents, but that had been hours ago, and with each plodding step, they became painfully aware of the weight.

"You think we've gone far enough we could cool it a bit, take a break? My ass is dragging," Andre wheezed.

"You like your ass dragging, or do you want it shot? 'Cause that's what those guys'll do if they catch us. Shoot us about a hundred times, and then leave us out here for the wolves. Let's just keep moving. We gotta be near that damn pickup truck. Any minute now, I swear, any minute, we'll get to that road."

"Who you trying to kid? You said that over an hour ago," Andre whined. "What if we just buried these things and came back for 'em later?"

"Bury them? Look around, Andre. You got any idea where in the hell we are? 'Cause I sure as hell don't. We bury these, we'll never find them again."

"I'm still wondering where all this came from. I mean all this cash. It's gotta be thousands," Andre said.

"Well, I think it's a pretty safe bet whatever it was ain't too awfully legal. Drugs, most likely, I guess. Unless those guys maybe robbed a bank or something. We get to the pickup, it might be a good idea to listen to the news. See if there was a bank robbed maybe down in the cities or over to Duluth, or Grand Rapids, someplace big like that."

"We can't get to that pickup too soon for my taste," Andre groaned.

"Like I said, should be any minute. Maybe just a half-hour, tops. It's gotta be."

Four

Cecil had all five of them fanning out from the armored van with instructions to yell as soon as anyone found something. He was guessing they might find a flare that had signaled a helicopter or maybe a mark on the beach where a speedboat pulled up on shore. There was desolate wilderness all around, but maybe they'd find tracks, some sort of trail. Something. Anything.

They did find a twelve-gauge shotgun lying next to the driver's seat, recently fired. Quite effective, not surprisingly, because when someone points a shotgun at you, all you see is a very large barrel with a pair of feet. Impossible to identify anyone, not that they could anyway since the team had been wearing masks.

Someone whistled, and they all ran toward the shore of the lake.

"See these footprints? It's like a trail or something."
Izzie Erdman pointed and then repeated as one by one
they arrived.

"Looks like they're going that way." This from Da-
Luca, almost four hundred pounds of him, sporting
groomed hair, Coke-bottle glasses, and usually spotless
clothes. Except that, this morning, his clothes were covered with mud splatters with a number of burrs clinging
to his dark trousers. The left knee was slightly torn. "Like
this helps. They get in a damn boat or something, we got
these footprints here, and then they're just gone, disappeared." He did not sound happy.

"This is absolutely useless," Cecil said, shaking his
head. "They could be anywhere, including watching us
right now, and there's no way we'd know. Let's get back
to the building, come up with a plan. Jimmy, grab that
damn shotgun and bring it along. Izzie, get hold of a tow
truck or whatever the hell they use. We need to get that
armored van outta here."

Celeste looked out from beneath the pillow and
peered at the green numerals on the digital clock. She
had a couple of hours before she had to get ready for
work. She read Rodney's sweet little note telling her to
help herself to fresh coffee and chocolate doughnuts on

the kitchen counter. He had signed it with a happy face and a pair of boobs drawn beneath the face.

She looked around his bedroom. There were lace curtains on the window, a double dresser, a full-length mirror, a headboard on the bed, no clothes on the floor, not a beer bottle in sight, and no Austin. It wouldn't take her very long to get used to coffee and doughnuts with a love note waiting for her every morning. Snuggling down into two pillows and pulling the covers around her chin, she wasn't even sure that idiot Austin could read, let alone write. Not that she cared. A couple of hours this morning would give her enough time to investigate Rodney's bedroom. Who knew what she might find?

* * *

It was twenty hours later and just about twilight when Austin and Andre finally stumbled onto pavement they could only hope was County Road 12. The sky had slipped into a final hazy pink. Part of the problem had been the lack of a decent trail, or any trail, for that matter. They'd had to hack their way through the dense forest using their bare hands. They had taken turns leading, attempting to clear at least the semblance of a path. It had been a very long, dreadful day. They'd had nothing to eat, nothing to drink, and had been driven almost insane by clouds of hungry mosquitoes until, virtually at wit's end, Andre had collapsed onto a fallen, rotting, moss-covered log.

"Yo, that's it. I give up. We are totally lost, man."

"Give up? Andre, you're carrying more money than we ever dreamed of. You can't give up."

"I sure as hell can. This shit don't spend all that well in the middle of the wilderness, man."

"Look, we're almost there. We—"

"You said that hours ago. Hell, a hundred miles ago. Come on, man, admit it. We've been lost since before sunrise. Why in the hell did I ever let you talk me into this? Face it, Austin. We've been wandering in damn circles. We're probably closer to that stupid armored van, or that damn Knox Security building and that gang of killers, than when we started this death march. We're liable to get eaten alive out here, and no one will even know the—"

"Shhh. You hear that?"

"Oh, great. Now what, a bear? I knew it. We—"

"No. Shut up, Andre. Listen, it sounded like a truck or something. Didn't you—shhh, shhh. There it is again."

"Sounds like it's coming from over that hill. Come on." Andre groaned to his feet and stumbled off to the right, snapping branches and climbing over deadfall logs as he staggered up a small hill. On the other side of the hill, muddy, scratched, bruised, and half-eaten by insects, they suddenly stumbled onto a paved surface.

"I knew it, man. I knew we'd find the damn thing sooner or later," Austin said, kneeling on the shoulder of the road. "Look, we'll follow this to my truck. You hear anyone driving toward us, say something. We can't afford to have anyone see us now. I'm guessing whoever these bags belong to will be looking mighty hard for us."

"I just hope we find your pickup."

"We will. It can't be too far. It just can't."

It quickly grew dark. They continued walking for the better part of two more hours. Eventually, they spotted Austin's truck, right where they had left it almost twenty-four hours earlier.

"Oh my God, I don't believe it. Please make it so," Andre pleaded.

"Toss them bags in back there," Austin said as he pried open the driver's door with a loud squeak. "Man, it feels good to get rid of these damn things."

"Oh, what a nightmare," Andre said. "I just want to sleep. Drink about a case of beer and eat a great big old steak, not necessarily in that order. But most of all, I just want to get the hell out of here."

Cecil and company were attempting to come up with a plan. They were sitting in Cecil's room on the second floor of the local Best Western with the drapes drawn, sipping his scotch and arguing.

"Look, it seems pretty obvious these guys are in one of four places, the East Coast, the West Coast, back in Chicago, or already outside the U.S." This from DaLuca, who had showered, shaved, changed clothes, and reeked of aftershave. His fat body oozed out of the chair. He sipped from a healthy glass of Cecil's single-malt scotch on the rocks. This was not his first.

"Let's be honest. They're just in one place—you know, not around here. When you gonna call Chicago? Tell 'em what happened?" Jimmy asked.

There was a long pause before Cecil answered. They were all watching him intently, as though their lives hung in the balance, because they did.

"I'll call tomorrow night unless we get something before then."

"So you're just planning to sit here with your thumb shoved up your ass? That's your plan?" Skoog said.

Leonard Skoog was bald, with a thin, dirty blond ponytail, scruffy goatee, and a pockmarked face. He served as the local connection since he'd spent ninety days in the county jail back in 2014 on a sexual assault charge brought by a first cousin named Connie. In an underworld where virtually everyone is identified by a catchy name worthy of Hollywood, he was known simply by his last name, Skoog. He had been the most aggressive in wanting to search for the two shotgun-wielding robbers but offered no suggestion on where, or even how, to begin. He didn't know it, but he was Cecil's first choice for the role of informer.

"Calling tomorrow night" was correct, technically. Cecil did plan to phone Chicago tomorrow night. What he hadn't told the others was that he already called Chicago, not ten minutes after he had returned to the hotel, telling Massimo Saventinni, and by extension older brother Salvatore, that two problems existed. The money had been stolen. And there had to be an informer in their midst. Find the informer, and they were halfway to getting the money back. Cecil went on to explain his misgivings regarding Skoog, and Massimo promised help was on the way.

Massimo and Salvatore Saventinni's nephew, Gabriel, arrived just before noon the following day. He went directly to Cecil's room. They had worked together before, and Gabriel wanted to assure Cecil no doubts existed where he was concerned. That wasn't exactly true, but getting to the bottom of things would be a lot easier if Cecil remained comfortable.

Gabriel served as a jack-of-all-trades for his uncles. He'd begun as a teenager running numbers, graduated to running women, from there to enforcement, before moving up the ladder once again and securing a majority of the Near North Side drug trade. He was a pleasant enough psychopath, enjoyed a good joke, fine food, excellent wine, country music, and underage sex partners. He was a tall, muscled man with a teenage girl's voice.

"So, Uncle Massimo said you got an idea who might have been talking. Tell me about him." Gabriel was sitting in a chair alongside a round, Formica wood-grain table, sipping his second cup of coffee. He held the cup with an extended little finger when he wasn't rubbing his eyes to stay awake. He had driven all night from Chicago up to northern Minnesota, a journey that took him a good twelve hours behind the wheel.

"Not a hundred percent sure who has been talking, exactly. I know it ain't me. We got Carlo DaLuca, Jimmy Brennan, and Izzie Erdman. You tell me. Man, they're all rock solid. Any of 'em would rather have his right arm cut off than talk. The other thing is, for what? Three million plus, split with the two guys that hit us? None of those guys is gonna roll over for that kind of dough. It ain't worth it. Hell, they know we'd hunt 'em down. No, it ain't any of them. But there is this other guy we sort of inherited, named Skoog, Leonard Skoog."

"Skoog?"

"Yeah, Skoog. Somehow he got to your uncles. Convinced them he'd be a good connection up here. Told them he knew everyone, knew his way around. Hell, I can read a damn map, so what do I need that jerk-off for? Far as I'm concerned, he ain't done shit since we got up here, 'cept be a royal pain in the ass." Cecil sprinkled aftershave in the palm of his hand, rubbed his hands together, then across his cheeks and neck before continuing.

"You wanna check him out? We got this place out in the middle of the woods. The security building, same place they hit us. As a matter of fact, it would probably be good for you to see the place. It's far enough out there's no one around to hear anything. If he knows something, you'll have him singing in no time."

Austin and Andre decided the safest place to hide the money would be to keep it under the bed in Austin's cabin. They parked the truck behind the ice-fishing house and stumbled into the cabin. They kicked the nylon bags under the bed and opened two bottles of Leinenkugel beer from the orange plastic cooler. Then they stretched out on a shabby, dog-eared, mouse-infested couch, took a few long sips of beer, and promptly fell asleep.

Just before noon the following day, Andre groaned and stretched, knocking a bottle of warm beer onto Austin's lap. Austin's eyes gradually blinked open as the warm beer slowly ran down between his legs.

"What the hell you think you're doing, Andre?" The empty beer bottle clattered across the wooden floor as Austin leapt off the couch.

"Murumph, umph." Andre stretched and slowly began to wake. He cast a questioning eye in Austin's direction, focusing on his soaked jeans.

"See how you like it, dumb shit," Austin yelled, grabbed the other bottle of beer, and poured it over Andre.

"Stop, stop. What are doing? Are you nuts? What the hell's wrong with you? Wasting beer, are you crazy?"

"Who the hell cares, man? Listen, Andre, rich guys like us, it can be Cold Duck or wine coolers from now on."

"You idiot," Andre said.

"Come on, man. Let's count that dough. Give me a hand hauling it out here," Austin called from the bedroom.

Two hours later, Austin's dinner table, actually a hollow core door on sawhorses, was covered with stacks of currency.

"Man, I've got a hell of a headache," Andre said. "Whoever knew trying to count so much money could be such a pain?"

"I'm not sure I can even add it all up. All I know is, this is one helluva lot," Austin said. Andre continued massaging his temples with his eyes closed. "This makes me wonder a couple of things," Austin said. "Where was Chester? Where were the damn Gleeson's? More important, what the hell are those guys gonna do? They gotta be out there beatin' the bushes trying to find this money, and us too."

"You think?"

"Those guys are gonna kill us, sure as shit. I mean, at least try to, and they aren't gonna give up. This ain't blowing over in a couple of days or even a couple of weeks, Andre. I mean, look at all this. We better figure out a pretty damn good plan. Anyone gets wind of this, we're as good as dead."

"A plan?" Andre asked.

"Well, I know a couple of things. We can't put this in the bank. We can't go out and buy new trucks or fishing boats. And we better not start buying drinks for all our friends or paying off all the debt we owe. We better continue going to work, and we—"

"Austin, we don't have jobs."

"Oh, well, yeah, but if we did. Anyway, you get what I'm saying. Right?"

"Yeah, I get it, sorta. I mean, should we just bury this stuff and forget about it?"

"No, no, I don't mean that, but if someone picks up on one of us suddenly walking around with a lot of dough, it will take them about five seconds to put the two of us together, and about a minute after that, those badasses will hear about it. We gotta be really careful, man, really careful."

Andre nodded, not looking too sure.

"Look, I ain't saying we gotta starve or anything. Go ahead and grab a hundred bucks if you want, maybe even two. But let's not go attracting attention to ourselves."

"Yeah, I get it," Andre said, thumbing a dozen bills off a stack of twenties and quickly stuffing them into his front pocket.

"Now don't go drinking all that down at some joint like the Lumber Yard and spending it on cheap broads."

"Yeah, sure, like I'd do that. Come on. I get it, okay? Quit worrying."

To be continued...

Looks like Austin and Andre pulled it off, maybe. I wouldn't sell Cecil and his crew short just yet. One can only imaging the pressure they'll be facing from the powers that be. It might be a good idea to get a copy of *Finders Keepers* and see what happens.

Enjoy!

Books by Mike Faricy

The following titles comprise the Hotshot series.

- **Reduced Ransom!** 2nd edition
- **Finders Keepers!** 2nd edition
- **Bankers Hours** 2nd edition
- **Chow Down** 2nd edition
- **Moonlight Dance Academy** 2nd edition

Contact the author:

- Email: mikefaricyauthor@gmail.com
- Twitter: @Mikefaricybooks
- Facebook: Mike Faricy Author
- Website: http://www.mikefaricybooks.com

Published by

MJF Publishing